Boundary

THE OTHER HORIZONS TRILOGY:
BOOK ONE

Boundary

THE OTHER HORIZONS TRILOGY:
BOOK ONE

Mary Victoria Johnson

LODESTONE
BOOKS

Winchester, UK
Washington, USA

First published by Lodestone Books, 2015
Lodestone Books is an imprint of John Hunt Publishing Ltd., Laurel House, Station Approach,
Alresford, Hants, SO24 9JH, UK
office1@jhpbooks.net
www.johnhuntpublishing.com

For distributor details and how to order please visit the 'Ordering' section on our website.

Text copyright: Mary Victoria Johnson 2014

ISBN: 978 1 78279 918 4
Library of Congress Control Number: 2015947760

A CIP catalogue record for this book is available from the British Library.

Design: Stuart Davies

Printed in the USA by Edwards Brothers Malloy

We operate a distinctive and ethical publishing philosophy in all
areas of our business, from our global network of authors to
production and worldwide distribution.

To Annabel

Shadows, nightmares,
I can keep them all at bay.
So come, little ones, come and play with me.
The day is long, yet the nights are longer.
Danger lurks at every corner of your mind.
So come, little ones, come and stay with me.
If there is no sunshine, you will not be afraid of the dark.
One lifetime is just about enough.
So come and dream awhile.
Just be aware, little ones, be very aware, the true terror is
    hidden
where you cannot see.
Fairy tales. Happily ever after.
I will make sure they stay away.

Part One

1

"I'm going to hide upstairs!"

"You mustn't, Penny! He'll skin you alive for simply saying the words!"

"I'm only fooling with you. Come on, I know a fantastic spot outside by the old cedar. They'll never ever find us there!"

I giggled at the grumpy expression on Evelyn's face. She could be such a worrywart! I could understand why she wasn't showing any enthusiasm, since hide-and-seek was beginning to become childish for a fourteen-year-old, but we didn't really have many alternatives.

She was fiddling with the purple ribbon tied in her black wavy hair, a satin piece that matched the shade of her gown perfectly. "Do we have to go outside? After all the rain, the ground is sodden and the mud will ruin my stockings. Why can't we hide inside? Behind the curtains, perhaps? It took Fred ages to find Tressa there last week."

I tapped my foot impatiently.

"If you want to hide yourself, be my guest," I said bluntly. "I'm going outside."

I turned purposely and ran down the long hallway towards the large double front doors. If I wanted anything done around here, especially with Evelyn beings as awkward as she was, then I would have to act as though I didn't care and hope that she didn't call my bluff.

I could feel my auburn bob bouncing as I hopped down the steps of the grand staircase with deliberate slowness, waiting for the voice behind me, which would surely come.

Just as expected, my leaving had the desired effect on Evelyn. She was not content to ever be by herself, and she wasn't particularly good at this game. Primness and dignity were her virtues, and hide-and-seek did sometimes have the habit of compromising those. I thought with a chuckle back to that time when she had become stuck in the airing cupboard, and our friends Lucas and Fred had been forced to use scissors to cut a tangle of corset lace free from the floorboard nails…she hadn't agreed to playing again for months.

"Penny! Wait up!" Evelyn called as loudly as she dared.

I slowed down to wait for her, and then continued my run at a pace I knew my delicate friend could easily keep.

We reached the grand hall in no time at all. It was the largest room we knew of in the house, a full three floors tall, completely paneled with oak like the rest of the manor save for the thick plum velvet curtains that ran from floor to roof, covering the massive front window. An imposing chandelier made of bronze and solid pearl graced the ornately carved ceiling, casting its soft glow about the room, which received no natural light thanks to the curtains.

We sneaked through the huge carved doors, making little noise, and stepped out in the gardens. A strong smell of dampness and wet grass immediately filled my nose, a result of the excessive rainstorms that had been plundering the manor these past few weeks. It made the plants lush and healthy, but was quite a hindrance for us when we wished to both play outside and remain somewhat clean.

As soon as the door was safely shut, I ran like a bullet across the lawns, making a beeline for the ancient cedar tree on the edge of the woods that surrounded the Boundary. The wet ground under my feet squelched deliciously as I ran, sending splatters of muck up the back of my pristine gown and stockings. It took a lot of concentration not to slip over. I wished that I could run barefoot, and considering the circumstances I didn't think it was as scandalous as it sounded.

Whilst my feet drummed in harmony with my heartbeat, I could hear the wheezing that was Evelyn fall further and further behind, yet I did not contemplate waiting as the adrenaline coursed through my veins. The others could complain that we were too old, that we should be spending less time messing around and more time focusing on our studies, but I didn't think that the thrill of such games ever truly went away if you didn't let it. There were still places in the estate that we hadn't explored, and age wasn't going to stop me from finding them. We had found some of our favorite haunts whilst trying to search for a hiding place.

In no time at all I was at the edge of the Boundary woods. They surrounded the manor, creating cover between the lawns and house and the Boundary itself. Surprisingly, they were not at all sinister like some other areas of the estate, contrarily consisting of tall, thick, moss-covered trees, deciduous and evergreen alike, all evenly spaced out with little density and only minimal undergrowth. Naturally, they were void of life other than that of the plants. For some reason, there were never any animals I had read about in the manor, like birds or squirrels. I supposed that they couldn't get around the Boundary.

I found my target, the cedar, and wrapped my hands firmly around an overhanging branch. I was glad my hands were more sturdy than dainty as I took a deep breath and hauled myself up onto the branch, brow furrowed in effort. I moved slowly and carefully, wriggling along the slippery wet limbs by winding my arms and legs all the way around the middle and pulling myself along.

"Why...did...urgh!" A wheezing Evelyn had appeared a few feet below me; her face flushed a deep pink from running, yet still managing to look beautiful.

I sat up straight to talk to her. Evelyn covered her mouth with a delicate gloved hand in horror, pointing at me as if I'd suddenly sprouted an extra head and large antlers.

"Goodness me!"

I glanced down, and almost burst out laughing. All down the front of my pale blue-grey bodice and petticoats was a thick line of muck caused no doubt from sliding around on the bark, not to mention the damage on my shoes and white stockings. To me, it didn't matter, but to Evelyn, it was murder. The death of a perfectly good dress.

"Never mind." I shrugged, laughing airily at the look of increasing horror she sported. "Here, give me your hand and I'll pull you up."

"Are you joking?" Evelyn gaped. "This is ridiculous! This is the only frock that goes with my amethyst necklace, so I will *not* ruin it for the sake of winning hide-and-seek! Besides, *He* will get suspicious."

With a haughty shudder, Evelyn raised her chin to the clouds and flounced off the stand conspicuously behind a birch only a couple of yards away.

I smirked to myself and resumed my wiggling to reach the prize hiding spot. When I reached the massive trunk, I jumped without thinking about it too much into a hollow just large enough to hide my whole body. This had been easier a couple of years ago, but it was curved so that if I leaned hard against one side passers-by would not be able to see me. All I had to do now was wait.

I thought about Evelyn. She was mortally terrified of the Master, and I supposed that even I had a part of me that feared His wrath. You would have to be inhuman, like Him, not to fear.

I closed my eyes and rested my head against the smooth, woody inside of the cedar, breathing in the fresh damp smell contentedly. I was pretty sure that I would be the last one found, as usual, so I had time to doze off while one by one my friends joined the hunt.

The woman was crying. She could hear them approaching from the outside, surrounding the house and blocking off all possible escapes. Though part of her was screaming in denial, deep down she knew that this would be it, that her brief life as a fugitive would be over in this very room. Had it been worth it? All the hiding, all the fear...had their motive been justified?

She wrapped her arms tightly around the bundle, which was wet with her tears.

"Bernard," she whispered hoarsely to her husband who was trying to bolt the door. His hands were shaking so much that he could barely fasten the lock as he bent down out of sight from the windows. He turned around and she saw his white face fill with the same despair as hers.

"Bernard, my love," she sobbed softly. "Don't. It will do nothing."

The man choked back a sob of his own, but sank down beside the woman and drew her close to him while placing his other hand on the bundle. He kissed her matted hair long and hard, and her heart fluttered as it always did when they touched.

"Elisabeth. I don't regret this choice one bit, you understand? So dry those tears and let us face whatever is to come knowing that we have at least made a fighting attempt to stand up against them."

Even as he said it, his voice wavered and broke. Elisabeth buried her face in his arms and tried to blank her mind.

A loud explosion blew the door open. Though Elisabeth's screams were muffled by her husband's tense arms, they were unstoppable, as she clung to him, refusing to look up at whoever was there. She could feel the judders now, wracking Bernard's body.

Sensing people coming closer she lost all sense of sanity as someone grabbed her bundle and began to wrest it from her. Thrashing and resisting with every ounce of strength, her screaming rose an octave.

"No, no, no, no!" she cried hysterically, eyes stubbornly shut against the enemy. They would not have the satisfaction of seeing the light leave her eyes when they killed her.

They gave one final wrench, and the bundle flew from her clenched hands. She could hear her husband yelling too, now, and the triumphant shouts of the enemy.

"Bernard and Elisabeth, you are hereby charged and convicted of—"

Elisabeth did not wait to listen to the death sentence spoken smoothly by people who were obviously untroubled by the present events. With her eyes still closed, she lunged blindly out at them, trying to grab the bundle, ignoring the shouts from her husband or the warning sirens in the coherent part of her mind. A wave of what felt like static buzzed for a moment through the room, and her head snapped back and one final shriek escaped her lips. She was dead before she hit the floor.

Her last thought was of the bundle.

I woke up with a start, my breathing as fast as it had been when I ran. The dream had been so vivid, so real! The oddest thing was that I had seen the entire thing through the eyes of the woman, Elisabeth, as if I were actually her. I had felt her strong emotions and when she had died, I had felt the world fade before I woke up.

I was slightly unnerved by its clarity, but to be honest I wasn't too fazed. Avery, one of my friends, sleepwalked, and Lucas would have bizarre dreams that he could remember the next morning, so having realistic ones myself was not an unusual occurrence. Still, I decided to commit it to memory – there was something about it that I couldn't put my finger on, something important. Oh, well. I would remember soon enough.

The thing that bothered me the most was how long I had been asleep. Had anyone found the others yet? Had they given up, or had it only been a few minutes? Then a new worry sprang into my mind: would Evelyn spill the beans and blurt out my hiding place? It was exactly the sort of thing she would do if she were to get bored or cold.

I poked my head anxiously out of the hollow to get some idea of the situation.

Immediately, I whipped it back inside and pulled my legs closer to me while scooting back against the wall of the tree in excitement. A grin of anticipation curled on my lips as I waited for the four figures I had seen slowly approaching through the evening mist to find me.

"Trust Penny to make us come outside after it's been raining," someone was saying. I was pretty sure that it was Avery. "Though how she brought Evelyn with her I might never know."

"It would be a trick worth knowing," another child noted. Fred, the seeker. "Then we could come out and play cricket more often – oh, there you are, Evelyn."

I heard Evelyn give an exaggerated sigh as she stepped out from behind her birch tree.

I counted four figures, so I knew that someone had found Tressa and Lucas as well and I had officially won the game. I could have revealed myself, but I decided to wait and see how long it took them to find me.

"Penny! You win! Come on out!" Avery called.

I held my breath and waited.

"Penny, please! It's nearly dinner time!"

The emotions immediately changed inside my hiding place as I yelped in surprise and jumped out of the hollow, bumping my head in haste. Had I really dozed for that long? Normally my body clock automatically told me when it was time to congregate in the dining hall, an acquired sense from all those times I had been late.

I swung down off the branch and landed with a thud in front of my friends, frantically dusting off the filth from my dress.

"Oh dear," I hissed to myself. "Stupid! How long do we have?"

I raised my head to meet the eyes of the group and was shocked to see they were all trying very hard not to laugh. It was then I knew they had duped me.

"It isn't time for dinner yet, is it?" I sighed, annoyed at myself for falling for such a clichéd trick.

Avery shook his head, smirking from ear to ear. "We couldn't be bothered to search every nook and cranny of the estate for you…besides, seeing that reaction was *much* more amusing."

"That's a rotten thing to do!" I scolded, only half joking. "You just can't lose, can you?"

"Who has time for losing when they could be winning? If you're not cheating, you're not trying."

"It isn't funny, Avery," Lucas piped up. Avery wiped the smirk from his face and gave us all a 'here-we-go-again' look. "No, seriously. I read this story, *The Boy Who Cried Wolf,* about—"

"Lovely. And I'm sure there will come a time when we have absolutely nothing better to do, in which case I'll be more than happy to hear about it." Avery switched his attentions, bored already. "Just because you're petrified of Madon, it doesn't mean we need a lecture every time I try to lighten the use of His name."

With that one word, the whole atmosphere seemed to chill slightly, running from playful and teasing to menacing in a second. A cold breeze swept through the trees, raising goose bumps on my exposed arms, as the branches on the previously tranquil cedar swayed as if they were possessed.

"Shut up, Avery," Tressa said tersely, putting an arm protectively around Lucas, who turned white with a mixture of irritation and fear on his face. As the last one punished, it was still very fresh in his mind why punctuality was essential.

"Yes, Avery, be a darling and shut up!" I tried to lighten the mood unsuccessfully, receiving only a few raised eyebrows at the terrible attempt at humor.

A heavy silence descended until Evelyn announced, "I'm going to dress for dinner now. Actually, I wouldn't mind some help from you girls: I lost a pair of earrings last week and can't for the life of me remember where I saw them last!"

"Quite the emergency," I mumbled, half to myself.

Still, glad of the excuse to do something other than stand around twiddling our thumbs, we plodded our way across the lawns to the manor without any more hesitation: Evelyn holding her skirt primly above the wet grass; Tressa with her jaw set and expression deep in thought; and then me, galumphing in an ungainly manner at the rear with my shoes sloshing uncomfortably.

2

A while later, our trio descended the grand staircase from our rooms in the south wing to meet with the boys, Lucas, Fred and Avery, in the entrance hall.

Lucas looked up at me as I came down the last few stairs, his ice-blue eyes squinting, straining to see properly after so many hours reading under a dim candle. He smiled, though the tension in the hall was palpable. We had to rein in our natural energies, and it was difficult acting formal. Lucas, I knew, tonight, did it out of fear, though he was generally quiet anyway, and content with his own company. To any new people he might have been difficult to get to know – luckily, there were never any strangers. Just us.

I smiled back in the hope of allaying some of his fears saying a formal, "Good evening," showing I could behave when I wanted to.

Tressa meantime, passed us with long confident strides, but still managing to look elegant. She was only a breadth shorter than Lucas, and towered over us other two girls. She carried an air of confidence and leadership wherever she went, but her angular face was gentle. She made her way over to Fred, a rather plump being with a contagious smile and handsome features that were usually partially covered by his flop of hazelnut hair.

"You look delightful, ladies." I turned and Avery mock bowed, eyes fixated on me for my reaction to his insincere compliment. Even he was reining in his usual loud and obnoxious self, I thought, but I could see tonight that he was having as bad a time as me behaving well. He could be a good ally in plots or games of strategy and we made a good team with our combined energy and enthusiasm. He often got on all our nerves though, but we all knew he was just compensating for being slight in build and height.

Evelyn blushed but looked faintly pleased, Tressa just

ignored him, and I stuck my tongue out at him and pulled a face. He raised his hands into the air in surrender, the permanent smirk still etched onto his face. The others had pointed out to me many times that perhaps Avery and I clashed only because we were so much alike, but both of us discarded this as nothing but a coincidence.

"Oh, stop it, you two!" Tressa commanded, playing the adult as usual. "Carrying on like a bunch of babies. You should look at yourselves!"

"Oh, I do. And I like what I see...well, for myself at least," Avery drawled arrogantly, receiving an involuntary snicker from everyone except Tressa, who merely rolled her eyes. Immaturity was always rampant when we were hungry. And already our acting formal was deteriorating, which was dangerous.

We mulled around in the hallway for the next few minutes, chattering, bickering, and fiddling with our splendid dinner clothes whilst waiting to be escorted to the dining hall.

I wandered over to a claw-footed chair over by the staircase. In my poufy onyx-colored dress I knew I must look like a collapsing soufflé as I sat down. The cushion had been widened and elongated to accommodate such voluptuous skirts, enough so that my legs dangled a few inches above the ground when I pushed right into the back.

Then it came. It had taken years for us all to get used to it. First, my heart began to race and kept skipping beats, followed by the sudden feeling of breathlessness, which left me faint from the brief lack of oxygen. A familiar chill crept up my spine as if the very fabric of the air were shifting around me, like an unnatural, invisible storm. My ears popped uncomfortably, accompanied by a ripping sound.

It was disconcerting, and told us all something. He had returned.

I stood up again, still reeling from the overwhelming sensation. This had happened nearly every day of my fourteen years on the estate, but I could never shake the feeling off. We just had to let it happen. It was useless to try to fight it.

As I joined the main group, another familiar silhouette emerged from the smaller corridor that twisted out from behind the stairwell.

Beatrix was an older lady who had taken care of us our whole lives. She was perhaps sixty years old, with a trim figure that was slowly beginning to expand with old age. She took the roles of governess, housekeeper, and cook, although no one ever saw her about the estate working.

"Hello, my lovelies." Beatrix smiled through crooked, white teeth, something she'd always managed to do through all circumstances. "How has your day been?"

"We played hide-and-seek," Fred told her, trying and failing to hide the resignation from his tone.

"I won!" I acknowledged proudly, the only one who wasn't embarrassed to still be playing children's games.

"Again, Penny? You must remember to give your friends a chance."

The corridor was claustrophobic compared to the rest of the house, with the walls only nine feet high and the elaborate molding around the top making them seem shorter than that. I could scarcely make out the pattern on the wallpaper, as the candles embedded subtly into the walls were fewer and dimmer in the hallways, and there were no windows to let in light. It was wide enough for three to walk comfortably side-by-side, so Fred, Beatrix and I walked ahead while the others followed in pairs.

Beatrix was talking cordially to Fred. I wasn't really paying attention though I was right there, as it was no secret that no matter how she tried to hide it, Beatrix preferred Fred to me. Honestly, I couldn't blame her. Fred was so genuine and pleasant, whilst I could be quite sassy.

"...very special day. You're all wearing the new outfits I gave you, which is perfect," Beatrix was saying.

I paid her no heed, and dragged my finger along the textured walls, roughly wearing my nail down, and making a funny squeaking noise as it ran over the grooves.

Then we entered the dining hall. It was a room I both adored and dreaded. The gothic vaulted ceiling was impressive as was the chandelier, many times my size, that hung glowing from the exposed wooden beams, which supported the roof, its hundreds of crystal drops sparkling in the candlelight. The ceiling itself had been expertly plastered right down to the tiniest detail, though what the design was remained a mystery as it was too high to see. Huge floor to ceiling windows, like the ones in the entrance hall, allowed dusky evening light to peep in between the heavy thick velvet curtains. The echoic room was void of anything save a massive oaken table that was centered perfectly with seven straight-backed chairs and one formidably winged throne-like piece, which was isolated down at the head. This was where the Master sat, and was the reason why I didn't like the room.

Beatrix moved away so that she could go and sit in the most uncomfortable of the chairs, one that had no fabric padding, a couple of yards or so away from everyone else in the no-man's-land between us and Him. We never questioned if this was unethical: that was her place.

I took my usual seat facing the wall with the windows, in between Tressa and Evelyn. The boys sat down with Lucas opposite me; Avery with Tressa, and Fred with Evelyn.

"I'm starving!" Fred exclaimed, licking his lips. "We must have walked miles searching for you and Evelyn! "

"Tell me about it," I agreed, copying custom and unfolding a crisp white napkin over my dress to protect it. "Try walking about in a corset all day."

My stomach rumbled in agreement as I surveyed the fantastic feast Beatrix had whipped up for tonight. It was even more scrumptious than usual: roast pork chops, buttered potatoes (mashed, boiled, or roasted), a gravy boat the size of a several stacked textbooks, salted cabbage, onion soup, wild mushroom rice, and a large assortment of seasonings and vegetables.

Even Evelyn, who refrained from eating too much in effort to keep her perfect figure, eyed the food hungrily and shuffled around her chair in anticipation.

There was silence in the room save for smacking lips and rumbling stomachs. We all waited in fearful anticipation for Him to show up so we could get the tough part over with and dig in. Beatrix had her head hung, her lips moving in her routine silent prayer.

Then He came.

The air turned icy, the candles flickered, and the pit in our stomachs twisted nervously, our eyes carefully trained to our laps. A breeze made the hairs on my neck stand up as I felt Him billow past me to the winged-back chair, with all the subtlety and danger of smoke. Madon. I would not think his name again.

He greeted us coolly. His voice was lilting and clear, soft and deadly. "Children."

"Master," we all chorused, voices wavering slightly.

His presence filled the room like a heavy weight – pressuring my mind and filling my ears with pounding blood. If sinister had a face, it would be His. To picture the Master, one must only give darkness a human form and they would have a spitting image. Dressed in the highest quality materials, which hung off Him like mist, with pupils and irises that pierced the very soul of whoever dared challenge the obvious aura of authority and utter control.

"You may begin."

Letting out the breath I had been holding in, I reached for a silver serving spoon and helped myself to food. The others followed suit. He didn't reach for anything, only watching us intently, drumming slight fingers against the arms.

When my plate was full, I avidly shoved the succulent food into my mouth, chewing and savoring every bite.

"T-t-the food is particularly good tonight, sir," Tressa spoke up hesitantly, not making eye contact but directing her voice to where He sat.

I was shocked. We never spoke to the Master if we could help it, trying to avoid any attention that might trigger anger or punishments. I had to admire her bravery, though.

"It does mark the fifteenth year of you being here," he answered as if it was a minor detail not worth saying much about. The trail of amusement in his voice was probably the same surprise that someone had spoken up.

"We're fifteen now?" I gasped, unsure about how I felt about that. There was a round of forced shushing. I had talked too loudly. "Sorry."

Instead of being excited at the prospect, I felt curiously empty. Ten years later, we were still here doing the same things we'd been doing as five-year-olds, and were no closer to knowing why.

"I said you are fifteen, so it must be so. Do not question me!" he snapped, and I felt my throat tighten.

"I'm very sorry, sir," I squeaked miserably.

He didn't answer.

No one spoke up again.

In the end I was one of the last ones finished as I didn't want to be reprimanded for being a pig and risk punishment.

"Thank you for the meal, Beatrix!" we sang after every plate had been cleaned.

"You're very welcome, my dears. Happy Birthday to you all!"

He shot her a meaningful look after that statement and she cowed. What was wrong with wishing us a happy birthday? I wondered. We never celebrated or got presents like the children did in books, so why the bother over a simple kind wish?

His icy indifference returned in a split second. With a lazy wave of a hand, I felt the air rip again as the plates and food faded away to be replaced with assorted mouth-watering puddings: Victoria sponge cake, sticky toffee pudding, vanilla ice cream, fruit meringue, and a trifle in a big crystal bowl.

I couldn't help myself.

"Penny!" Fred chortled as I dived like a madwoman for the toffee pudding and attacked it possessively.

"What? I'm the only one who really likes it!"

"Actually, it's my favorite too, but we just pretend we don't want it so you won't bite our heads off!"

"Liar. Pass the ice cream?"

Evelyn shook her head in distaste as I scooped some of the creamy white mass onto my huge pudding and licked my lips as it began to melt under the warm toffee.

"Can I have your gown after you grow too large wear it?" she asked scathingly.

I noticed on her plate she had only the tiniest slither of cake possible and rolled my eyes. The moist, sweet, gooey pudding was heaven. My waist could die in a hole for all I cared at that moment.

When we finished, me last again for different reasons, it was pitch black outside. He got up first as usual, pulling on His long travelling coat, which seemed to have appeared from nowhere.

"Goodnight," he said briskly, without emotion, buttoning His coat with another gesture of the hand.

I followed suit and scraped back my chair feeling warm, full, and satisfied. My corset was killing me though, and I cursed the stupid fancy frock for needing one. My day dresses didn't, thank goodness.

"I hope you enjoyed it, my darlings." Beatrix hugged us all tightly with her back to the Master. "I have left a little gift for you all in your rooms. You are getting a little old for playthings so I have given a card game to you boys and some jewelry for my little ladies, which I think you will find useful for supper times."

The others thanked her happily, but something played on the back of my mind. I was about to follow on out down the corridor when I changed my mind and marched right back up to her

"Beatrix, there is something else I – I would like for m-my birthday," I stuttered, confidence faltering.

"And what is that, Penny?"

"I would like...I would..." How to say it? "I want to have and look and see what is on the other side of the Boundary now I'm older," I finished with my voice growing stronger at the end.

It happened in a matter of seconds.

Beatrix looked at me with a mounting horror, not having time to open her mouth to scold me before He was there, raging like a silent storm cloud.

"What did you just say?" he asked, deadly calm.

"Nothing!" I shook my head frantically. "I – I was just— "

The pain came suddenly without warning. I threw my head back and screamed, falling to the ground and writhing like a worm. I was being stabbed with poison knives, my organs being ruthlessly cut out and my bones broken... The world swam before me and the agony redoubled, making my back arch involuntarily off the ground. A buzz filled my ears until I could barely hear my own blood-curdling shrieks for this to stop, for me to die and slip away from the feeling... I could see Him standing over me with a grim, untroubled expression, Beatrix looking away, my friends sobbing in terror. I tasted blood. I was dying. Finally.

Then I vomited and it was over.

Choking and crying, I curled into a ball on the ground.

"Pathetic," I heard Him sneer. "Get up."

He kicked me in in the ribs as I struggled trembled to my feet, shaking convulsively.

"I don't want to hear any talk like that again, do you hear? Or I'll make the pain last your whole miserable life and watch you go mad."

With a whirl of a coat and a rip, he was gone.

3

"Penny? Oh, thank goodness. I thought you were dead. You look awful!"

"Be quiet, Avery. I was just dozing."

Even Avery couldn't use sarcasm to completely mask the nervousness he too was feeling.

I had woken up that morning with a gigantic headache and clammy skin, the fever causing me to miss breakfast and stay in bed for most of the morning. I was still very shaky from my ordeal and was utterly dreading dinner, for although I had no physical scars to show from the torture, since we all knew that it was nothing more than an illusion, inside I was a nervous wreck. It had happened before to most of us, and took a few days to recover.

"I'm going out before lessons start," I announced quietly.

We were all dallying in our common room, a large area on the second floor with a fireplace, sofa, a patterned rug, and bay window with gorgeous views of the grounds. It had been our nursery when we were younger, and now served as a place to stage all indoor activities.

Avery, Fred, and Lucas were using the table on the rug to set up the game they'd received yesterday, setting out rectangular cards and trying to figure out what to do with them. Evelyn was curled up in a chair by the roaring fire with Tressa affectionately braiding her pale blonde waves.

When I voiced my idea, every head turned to the window, which was being viciously pelted by a steady rain.

"Don't be silly, Penny," Evelyn scoffed, turning back to Tressa's hair. "You'll catch a terrible chill in this weather, especially in your state. Stay in and I'll plait your hair next if you'd like."

"Why do you even want to go out?" Lucas piped up.

"I need some fresh air." I shrugged, eyes pleading for them

not to push further than that.

None of them had mentioned last night, but they mutually understood the reason for my needing to clear my head, and so they questioned that no further.

"Make sure you stop and get a coat out of your room before you go, and be back before noon. Don't expect us to come out and remind you," Tressa told me with authority.

"You're letting her go?" I heard Avery gasp as I got up to leave.

"You should know better by now than to try and tell Penny not to do something once she's set her mind on it," Tressa said philosophically, flaunting her excellent ability to judge character again.

My bones ached, and my eyelids felt heavy from the few hours of turbulent sleep I had managed. I did not take the detour to the south wing for my coat; instead, I headed straight down the staircase and out onto the lawn.

The rain had dulled to more of a drizzle than a downpour, but it was still not very warm. I headed straight across the grass with purpose for the distant Boundary woods. A light mist shrouded them, making them seem mysterious, though not threatening.

The air was fresh and there was a woody, earthen smell. Big fat drops of water splattered down from wet branches until my hair turned a dark, almost mahogany, red, which plastered to my scalp, my sodden dress clinging to my arms. I stepped quickly over twisting roots and piles of mulch, not really trying to minimize damage to my already-soaked stockings and shoes. There was no marked path as we didn't usually travel this far into the woods, but the widely-spaced trees and limited undergrowth allowed me to easily make my journey.

The fog grew denser as I walked and the trees began to close up and become more spindly than the massive giants that bordered the lawns. I stopped all of a sudden, feeling the surreal buzzing all around me. I looked down, and sure enough there was a tiny, barely noticeable dribble of water, nearly too small to be called even a creek. Though not particularly wide nor deep, it circled the entire property like some trickling little fence. On the other side, the fog and trees grew so thick that I couldn't see more than a few feet. I had reached the Boundary.

I closed my eyes and inhaled deeply, ignoring the unpleasant feeling of the rain seeping through my clothes and the foreign will inside my mind egging me to turn back, perhaps caused by the static pulse that crackled through the nearby air.

As I stood, the wind picked up a few oak leaves and carried them in an unsteady line towards the invisible wall. As the leaves crossed above the creek, there was an odd ripple as if they had hit a vertical body of water, and the leaves fell to the ground at my feet as no more than a pile of ashes.

I remembered when I was six: I had been punished just like I had been last night, and I had wanted – no, needed – to get out. Luckily, I had tripped on a root and fallen just before the Boundary, and only my outstretched hands had touched the creek. The tips of my fingers were burned black, my nails worn down to tiny stubs, and it had *hurt!* I'd put on gloves in hopes no one would notice, but I should have known better. Nothing got past the Master. I had been punished again for trying to get out, trapped in my room for ages, and confined to the house for even longer.

I wasn't stupid enough to try to cross the Boundary again.

An angry tear trickled down my cheek. I knew that a world outside mine existed, since I had read about it and learned about it from Beatrix, though it was forbidden knowledge. Somehow, Beatrix got away with talking about things against the rules when we never did, but I was glad instead of jealous. It was as if she were a window.

When I was younger I never questioned why the Boundary was there, or why we lived in the restricted environment of the estate. Now it felt claustrophobic. Fifteen years I had been stuck trying to scrape together a somewhat enjoyable life, but we couldn't go on playing games forever. Time was ticking, and the older we grew, the more strangling the Boundary became. This wasn't anything I could fight against, and it killed my pride.

I collapsed down onto the mucky ground and wrapped my arms around my knees. "I hate you," I spat into the air in front of me.

Who was I talking to? The Master? The Boundary? My life? Maybe all of them.

Why were we here? How could we get out? I had lived in compliance for too long now, and had no intention of staying on the estate for my rapidly approaching adult years, yet I had no idea where to even start. My friends got frustrated sometimes, definitely, but not enough so that they would do anything about it.

I knotted my fingers tightly within my hair the powerlessness absolutely driving me past insanity. How much torture would we have to endure, and for how much longer would we remain in constant fear of Him?

I remembered my dream. Perhaps it had been some sort of message: stand up, or be conquered.

It took two sides to play a game. I knew what side I was on, and who my opponent was.

The only question that remained, was would the threat and fear of being caught be enough to keep my friends from joining me, or would we finally be able to unite for a freedom that surely existed, if only we were brave enough to fight for it?

4

Evelyn almost died when she saw my dress.

"Penny! How could you? That was one of your most flattering gowns! Not many shades go with your hair, but that one looked exquisite and you've *ruined it!*" Her voice rose hysterically. "Oh, I'm sure I can live without it." I shivered, my teeth chattering. Tressa was equally appalled, but more for my lack of common sense. "You're a fool, Penny," she scolded, after returning with a pottery basin full of steaming hot water, which she had fetched from the bathroom. I had to agree with Tressa on that one, perched in my bed with a blanket thrown around my shuddering shoulders.

I dipped my feet into the basin and sighed with pleasure. I had taken off my shoes, stockings, and outer dress so I was wearing only my camisole and petticoats under the shawl. "Thank you, Tressa," I murmured contentedly.

She didn't reply, instead sorting through my wardrobe for another item of clothing for me to wear.

"Where did you go, anyway?" Evelyn inquired, sitting down beside me frowning curiously.

"The Boundary," I admitted, squirming as I waited for the reprimand from Tressa.

Sure enough, she whirled around and shouted, "You utter *idiot!* How could you? After being punished last night, it's *not* a good idea to go galumphing around in an area you know He hates us to be! It's dangerous!" She threw her arms around like a windmill.

"You're not in charge of me, Tressa," I challenged. "I can do whatever I please. I needed to be alone and I just walked until I had to stop, and then plopped right down there. It's not a crime."

"No, but suicide is."

"Oh, forget it. I couldn't expect She-Who-Can-Do-No-Wrong to understand what punishments do to you." I gave up arguing to savor the heavenly luxury of the boiling water in the basin.

Tressa was the only one among us who had not been through punishments more than once or twice, largely due to her ability to keep her mouth shut and read people's moods better than we did.

"Well, it's done now," she harrumphed, changing the subject. "You're out of decent day dresses. Mine will be much too long on you, as I must be at least a foot taller... Evelyn, could you be a darling and lend Penny something to wear for the afternoon? We'll talk to Beatrix and see about getting her a few hardier garments made, but she needs something without ruffles and lace for lessons."

Tressa might have well suggested Evelyn go and set fire to a litter of kittens for the response she got.

"You *can't* be serious?" Evelyn jumped off my bed, getting into a bigger and bigger fluster as she paced around. "She'll be fine in a dinner frock, or we could at least turn up one of yours! Please, Tressa, you know she'll just scuff and stain it something awful!"

She started to blabber, oblivious to Tressa's and my unimpressed expressions.

"Your generosity and selflessness continue to inspire me," I said sarcastically.

"I can't force you"—Tressa shrugged—"but it's the only option. Either you grow up and lend poor Penny a dress, or she'll simply have to go naked and *you* can explain to the Master why."

*

Tressa's threat worked like a charm. I found myself wandering down the lower hallway towards the library in one of Evelyn's most old and distasteful dresses. It was dusky pink with a silver rose pattern, and it clashed horribly with my red hair. The worst part was that I was a few inches wider than Evelyn in several places, so the seams around the shoulders and waist were straining and sucking me in worse than a corset. I could barely breathe.

I was sweating by the time I fumbled into the library, having let Tressa and Evelyn go ahead without me under the pretense of a bathroom break.

The library was, compared to the rest of the house, nothing particularly special. I had seen a picture in a book of a library in an estate the size of ours: masses upon masses of books piled from floor to ceiling, on shelves three stories high, with painted cherubs smiling down from a roof mural…but not here.

Only slightly bigger than our common room, it contained a single bookcase, a few worn wooden desks, and a ceiling that sloped downwards towards a stained-glass window.

The others were already sitting at their individual desks, getting out new ink pens and thick sheets of creamy paper to practice our usual thirty minutes of handwriting.

"Penny, dear, please make sure you arrive with everyone else on time, please," Beatrix scolded from her stool in the middle of the circle of desks.

"I'm sorry for being late." I sat down. A loud rip of material echoed, but not one of the supernatural kind.

"Oops," I whispered.

I looked down. The side seam had torn. Evelyn flashed Tressa an I-told-you-so look, and I blushed.

"I'll see about getting you some more dresses," Beatrix noted kindly. "For now, get out your supplies and start writing."

Beatrix really was an angel sometimes.

I pulled out my pen, paper, and the dictionary I was copying from and began to write. Long, elegant, curved strokes soon began to fill my paper as I started where I had last left off at 'lachrymiform.'

I loathed handwriting with a passion. It was so pointless! When would I ever need to write? Why couldn't we just read the dictionary and be done with it?

I had mouthed my opinions to Beatrix a few years ago, and she had told me that good penmanship was a becoming and necessary talent every lady must possess, and that writing down definitions was much more effective than pure memorization. I had told her frankly that I wasn't interested in becoming a lady, at which point she had snapped at me to stop complaining and to write for an extra ten minutes.

I always started with lovely neat strokes, but towards the end my words were blotchy and scribbled with the telltale signs of a writer with hand cramp. In fact, by the time I had reached '*mumpsimus*,' my letters were barely distinguishable.

"That will do," Beatrix called, after what seemed like forever.

With barely concealed whoops of relief, we all dog-eared the dictionaries and tucked all the stationary into little cubbyholes fitted under our desks.

"I've reached the Rs now," Avery boasted, surveying us in a way that dared us to challenge his superiority.

"Well done," Beatrix said vaguely.

Avery, like me, was too much of a handful to be very close to her heart, but he didn't care. I had a feeling that he would have been more disgusted if she had showered him with hugs and mushy compliments instead of a polite, reserved affection.

We all edged hopefully towards the bookshelf, but Beatrix had other ideas. "Boys, retrieve your numeracy workbooks and continue wherever you left off last time. Girls, fetch your tapestries and try to make some progress on those."

Flexing my sore fingers carefully, I pulled out the fine cloth on which I had been embroidering a fancy likeness of the chandelier in the foyer. I had originally chosen the design because I had thought it would be simpler than doing a landscape like Evelyn and Tressa, but it had turned out to be most difficult with all the little details.

Tapestry was, though, one of the perks of being a girl. Despite the fact it sometimes frustrated me to distraction, the end result seemed a lot more useful than the pointless juggling of numbers that the boys did. We ended up with a beautiful (though imperfect) representation of an aspect of the estate, whilst they ended up with nothing but a calculation of figures scribbled on paper. Why grown gentlemen needed the skill, I would never understand.

I fiddled with the needle and thread for another half an hour, succeeding in only pricking my fingers once. I fumbled with a knot in the last few minutes and had to get Tressa to help me untangle it, but apart from that, I thought I had done rather a decent job.

Beatrix was too preoccupied by something, it wasn't clear what, to notice my little hiccup, toying with her apron distractedly, occasionally glancing up in nervous, jerky movements. She clearly had a lot on her mind. I supposed it must be hard work being the sole servant of such a grand estate, in addition to tutoring every day.

She even made us work for an extra few minutes before jolting out of her reverie and checking her pocket watch.

"Sorry, my dears, I was daydreaming! Good on you all for working so well. You may have a few minutes of reading before luncheon."

I tore towards the bookcase happily, desperate to have first choice of material.

Beatrix retreated into her mind, the worried expression still fixed upon her brow.

Besides Beatrix herself, these books were our best source to what life was like outside the Boundary. The shelf itself was mainly full of reference textbooks for our studies, but if you knew what you were looking for, then you would be able to find the three or four that contained information on outside life. Every couple of weeks they would be replaced by new ones. I was certain that the Master had no idea of their existence, either because he couldn't be bothered to censor what we were reading or because he actually trusted Beatrix. Although the latter was more likely, it was also quite a strange notion.

I grabbed a large worn book, which, like them all, I had previously read, and slammed it down on my desk. The others were still fighting for space and grabbing what books they could.

I pulled back the green leather cover and flipped to where I had left off, my heart pounding in anticipation. The more I discovered about the world, the more I ached for freedom, while equally my loathing for Him grew.

I had decent reading skills, but for me, the pictures and illustrations held more information than the tiny printed words. I poured over dazzling paintings of cobbled city streets in which masses of gorgeously clad men, women, and children walked or rode in boxes on wheels called 'carriages' sometimes pulled by several horses. I marveled at the density of buildings, which lined the streets, and at how small and rickety they all were compared to our manor. I puzzled over why there were no plants or lawns anywhere to be seen. And I learned about 'money' and how the amount of it people had decided how they lived, whether they were rich or poor.

"Beatrix?" I called, still enveloped in the splendor shown to me on the pages of the book. She jumped, looking around wildly for a moment, before relaxing and coming over to where I sat.

"What is it, Penny?"

This city," I said, jabbing my fingers at a sketch of the skyline. "Do we get to go there when we grow up? Is that why you teach us all these things?"

Everyone's head had slowly lifted at my questions. They had lowered their eyes but no longer scanned the words, as they listened intently for an answer.

"Why the sudden interest?" Beatrix retorted, uncharacteristically sharp. "Last night I would have thought you'd learned your lesson! I only allowed you to read such a book to stop you from asking questions like this, not to educate you about a future home! Have you no common sense?"

To my mortification, I felt tears pool in my eyes. Beatrix never spoke with such abruptness to anyone, ever.

"Then why teach us?" I managed to croak.

Evelyn gave a barely audible squeak, burying her nose in her book again to shield herself from such behavior. Apart from her and Lucas, who was deeply absorbed in his own pages, everyone else had dropped their subtlety and was watching our exchange thoughtfully.

"Would you prefer to know nothing?" Beatrix snapped, a flush winding up her neck.

"Yes," I whispered. "I would rather not know of what could be, if it will never be mine. It's like...like showing a pauper fabulous riches and jewels, and setting them before him only to say that he is never to touch nor spend the fortune, only look. He would rather not have that constant reminder of his poverty."

Out of the corner of my eye, I saw Fred had also, like Evelyn, averted his gaze but Tressa and Avery were nodding to themselves in agreement.

"So be it." Beatrix sighed. Suddenly, she seemed very tired. Though she couldn't have been much over sixty, she appeared a much older woman at that moment. "I shall remove the books from the library."

"No!" we all shouted in unison.

"Please don't, Beatrix, it's the best book there!" I cried.

"Don't do this—" echoed Avery.

"She's not herself after last night—" pleaded Tressa.

"Enough!" Beatrix thumped the desk. "It was due time I hid it away again anyway, since the Master is more suspicious than ever now you have grown older. If He ever discovered you had seen this book, then it would be death to all of us."

With a wave of her hand, more exhausted than ever, there was the tiniest of rips and our beloved books disappeared. We all gasped, staring at Beatrix in shock. Unaware of our reaction, she dismissed us and stumbled out of the library.

We all sat transfixed, staring at my empty desk. Avery, as usual, was the first one to speak.

"Since when did Beatrix have the same abilities as Him?"

We had no answer to that, no comment on the fact that she appeared to have the same power as the Master himself.

5

'Traitor' was a very loose term. I couldn't decide exactly how it applied to Beatrix, but the sting of pain I felt in my chest whenever I reminisced about that afternoon was most definitely the hurt of one betrayed. All this time, she had let Him bully us into submission using the threat of His powers, when she possessed her own! Poor, gentle, overworked Beatrix could have challenged Him when He tortured us and stood up for us, but instead she had cowed away from Him like the powerless servant she had led us to believe she was. It was infuriating.

"I don't see what all the fuss is about," Fred defended her, characteristically, refusing to see the bad in anyone. "Maybe she can only do little things."

"Fred," I confronted him, swinging from my comfortable position in front of the fire to stare him in the eyes. "She made the only blasted decent book we had disappear into thin air."

"Don't swear, Penny!" Tressa reprimanded me sternly.

I stuck out my tongue when she turned away.

It had been five days since that dreadful afternoon. We had all been significantly more distant towards Beatrix during lessons and walking to dinner, though she was so tired lately that she never seemed to notice.

Lessons had become duller and more of a chore than ever now. And without my trust for Beatrix I felt more trapped inside the Boundary than I thought previously possible.

The persistent rain had started again, confining us to the house. With the attic floor forbidden and the lower containing nothing of interest, we had spent most of our time in the common room. Today was no different.

Tressa, Fred, and Avery were half-heartedly matching their wits at cards, whilst Lucas was curled up on the window seat reading. Evelyn was still in our bedchamber mending a bracelet. I stared into the fire. The hissing and flaring of the quietly destructive flames rather reminded me of my thoughts, and perhaps that was why I was drawn to it as my place to brood.

"You know, as much as I hate to admit it, Penny does have a point," Avery piped up. I was too glad of his support to gloat. I tried to catch his eyes, but they were fixated on his hand of cards. "If Beatrix could only do party tricks, then why hide it from us? If there was nothing she could do to protect us, why keep it a secret? You'd have thought it would have been so much simpler to say, 'Oh, I can rip, too, but don't pester me because I can't do anything useful.'"

Tressa cursed under her breath as Fred slapped a card joyously onto the playing table, taking another from their huge deck. "I know, I know. It's hurt me as much as any of you, and don't think I'm not suspicious of why she hid it for so long. Actually, I'm more interested in what was going on in her life which caused such a slip in discretion, but anyway"—she sighed still not looking up from her game—"what can we do? Sulk about it for the rest of our lives?"

"Confront her," I suggested.

"And then what?" Fred said, eyes widening as Avery flashed his hand with a smirk. "I think you're all making a mountain out of a molehill. Poor Beatrix never meant to deceive us like that; she's been so preoccupied that she probably never gave it second thought. Why can't you just leave it alone and continue like normal?"

I clenched my fist as the maddening thought that had been bugging me for five days finally turned into low, emotional words. "What if Beatrix has the power to open the Boundary?"

Silence followed.

Slowly, the three placed down their cards and raised their heads to gape at me. Even Lucas ceased reading for a moment.

"Penny...no one can open the Boundary. I doubt even He can. It's a solid part of our world, not an illusion," Tressa said quietly.

"Why are you so blind?" I uttered bitterly. "Do you want to

stay here forever? Somehow, we got in here and there has to be a way back out again."

"Penny, I…"

I didn't wait to hear whatever pathetic, reasonable excuse Tressa had come up with this time. Instead I got up and ran out of the room, slamming the door behind me for good dramatic measure.

Tearing into the corridor, I began to pace up and down the worn patterned carpet with a fury boiling through my mind. I had expected a shocked response to my suggestion, but had been certain it would be followed by mutual agreement and serious discussion. Instead they had treated me like a blabbering toddler! Especially Tressa, who I had thought to be clear-headed about everything.

Fuming, I ran to the girls' bedchamber.

It was cold. Someone had opened the window and rain pelted though soaking the curtains. A chill wind gusted in, a huge contrast from the toasty common room. Maybe it was also the shadows on the walls, and the candle flames wildly flickering, which caused the room to look so threatening, but whatever the case it stopped me in my tracks.

I shook the feeling off and ran to the shutters to close the window. The pane was icy to the touch, and I shivered. I wiped my damp hands on my frock before pausing, listening. From the corner where Evelyn's bed was, I could hear a muffled sobbing.

"Evelyn?" I called testily. The weeping stopped for a moment, and then continued with renewed sorrow.

"It's me, Penny!" I tried again. When she refused to respond, I went over to her bed and none too gently pulled back the covers.

Evelyn's tears plastered her hair to her porcelain face. Her eyes were wide with terror and her whole body racked with deep sobs.

"Whatever's the matter?"

"I don't know!" she wailed, trying feebly to prop herself up on her elbows. Another bout of her mysterious afflictions claimed her at that moment and Evelyn doubled over with a loud hacking sound, her slender arms wrapped tightly around her middle.

Rocking back and forth like a helpless child who had just experienced a nightmare, I felt all my previous anger melt with sympathy for her, and I bent concernedly down by her bedside to clasp her shaking hand.

"It's all right, Evelyn," I soothed, stroking back her damp curls. "Don't fret, now. It's nothing but...an, er...bout of indigestion. Nothing you should worry about. Takes some deep breaths."

She did as she was told. I squeezed her hand in support, and at last the crying subsided into snuffles and moans of discomfort.

"Oh, Penny!" Evelyn spoke into her pillow as she rolled over on to her stomach. Her voice sounded distorted. "Whatever shall I do? I've suffered from a bad tummy before, but it was nothing like this!"

To be truthful, I wasn't entirely certain how to handle the situation. I wasn't the first person anyone asked for when they were feeling under the weather due to my lack of compassion and patience, also Evelyn did have a habit of blowing things out of proportion. Yet she did look very uncomfortable to say the least, and I wasn't about to go begging Beatrix for help. Not now.

"What are your symptoms?" I inquired hesitantly. Evelyn turned back over with a groan to face me, a sparkle of relief in her eyes now someone had taken control.

"I fear I've contracted some sort of plague," she complained. "My throat is so sore, that it feels like I'm swallowing shards of glass! My nose feels stuffed, my eyes are watering, my ears keep popping, and I feel I'm burning up. I don't suppose you'd be an angel and open the window agai—"

Before she could finish, she sneezed and froze in alarm as mucus began streaming from her nose, which she dabbed away with the bedding. She had my hand in a vice-like hold now, and I had to strain to wrench it free.

"Ouch!" I hissed, rubbing my pinched fingers tenderly. "Right, I'll go and open that window now." Giving one last worried look over my shoulder, I hurried to do her bidding. The shutters had blown open again and a gust of wind whooshed in on cue, instantly raising goose bumps on my arms.

"There," I crooned through chattering teeth. "That's better, hmm?"

"Much, thank you." Evelyn sighed, cringing at her nasally tone. "The rain is such a tranquil noise, it helps calm me down. Oh dear, to merely keep myself from panicking is sapping all my strength! What if I'm dying? Surely this isn't natural?"

Her voice rose, her eyes widening into two pools of horror at the thought.

"Don't be ridiculous!" I said. "Now, you rest here whilst I go and fetch everyone else. No dire thoughts, all right?"

Evelyn nodded meekly. I gave her an encouraging smile on the way out.

Once I'd shut the door, I ran.

I had no idea what was wrong, if anything, but compassionate or not I hated seeing any of my friends in such discomfort. We had read about the terrible maladies that occasionally plagued the outside world, but not in any detail. The worst sickness that ever happened here was a bad stomach after eating too much, so actually having illness in our presence was frightening.

Just as I rounded the corner, my foot caught on a bump in the carpet, sending me sprawling to the ground with an ungainly thud.

I heard scuffles as everyone inside the common room scrambled to see what the commotion was, muffled voices growing louder until the door burst open and a surprised group encircled me.

"Penny, are you all right?" Fred asked, bending down to help me up. I took his offered hand to haul myself off the ground, wobbling a bit and rubbing my knee tenderly.

"Yes, I'm fine, but—"

"I'm sorry about what I said, by the way," Tressa blurted out, taking my hands. "Please don't be angry at me! I was only...I didn't want you to be—"

"It's fine," I interrupted hastily, although it most certainly wasn't. "Look, can we argue another time? It's Evelyn. She's ill."

A collective gasp rippled, and everyone bombarded me with a tide of individually indistinguishable questions about her welfare.

It was Tressa in the end who having enough of talk, broke out of our circle to stride back down the corridor to the girls' bedchamber. We stampeded after her, but only I entered the room as the boys were forbidden.

"Dear me, it's absolutely frigid in here!" Tressa commented, arranging her hair around her lace-covered shoulders for more warmth. "I'll go and shut the window before we all fall sick."

"No!" I stopped her reluctantly. "She wanted it like this. She has a fever."

"Tressa? Have you come to help me?" came a feeble croak.

"Of course! Are you all right?" Tressa cried, jolting back into the situation at hand and hurrying over to the bedside.

Evelyn was as pale and sweaty as before, clutching an old pillowcase to her nose with forlorn sniffling.

"Oh my goodness, why didn't you tell us this morning something was wrong? Lucas might have been able to tell what it was and—"

"I was fine then," she replied quickly. "But my nose started getting stuffy just after luncheon so I decided to rest. But now..." Evelyn hiccupped miserably, wiping tears from underneath wide eyes.

Tressa pulled out the silk ribbon holding her own hair back

and tied Evelyn's locks away from her flushed cheeks.

She turned to me and said sternly, "Tell one of the boys to fetch a dampened cloth from the bathrooms, will you, Penny, and then nip down to the kitchens to ask Beatrix if she has anything that might help."

I folded my arms firmly across my chest. "I'll not talk to Beatrix. And I won't let anyone else, either."

"Penny, you can be so awkward sometimes!" Tressa groaned in exasperation, but I could barely hear her over Evelyn's constant whimpers and coughing. "Fine, just get the towel, but be quick about it. And shut the window, for heaven's sake, we'll keep her cool in other ways!"

I consented, flying to the door. Fred, Avery, and Lucas were crowded about it anxiously, straining to hear what was going on.

"Go and fetch a bowl of cold water and a cloth," I instructed, before anyone could speak. "I'll explain when you get back."

They scooted away, leaving me free to return to Evelyn.

Tressa was murmuring words of comfort to her, only faltering whenever she sneezed, instinctively recoiling. The scene was so tranquil though that I felt bad disrupting it, and decided instead to sit by the now closed window until someone needed me.

It was a shame, really, that Beatrix had chosen to betray us all now. Whenever one of us felt poorly or hurt ourselves before, she would cure us that very same day with her infallible store of medicinal herbs and remedies that stopped any kind of ache or pain.

Now looking back at it, I wondered whether her miraculous talent was due to her powers rather than an adept skill at healing. Where else had she deceived us?

Bitter thoughts mixed in with ones of concern and sympathy for Evelyn, making my head spin as I rested my head against the window frame, the cold grooves biting my skin. But where my mind had wandered off too there was no feeling, no trouble, just a blissful dreamland…

6

I groaned and opened my eyes. The wooden frame had left a deep red imprint all over the left side of my face, and my body ached from sleeping in such an uncomfortable position. The bright light poured in from a faint morning sun shining bravely through the mist, reflecting off the walls with a blinding furor, and causing me to squeeze shut my eyes again to block it out.

Stretching out with a yawn, I uncurled myself and stood up. Then I remembered my dream. Exactly the same one I'd had before. I was Elisabeth having my baby snatched from me.

Tressa stood beside me, hands on her hips and a poisonous expression on her face.

"I'm up, I'm up!" I muttered with another yawn. "You woke me from such a vivid dream..."

"I should think so. You slept on that ledge so soundly that I couldn't wake you for dinner!"

"What?" I gasped in alarm, now fully awake. "Then how come He didn't come right up here and punish me?"

"I told him you were also ill," Tressa said, jutting out her jaw bravely. "Beatrix backed me up."

"Thank you!" I exclaimed in awe, choosing to ignore the last part. It took a lot of nerve to lie directly to the Master, and I suspected the only reason Tressa had gotten away with it was because of – if I had to address her – Beatrix.

"You'd better be," Tressa said grimly. "It took a lot of work from Beatrix, and a lot of guts from me. Anyway, come on down to breakfast. Evelyn only just fell asleep, poor darling; she was tossing and turning all night so I expect she'll be tired today."

I hopped off the ledge and tried to straighten the creases from my skirts, and then made a feeble attempt to pull my fingers through my hair in lieu of a comb, with an equal amount of success.

"I hope she feels better soon," I commented. My ankles creaked in protest as I began to walk – punishment from sleeping in shoes. Never again would I fail to change into my nightgown.

"Yes, so do I. Hopefully it's just a little thing that will pass quickly." Tressa nodded.

I noticed bags under her eyes, signs of her staying up all night by Evelyn's side. Tressa could be very blunt and bossy sometimes, but never could you ever doubt her loyalty to her friends.

We didn't eat anything but dinner in the dining hall, so breakfast and luncheon were always served in the small room that could be accessed on one of the split-levels where a smaller staircase diverged from the grand stairway about halfway down..

The breakfast room itself was more of a cavern dug out of thick brick, with a low arched door opening into a circular turret. One thing I did like were the doors leading to a balcony, which wrapped one side of the turret and overlooked the western Boundary woods.

"Hello, you two," Fred greeted us from inside. The three boys were already sitting munching warm porridge oats sprinkled with brown sugar, eyes flicking over to us briefly in case Evelyn had made a miraculous recovery before turning back to the food.

Tressa and I sat on stools beside them and helped ourselves.

"Lucky escape last night, Penny." Avery smirked, peering at me over the table and egging for a reaction. "Thought you were in for it, snoozing through dinner."

"I was tired," I said shortly, not in the mood for his antics.

"I'll bet, holding a grudge is very exhausting." He nodded wisely. "Even when—"

"What book is that, Lucas?" Tressa asked, deciding with good justification to stop Avery before he went too far. "I thought we weren't supposed to take them out of the library?"

Lucas jumped and shut his book with a start, tucking it under the table guiltily.

"It's only numeracy. I'm sure she won't mind."

"It looks like the weather is starting to perk up," Fred noted conversationally. "Thought it never would!"

"It never *does*," I said bitterly, staring at my porridge with an accusatory frown. "The blasted mist is always hanging over us the whole darn time."

"I beg your pardon?!" Tressa gasped. "Where are your manners? Don't say those words ever, least of all at the table!"

Avery's mouth twitched a little at the edges and he coughed as if to hide a laugh. I hadn't even properly cursed, but to Tressa, there was no difference. Good words, bad words, and nothing in between.

"Oh, I had a dream last night!" I remembered, as if I hadn't heard what Tressa had told me. She ground her teeth in annoyance but remained silent, stewing as she ate her oatmeal.

"Oh?" Fred inquired with a genial curiosity, though no one else seemed at all interested.

"Yeah…it was really strange. The odd thing is, I've had it before. Do you reckon it means anything?"

"Not unless you're living in a novel," Lucas muttered under his breath.

"I had a queer one about the ocean – remember, from one of those books, it's this massive body of salty water? I had a dream that I was doing my numeracy whilst floating along, and you were all…"

I – and I was sure everyone else did too – blanked out as Fred genially launched into a full-blown description of his nonsensical dream with an enthusiastic energy, spurred along by our occasional 'oohs' and 'ahhs'.

I did not grow bored; contrarily, this excuse to sit with my eyes unfocussed and blank at the table gave me a chance to mull over my own dream some more in hopes of fishing out another detail. I wanted to know the story! Having only seen two adults, one of whom hardly seemed human and the other I distrusted too much to even think about, I was very interested in seeing the mysterious characters' faces.

Then Tressa stood up, so suddenly that she knocked over her stool. I removed my elbows from the table and wiped the corners of my mouth, but she wasn't looking at me.

Wordlessly, she excused herself and left the room without second glance.

"Any clue what that was about?" Avery craned his neck to glance behind her.

"None at all." I shrugged, equally puzzled.

A stickler for manners, it was odd she should behave so out of order. Odd enough that I decided to also leave my now lukewarm porridge to chase after her.

The boys followed suit, trampling back up the stairs to the girls' common room. I was a few feet away from the door when I began to hear the muffled cries coming from inside.

White-faced, heart hammering, I burst in. Evelyn must have taken a sudden turn for the worst.

I bumped into Tressa on my way in. Her face was ashen with worry, normally strong features seeming weak and powerless.

"What is it? What's happened?" I gasped, taking her shaking hands in mine. "Is Evelyn all right?"

"I don't know. I had a horrible feeling that something was wrong with her. And I was right." She led me to Evelyn's bedside.

Hardly daring to look, I took in the surroundings.

Evelyn was standing in her flowing white nightgown like some sort of specter. Wild curls tangled in ribbons, tears falling down her pasty cheeks as she explained.

"I couldn't breathe!" she moaned through a very blocked, very red nose. "Then I got so flustered I – I passed out!"

"Oh my goodness!" Tressa bit her nails. "This is awful! She must be very seriously ill for this to happen."

"What can we do?" I clutched at the iron bed frame to keep myself from laughing. Yes, it was serious, no, it hadn't happened before…but that red nose just make me want to giggle, and giggle, and never stop. Was that wrong?

"Get Beatrix," Tressa decided. I did a double take and stopped chuckling to myself.

"What?"

She repeated herself, gaining confidence.

"No!" I refused, leaving no room for negotiation. I was not going to reconcile now, nor ever for that matter. My protest would mean nothing if I went begging for help a mere week after she had betrayed me so.

"Don't be selfish!" Tressa yelled. I took a step back, alarmed by her sudden anger and the tears spilling down her own cheeks. "How will you ever forgive yourself if Evelyn gets worse or even dies because you couldn't conquer your stupid pride? Pull yourself together and think of someone other than yourself for once! It isn't all about you!"

She broke off into a sob, turning away to wipe her eyes. I bit my lip.

"Can't you do it?" I pleaded in one last feeble attempt.

"No," Tressa said, nothing more than a whisper now. "No, I don't want to leave her in case it happens again."

I fought within myself, weighing the options. I hated being the first to surrender, even when the opposition didn't realize there was a battle, but my friends were everything to me. More than that, they were my life.

"Fine," I uttered through my teeth. "For Evelyn, I will."

She blew her nose in gratitude, giving me watery smile

Tressa, on the other hand, didn't sing praises or thank me. She just mutely nodded and adjusted Evelyn's pillows into a more comfortable position

"What's going on?" Fred asked the moment I appeared.

"Don't press me," I growled, in a foul mood. "I have to go ask B— I have to go get something."

"You're going to get Beatrix?" Avery gasped incredulously.

As I thundered down the stairs, I heard him whisper to Lucas, "Bet you the answers to numeracy that only one of them comes out alive!"

The kitchens and staff quarters were located down a steep but small staircase behind the foyer and next to the tunnel leading into the dining hall. They took up most of the lower floor with their stone simplicity, yet I had only visited once or twice for the odd cooking lesson.

I found Beatrix, not working, but dozing in a rocking chair outside the locked kitchen door. A recipe book was lying open in her lap, and I wondered for a moment whether she had accidentally locked herself out. My face hardened as I remembered her abilities. She could unlock any door.

"Beatrix," I said, as tonelessly as I could.

She started and looked around wildly, slamming her book shut.

"Oh, Penny, it's only you! I thought you were... Never mind. What is it, dear?"

I took a deep breath, stopping myself from spilling into a full-blown rant of hurt and betrayal. I wanted dearly to see her crumble with the same pain she had showered over me. But at the same time, I wanted her to present me with an explanation that would solve the whole thing and bring me back the Beatrix I had known and loved for fifteen years. Instead, I managed to keep my head and stay with the matter at hand.

"Evelyn is not well," I explained. "She has a blocked nose and can barely breathe, and then just a few minutes ago passed out."

Beatrix's eyes widened. After a moment's thought, she seemed to have reached a conclusion and uttered a small laugh. "I suppose you haven't had any experience with colds before, have you? I only wonder..."

Her voice trailed off so that I couldn't quite catch the ending, but I was pretty sure it was along the lines of "who brought it in?"

7

"So you're saying it's not actually fatal or anything? She's just got something common?" Tressa probed when I returned to the bedchamber, hardly daring to believe it.

"How am I supposed to know? Beatrix just seemed very relaxed about it, so I'm guessing that Evelyn has come down with some perfectly ordinary...thing. Unless she wants us to all die," I added on afterthought. Tressa shot me a withering look and took to fiddling with her petticoats impatiently.

We were both perched on the edge of my bed, waiting for Beatrix to emerge from the washing room with Evelyn. It was tedious waiting, but our situation was certainly more bearable than what the boys had to endure, crowded outside our chamber door with no clue as to what was going on at all.

"Honestly, I think you're overreacting to the whole thing." Tressa sighed, shifting into a better position. I rolled my eyes; here we went again. I decided to enforce my point once again before getting the lecture for the millionth time.

"Before you plead her innocence to me—"

Yet I too was interrupted mid-speech. Beatrix appeared from behind a door, arm around Evelyn, who seemed pale and slightly fragile but with a less angry red nose and quieter breathing.

She had changed into a loose-fitting gown and had swapped her terrified grimace for an uncertain, sheepish half-smile.

Tressa leapt up and threw her arms around her. Evelyn stumbled back, but patted her shoulders saying, 'It's all right, now, I'm fine! Dear Beatrix has explained everything to me and I'm perfectly fine. I might of...erm...overreacted."

Dear Beatrix. Someone fetch me a bucket.

I gave Evelyn a wan smile when she looked my way, but did not embrace her. Instead, I led the way out into the hallway where Avery, Fred, and Lucas were waiting as they had been for the past few hours.

They had fetched their cards and were having a slow-paced game. When they saw me, they jumped to their feet.

"So is she all right?"

"I'm pretty sure, she is." I waved my hand vaguely. "She'll be out in a second, and then you can ask her for yourselves."

Sure enough, within a moment, Beatrix, Tressa, and Evelyn appeared.

"What was wrong?" Lucas asked, refusing to join me in my campaign to all but ignore Beatrix's existence. Clearly, he shared Tressa's view that I was being childish.

"Evelyn has merely contracted a little bug that is quite common in many places, but has never made its way here," Beatrix explained in her soft, patient, *likeable* voice. "She has a cold. Nothing dangerous whatsoever."

Avery snorted. It was so typical of her to panic everyone like this, but still, relief was evident.

"How did it get in?" Lucas inquired, echoing her earlier musings.

"I'm afraid I don't know."

"Oh, great. Another mystery. It was getting so very boring with all this consistency," I said, under my breath.

Beatrix frowned, not understanding.

I shut my mouth, instantly regretting the words and wishing I could take them back.

"I – I don't understand, Penny. What do you mean?" She surveyed the others to try to find some sense from what I was saying.

I folded my arms, face stony.

"She's been furious with you for the past week or so," Avery enlightened her, smirking at my murderous glare.

"Why ever is that? You never told me something was wrong?" Beatrix approached me anxiously. I debated spilling my accumulated anger right there and then but decided against it, pursing my lips instead.

"To tell you the truth, we all felt rather put out by what you did," Tressa explained, as collected and rational as ever. My face flushed a deep red, the same shade as my hair, loathing at how immature I came across in comparison. "Remember that one lesson where you removed all the special books because of Penny's questions? You – well, made them disappear into thin air. Like He does."

The silence that followed was so heavy it was almost suffocating. If a bobby pin from my hair was to have dropped to the carpet, it would have been deafening.

Her eyes widened, as if she'd completely forgotten about it. As if she was waiting for something, anything, to appear and undo what she had done. She bowed her head.

"I see. You'd better come with me."

*

The mug was painfully warm. I adjusted it in my hands, thinking in the back of my mind that I should probably place it down on a side table until the cocoa inside was cool enough to drink. If I did that, though, I would break the eerie stillness that had settled. We were in the breakfast room again, sitting on our stools waiting whilst Beatrix composed herself outside on the balcony. We made no eye contact, no attempt at conversation, nor jokes. I had no idea what Beatrix was planning to reveal, only that it must take lot of courage to admit, as she had been sitting with her head in her hands outside for quite some time. My heart was still cold where she was concerned, but the promise of truth rivalled all petty emotions.

The only person who moved was Evelyn, coughing once in a while to remind us that she was sick, in case we'd dared to forget.

Beatrix came in after a few more minutes. She sat down.

"You are all very, very clever. Wise beyond your years in many ways," she began, her voice thick with emotion. "And yet, there are so many things that you do not know which others of your age must live with. This being said, with what you have, you are extremely observant, and you've picked up details which I hoped to hide from you for a good many more years."

Beatrix waited for us to comment, but we said nothing, frozen in anticipation. My attention was on her one hundred percent, a feeling of subdued triumph that she was finally owning up. Part of me wanted to point out that observational skills had nothing to do with it, since even the dullest person would've seen a trick such as the one she'd betrayed, but I forced my mouth shut.

"I wasn't thinking that day. It pains me greatly to see any of you punished in such a fashion, and Penny, sweetheart, I am sincerely sorry that I couldn't stop what happened to you that night, and how I sharply spoke to you the next day. It was insensitive of me."

I didn't tell her it was all right, or even smile. I didn't want an apology. What was done, was done. I wanted information.

"You all saw me make the books disappear. I can imagine how shocking that would have been for you! Having always assumed me completely ordinary, I understand why you chose to take deep offence that I hadn't explained myself earlier. But let me make a few things clear..." She took a deep breath and we all leaned forward. "I am by no means anywhere close to having the same power as Madon. I can only do things that involve the upkeep of the estate such as cleaning, and preparing food."

A little spark of hope flickered and died as Beatrix spoke those words. She couldn't open the Boundary.

Her voice was clearer, more assured now, and the nervous crisscrossing and uncrossing of her legs had stopped as she continued. "I just want you all to know that I'm sorry. I love you all so dearly, as if you were my own children, and I never wanted to hurt any of you."

With that, Beatrix's voice faltered and a single tear leaked out of the corner of her wrinkled eye. I had a peculiar feeling that she was apologizing for slightly more than a lapse in cover and the removal of some books, and I was anxious to find out exactly what else she'd kept from us.

"So…how *can* you do those things? Why can't we?" I asked, admittedly half won over by her tears.

"That's not something I can say, I'm afraid."

"Beatrix?"

"Yes, Penny?" She sighed, waiting for another unanswerable question.

"Who looked after us before you?"

It was a simple enough query, but Beatrix looked as if I'd asked permission for murder. "How many times do I have to tell you? If Madon ever hears you saying such things, he'll punish you past sanity!"

"But he isn't here."

"I wouldn't mind knowing," Avery offered, to nods from the others. "I mean, we must have had proper parents at some point."

"I don't know!" Beatrix said, her voice rising, her frustration evident. She took a deep breath before continuing. "I really don't know. I was asked to care for you, and so I did, as though you were my own children. You'd be surprised by how little I actually know compared to the Master, and so you'd all be better off not risking your skins by asking."

"Did you ever have children of your own?" Tressa asked quietly, sensing something behind her tortured tone that I hadn't picked up on.

Beatrix lowered her head, her hands starting to shake again.

"Yes," she whispered, barely intelligible. "Once, a long time ago, I had a son. I had him before I was married, when I was only eighteen, and so customs meant I had to give him up to be raised by another family."

"How tragic!" Evelyn gushed, and I could see a romantic story forming its way into her mind with a young Beatrix, handsome stranger, and illegitimate son struggling to stay together in the mysterious realm beyond the Boundary.

"It was. By the time I managed to track him down again to introduce myself, it was too late. He was all grown up. Sometimes I wonder if I had made more of an attempt to fix the situation, how different my life – all of our lives – would be today."

There was an odd little thought working its way into my churning brain. It couldn't possibly be correct, and yet it gave me the chills every time I mulled it over as if I had stumbled onto a very important morsel of information. A quick glance at my friends and their identical masks of pity confirmed that I was the only one with the notion, but it didn't eliminate my idea.

Could it possibly be?

Beatrix got up and hugged each one of us in turn, murmuring apologies in our ears. When she reached me last of all, she breathed, "I hope we can once again be friends, Penny. I never meant to upset you."

Her soft cheek was wet with uncontained sadness as it brushed my own, but she was gone too soon for me to voice my question. I decided I would follow her. I had to know. So, as everyone solemnly discussed the turn of events and sipped at their hot chocolate, I excused myself and slipped after Beatrix.

Down the grand staircase, and down the narrow passage leading to the kitchens. I followed her like a shadow as she unlocked the door to her retirement quarters without touching anything. Only when she flopped, exhausted, onto her armchair did I make my presence known.

"Beatrix?"

"Penny?"

"Your son," I said, deciding to be direct. "What was his name?"

Her reaction was immediate. Recoiling as if I'd slapped her, jaw hanging in surprise, and lips moving wordlessly to try and find a decent response to my question. Eventually she just went still and stared at me. She knew I already had the answer, but to say it might have unimaginable consequences for us both. Certain she'd never admit it, but confident I had enough evidence, I turned to leave, just as she spoke.

"You don't – I can't – he'll never..." A rattling sigh came somewhere between defeated and determined, then, "Madon. His name was Madon."

8

Something in the air shifted then, just like a rip. I'd suspected it, of course, but hearing it admitted out loud was absolutely shocking. Never in a thousand years would such a notion have entered my mind before today, and I was still having a hard time processing what it meant. Beatrix just sat there trembling, emitting a feeling of dread so intense that it almost scared me into not asking more questions. If I'd been smarter, maybe I should have left it there. As it was, finally managing to crack a massive secret like this one only inspired me to push on.

"I can't believe I just— He said that if I ever…I promised on my life that I'd—" She struggled to string her sentences together, trailing off into a senseless gabble as the finality of what she'd done came crashing down. "Penny…"

"But…if He…" I just shook my head, equally stunned out of speech.

"He's going to murder us both for this, mark my words." Beatrix spoke faintly, trying and failing to stand. "Whatever you do, don't tell the others. We can't have them in danger too."

I collapsed into the chair opposite her. "You're His mother…" I stuttered, not really listening. The whole room seemed to be spinning around me, pieces of furniture a blur of subdued color with no form or purpose. Maybe I was dreaming, hallucinating, sick… "B-But how come? He's not human…you're His *servant*…"

"Oh, Madon is human all right," Beatrix corrected grimly, stronger now. Only her shaking hands betrayed the fear. "Only one of a very different kind."

"Why do you put up with Him?" I interrogated. "I thought mothers were in charge of their children, not the other way around?"

"When I saw him again"—Beatrix clearly docked the capital H, saying 'him' in a less reverential way—"he was an adult, with his priorities already decided and motives for the future set in stone. My early life hadn't been at all easy, and I was in desperate need of a purpose, so to speak. He was my son; I loved him, felt guilty about abandoning him and could never go against him. He took advantage of that I suppose, and I agreed to help him."

"What plans?" I probed with a new eagerness softening the alarm of the revelation.

"I can't say," she said with absolute certainty. "I've told you too much already, and I swore on my life that I would never divulge what happened outside of this estate. It is better you do not know anyway."

I picked myself up off the chair, not entirely trusting my knees for support. My head felt heavy and overloaded with information to the point I visualized secrets pouring from my ears, and I almost wished that they would. How I would ever be able to face my friends again with an honest face?

"Why don't you try to stop Him? You have power, and I could help you!" I implored desperately. "Together, with the others, we could overrule Him and pull down the Boundary!"

Beatrix shook her head in a defeated manner, as if she had given up long ago. I had to admit, she didn't appear a fighter.

"On this land, Madon is invincible. There is nothing that can be done, and even if there was I would not wish for it. You are young and naive, Penny, and you assume that real life is a fairy tale when it is far from that. Maybe I didn't stop him when I had the chance because I believed that you would all be safer here, sheltered from the perils of the true world."

"He tortures us!" I shouted, not standing for her defense of Him.

"I know."

There was a deep, infinite sorrow in her voice that brought tears to my own eyes, as I croaked, "But there has to be a way! Like you said, He is human."

The grandfather clock on her mantelpiece chimed rhythmically, signaling with its inanimate punctuality the impending start of lessons before luncheon. Today, I guessed, our strict schedule might be a little bit off.

I was closer than I had ever been to cracking the shell of unspeakable truths surrounding our estate, and for the first time getting out seemed like it was a feat that could actually happen. I was agonizingly close, to the point I could nearly taste my first gasp of freedom.

All I needed now was the others, primarily Beatrix, to help me. She pulled herself to her feet and was trying to fix her disheveled appearance, scooping her hair back into a neater bun and retying her apron a bit tighter. She was breathing quickly, and I could see a fierce determination slowly come to life in her weary eyes.

"There is one way," Beatrix voiced, more to the cluttered wall than to me. "But the outcome is not certain. It may end up harming you more than the Master."

I could have screamed for joy! I rocked on the balls of my feet, hardly daring to believe what was unfolding.

"Anything!" I gasped.

She raised an eyebrow.

"Remember, Penny, this is not something to be taken lightly. In accepting what I am about to give, you are jeopardizing not only your life, but all your friends lives too."

"Absolutely," I repeated with complete decisiveness.

I didn't hesitate nor pause to think of the consequences my brash choice might have on myself and my friends, only that I might finally be able to score a point in a game I had long believed to be lost. If I hesitated now, I'd regret it for the rest of my life; better to die knowing I tried, than live knowing I didn't.

Beatrix exhaled with deliberate heaviness, expelling all fears.

"Whatever happens next is meant to be," she muttered to herself. "It is out of my hands now."

She was still mumbling to herself as she turned and rummaged through a drawer, which at first glance contained nothing more than a packet of matches and many stacks of fresh paper. She found something and slammed the drawer shut, pausing for a few moments to stare at whatever she'd fished out. I craned forwards to see what exactly it was.

"Take and protect it," Beatrix instructed me. She took my hands in hers, and I felt a dull weight as she placed something in my palms.

I opened them up, and my eyes widened in surprise. She has given me a key, of all things, a massive black iron one with queerly shaped teeth jutting out at all angles along its heavy, rough stem. It was neither delicate nor intricate as one might have expected; in fact, it was lumpy, dull, and the length of my hand.

"What does it open?" I managed to utter. I wasn't sure what I had expected, maybe an enchanted sword, or a mixture that would give me powers, but an unimpressive key was definitely quite far down my list.

"The upstairs door," Beatrix answered with a sideways smile.

"There's only one locked door and that's to the upper floor? What's inside it? Why do you have the key? Why are you giving it to me?" I ranted, trying to get a hold of the situation. I felt as though something was missing.

"So many questions!" Beatrix shook her head, the smile still on her lips. "There is only one locked door and I'm in possession of the key because it is part of my duty as the keeper of this manor to account for it, and I'm giving it to you because you wanted a way to get across the Boundary and I'm done with seeing children held here against their will. As for what it unlocks and why, that is a blank you will have to fill in for yourself. If you are certain that you are prepared for what it will unleash."

I turned the thing over and over in my hand, thinking about her warning. I was at the point where I was willing to do absolutely anything to bring down the controlling world in which I had squandered my childhood, but the only thing keeping me from running straight upstairs was the effect it might have on my friends. They were not as obsessed with freedom as I was, and possibly were not prepared to pay as high a price.

If I told them the truth right away, then they would demand to know why Beatrix had given it to me and I felt it was not my secret to tell. Tressa would try to stop me, and knowing her, would succeed. I couldn't put them in danger though, so I was going to have to make a choice on their behalf. I needed to plan.

I glanced up at Beatrix. She was fiddling with some ornaments on her mantelpiece, moving a candleholder back and forth as if to get it precisely in the center.

I glanced down at the ugly key.

I thanked her in a hushed voice, and turned to leave.

I wasn't sure if she heard me or not, but as I stood in the servants corridor outside puzzling over where to put the key, I noticed the skirts of my gown had magically sprouted deep pockets that were perfectly sized to hide a specific iron key.

*

I felt like a criminal as I scurried back upstairs to meet with my friends again. The pockets were buried amongst the folds of my dress in such a way that no awkward bulges were visible to onlookers, but the key's heavy presence next to my legs was a constant reminder of what I was hiding, and what I was about to do.

The identity of Beatrix's son also added guilt to my conscience, and I had to avert my attention elsewhere when Tressa and Evelyn began to gush about her romantic past. Despite my unusual skittishness, they did not question me. I once caught Lucas throwing me a curious sideways glance, but apart from that all was as normal.

During lessons, Beatrix acted with an impressively

nonchalant attitude, which gave nothing of her conversation with me away, acting towards me as if nothing had happened.

But no one could miss my extreme nervousness when the time for dinner arrived.

"Dear goodness, Penny, you seem rather agitated. Is anything the matter?" Tressa asked me concernedly. We were in our chamber changing into our uncomfortable dinner gowns (like my day dress, mine also now had pockets, for which I credited Beatrix) and prepping our hair into styled plaits.

"Nothing at all!" I lied in a falsely cheery tone. "I'm just contemplating what Beatrix told us today, and how much better this will make everything now she's back on our side."

Evelyn held up two similar necklaces in front of her mirror indecisively, commenting, "Actually, it wasn't as much of a revelation as I had hoped for. She only confirmed what was to be expected and made amends, but apart for that, nothing has changed. Though it is awfully romantic, isn't it, about losing her son and eventually her lover for the sake of society?"

"Romantic? It's diabolical! What kind of a world would separate a family because they weren't married?" Tressa scoffed in disgust as she finished tying her own corset and stepped elegantly into the petticoats of her gown. "I'm not so sure I would want such restrictions."

Normally, I would have made some irritated comment about how restricted our life was now and how it couldn't get any worse, but instead I just kept out of their conversation and stared at my hands. They were coated in a fine black dust from the textured surface of the key. Hastily, checking over my shoulder with an expression of pure guilt etched on my brow, I scurried to a filled basin and tried to scrub them clean as discretely as possible.

"Do you need a hand tying your corset, Penny?" Tressa called.

My face burned, but I mentally reminded myself that I had done nothing wrong. Yet.

"Er, no thanks," I refused brightly, scrubbing so hard that my hands began to sting.

The water turned a dirty grey and I winced, praying that no one would notice until it was switched over.

"Hurry up, then! We'll be late!"

After scrambling into a new dress and quickly clipping in some dainty golden hoop earrings, I went with the girls down into the foyer. The key banged against my leg as I moved, stoutly refusing to let me forget its presence.

Dinner was, I supposed, one of the most relaxed and less tensional sessions we had had for quite some time, with everyone chatting merrily with Beatrix as though the episode before had never happened. It was as though a heaviness had been lifted from all our shoulders; only mine had been replaced by an even darker one.

I ate because I wanted to keep face, though I wasn't at all hungry. The normally succulent pork chops tasted dry and flavorless, scratching my throat uncomfortably on the way down, and the routine toffee pudding was too sickly with an odd texture.

Naturally, it was only my paranoid mind playing tricks on me as I debated, over and over again, whether I should use the key or not.

The Master was watching me. The entire mealtime, I felt his piercing eyes turned in my direction, though I never once caught him staring when I sneaked a peak.

When the ordeal was over, I was the first to jump out of my chair to leave.

Then I felt the hair on the back of my neck prickle, and whirled around in shock. He was right behind me, dashing in His tailored suit but terrifying in His menacing aura. Though I tried to bow my head and appear humble, I surprised myself by wondering in what ways He looked like Beatrix and concluding in no ways at all.

For a while, we stood facing each other as if sizing the other up, then He spoke.

"Watch yourself, Penny."

And then, He was gone.

9

"It's sunny! Finally!" Tressa sang as she threw open the curtains one morning. I would have thought 'moderately not-miserable' would have been a better description, but who was I to be the estate pessimist?

"Hurray!" I cheered bleakly. "It was starting to get my spirits down."

It had been nearly three days since Beatrix had handed over the key, and still I had done absolutely nothing with it more than peer curiously up at the north wing, which contained the door to the mysterious, forbidden upper floor. Admittedly, I had been rather shaken by the ominous warning from Him as I had no doubt He knew something was going on. I had no intention of being punished again anytime soon, yet if He so much as suspected that I had deliberately disobeyed a rule, let alone knowing about his mother...

"I can tell," Evelyn observed from her vanity dresser, applying powder to her naturally porcelain skin in attempt to cover her nose, which still shone a sore red, "you haven't been yourself lately. Perhaps you are coming down with a cold —"

"Enough!" I shuddered. I hated the mere thought of a cold! "I've just been a bit prone to daydreams lately, since with so little do to I haven't got anything more interesting to occupy my mind."

"How about we just be glad for the weather, hmm?" Tressa suggested, sweetly stabbing me a 'stop-being-so-darn-miserable' glance. "Let's get changed for breakfast and go ask the boys what they want to do with all this glorious sunshine!"

I changed out of my nightgown, clambered into a brand new day dress, combed through my hair, buckled my shoes neatly over my stockings, and sneakily removed the key from its temporary hiding place under the bed into my pocket.

To be perfectly honest, I was considering returning the

ghastly object to Beatrix and ending my whole dilemma for good, as neither a decent opportunity nor stroke of courage had presented itself to me.

I decided, as I doused my face with cold water, that either I would take initiative to act today, or I would give up completely. Tomorrow at this time, one or the other will have happened. It'd better be the former.

Breakfast was buttered toast with fresh berry jam.

"Have any of you ever wondered where our food comes from?" Lucas mused through a mouthful of toast.

"Nope." Avery shook his head a little too much, sending bits of chewed bread spraying at Evelyn, who squeaked in horror.

"I read last ni— I mean, a while ago, I read that our meat...well it comes from animals. Yet, we have no animals. It must come from somewhere, but where?"

"Don't be ridiculous!" Avery scoffed. "Meat is magically produced...He makes it appear."

"There are no wheat fields either, for our bread," Lucas argued, stung by being so blatantly mocked. "Or orchards for our fruit, or factories for our furniture, or anything of the sort! Everything must come from outside, including our meat. I mean, where else would chicken come from, but from actual animals? I've never read anything about it being magically made."

I was astounded. Lucas was beginning to question the outside world – that there must be a way in and out of the estate. I wasn't alone in this. Now that he had confirmed my own thoughts, my remaining doubts lifted.

Avery shook his head, refusing to back down. "Look, Lucas, you can't trust everything in those books. Some of them *are* stories you know, and anyway, no one leaves the state. No one can! Nothing comes in or out."

"So you're trying to tell me that no food is real, it's all magical. It's not grown by someone or the animals reared and killed for meat!" Lucas snapped in irritation. "Food can be transported magically from the kitchen, but how does it get into the kitchen? It's always there, and increases and decreases weekly. If it were magical, why just make it appear at the table on the spot? And why would the textbooks lie? So stop ignoring the fact—"

"Where did you get such a reference book anyway?" Avery interrupted, cocking an eyebrow. "I've never seen—"

"Does every morning have to start with bickering?" Tressa said, forcefully pushing her voice over the top of Avery's drawling arguments before it all got out of hand. "How about we make a plan for the day instead? It's so lovely and warm now. Cricket maybe? Or perhaps croquet?"

It sounded ideal, and I was about to consider the plan when another idea occurred to me. Finally, I might have the timing I needed.

"Or hide and seek?" I suggested slowly, playing absently with the antique butter knife between my jammy fingers.

Fred nodded consentingly as he helped himself to a fifth slice, but the other four wore identical expressions of reluctance. We weren't children anymore, and they weren't enthusiastic about such games now, but I was hoping to make it into something a bit bigger than hide-and-seek.

"We can hide in the gardens now, instead of just the manor," I prompted. "Come on; stop growing up for a moment!"

"Penny, it's just that…well…" Tressa looked to the others for support. "It's become slightly boring with you winning every single time, and although it is wonderful you have talent, the rest of us are beginning to question the point. It's getting rather tiresome."

I kept my eyes on the scarred tabletop and crisp purple-splattered napkin on my lap as I volunteered, "I can seek."

There was quiet, then a splat as a piece of drenched toast missed Avery's gaping mouth and landed face-down on the tiled floor.

"A-are you sure?" Tressa asked, not sure she'd heard right.

"You've never done it before, since you insisted you hated seeking more than anything."

"I can try new things!" I insisted, my heart beginning to thud with possibility. "What harm is there in that? Only, don't judge me if I take forever to find you all!"

For good theatrical measure, I threw in a silvery laugh and silently congratulated myself on arranging a scenario in which I would not only have the estate to myself, but could take as long as I needed and blame it on poor seeking skills.

"Well, in that case, I don't see why not. We have no lessons scheduled today, so we should have plenty of time to play hide and seek as well as another game afterwards," Tressa agreed, albeit unenthusiastically, surveying the others for objections. There were none, and with a slight edge of disappointment, she nodded at me.

The key was a magnet gluing me to my chair with the realization that this would be it. Today I would open the forbidden door upstairs and perhaps forever change my fate, and that of everyone else living in the manor too. If we were ever to escape our imprisonment, I had to. Someone had to. But by not involving them directly, I risked only myself.

Beatrix must have given the key to me for a reason, when she could have given it to another of my friends. But perhaps she thought they were too weak to act. She must have wanted me to act. She needed to escape too. The Master must be keeping us imprisoned on the estate for a reason but I wasn't sure I wanted to find out what that was. So perhaps I should leave well alone. Perhaps this was the best life had to offer. Perhaps I had this all wrong.

My dream suddenly popped into my head like a vision. Elisabeth desperately holding onto her baby. No, I convinced myself, fighting the doubts that crept in. I had made my decision, and no amount of 'perhaps' should change my mind.

*

"Remember, give us a good five minutes before you come looking," Tressa instructed, clearly regretting her decision to play. "But then, we all know the rules by now."

Don't question what you are told. Don't attempt to cross the Boundary. Don't open the upstairs door. Sure, I knew the rules. Not the ones for hide-and-seek, but the rules set down by the Master. I was preparing to break all of them: starting with the first, now the last.

We were standing in a huddle in the foyer, our mood twisted between light-heartedness and reluctance. Most of them had gotten into the spirit, eyes flickering about to try and remember where the best hiding places were, so that the only person visibly unimpressed was Evelyn, who stood a little to the side of our group with her arms folded resolutely across her chest, completely lost now that I was not able to find a place for her.

"Do try to find us all before luncheon, won't you?" Fred reminded me with a wink. "I hate missing a meal."

Avery gave a loud cough, which sounded suspiciously like, *"Pig!"* followed by another, which clearly covered up a snigger.

Automatically my arm ached to throw a punch into his superior little face, but I squashed the urge. I needed to get going as soon as possible.

"You're first, Avery," I whispered instead, flashing him a smile of all teeth and no warmth.

He shot me a nasty side-glance, sticking out his tongue, but I knew that deep down he enjoyed the extra challenge.

"Right then, everyone! Countdown begins!" Tressa called.

As the other five scattered in all directions, I obediently sat in the armchair by the staircase and buried my face in its velvet plush surface.

I waited for the customary five minutes until all their footsteps had pounded away into the distance before slowly raising my head. I took in a long draught of steadying air, and then my hand involuntarily moved to caress the iron key in my pocket. Finally, it was time.

I did a quick scan of the area to make certain I was alone, and then began one of the longest walks I had ever been on.

My feet seemed to clunk heavily down upon the marble and echo loudly for all to hear, my breathing a deafening racket announcing my location to every inhabitant of the manor. Or so it seemed. Really, I took utmost care to tiptoe silently up the grand staircase so not to alert the others of my presence.

I didn't see anyone as I padded along the second floor. The estate was massive and there were an awful lot of places to hide, most of the best ones outside or on the first floor, as many of the rooms on this floor were exclusive only to one gender.

To keep my nerves intact, I charged my overactive imagination to wonder about what sort of thing could possibly be hidden upstairs. It must be terribly important for it to take up the entire level and warrant such importance, but from what Beatrix told me it was also very dangerous. Perfect.

I took my time walking down the long corridor, past several brightly lit rooms to the darkened north wing. The candles grew steadily dimmer and spaced further apart as I approached the staircases, plunging me into near darkness though it was the middle of the day.

Seized by a sudden trepidation, I reached up to pluck one of the waxy sticks from its cove in the wallpaper for a source of light that I could take with me as I edged closer to my forbidden destination. The faintly dancing flame and its homely smell put me a little more at ease, though it only illuminated a mere few feet in front of me.

"Gosh..." A dazed whisper escaped my dry lips. Appearing abruptly in front of me was a tiny arched door perhaps four feet tall and crafted out of a thick, dark wood with black metal hinges. *Do not open the upstairs door, under any circumstances...*

I set the candle down by my feet with a shaking hand, fumbling in my pockets for the key. That was when I realized that the door had no lock on it. Swallowing the growing lump in my throat, I steadied my hand enough to take hold of the rusted iron handle (made of iron the same as the key) and pull. It was a little stiff and took quite an effort to loosen the hinges and pull it open, enough so that I stumbled backwards once it swung clear.

Tentatively, I bent over to peer into the darkness, holding my candle out in front of me. There was another staircase, as steep as the one leading down to Beatrix's quarters yet as finely carved as the grand one in the foyer, with thick oaken banisters leading upwards to oblivion. I was instantly glad of my trusty candle, though, as there was no light whatsoever.

"You can do this, Penny," I told myself sternly. "You have to do this."

With one last longing look over my shoulder, one last fleeting thought of simply playing hide and seek, I plunged into the tunnel and began the ascent of the creaking, unused wooden steps towards an unknown destination. Adrenaline coursed through my veins as I bordered on hyperventilation.

One step away from the top, a sudden draught extinguished my light. I cursed and debated turning back for a new one. The only issue with that was I wasn't certain I would be able to gather the bravery to come all the way back up!

Blindly, attempting to force my eyes to adjust to the dark, I found myself wobbling on a small landing area facing a huge...wall?

I squinted to try to make some sense of the scene, but even as I started to make out faded shapes in the blackness, the simple papered object in front of me retained its shape as a perfectly ordinary wall. No door in sight, no other passageway. Just a wall.

Disconcerted and dizzy in the murky light, I threw my arms out in front of me so I didn't hit anything as I approached the wall, then proceeded to run my hands over its smooth surface for any hints of extraordinariness. I hit the jackpot when I felt a cold brass plate under my palms, a plate with a peculiar hole in it that was roughly the same size as the teeth on my key.

I fumbled in my pocket for the key, nervousness making me lose hold f it. I struggled to put it into the keyhole.

It fitted.

I turned it.

I pushed open the artfully camouflaged door with my entire body and fell over a raised threshold into a huge room where out of the corner of my eye, something was glowing. For a moment, the light blinded me. Then my eyes adjusted and the iron key dropped out of my limp hands to clatter noisily on the floor.

I did not flinch. I was too busy trying to comprehend the fantastical thing standing in the large room opposite me.

It was made out of nothing I had ever seen, two gigantic silver rings interlaid with each other to form a sort of hollow sphere bathed in an ethereal glow. Each ring was at least two yards in diameter and yet only as thick as my forearm in its widest place (the thickness fluctuated around the circle), mounted firmly on something made with a million indescribable wires, all attached to an object that I could only say looked like an opaque window. Out from under the rings, there was a brass lever, which seemed much out of place amidst all the jumble of such incredible...things.

What on earth...?

I wandered over to the machine in a daze. I had that odd displaced feeling, when you feel as though you are in a dream and minutes away from waking up to the real world. Maybe I had fallen asleep in the armchair as I counted down from five minutes.

My hand hovered over the lever, eyes still turned to the strange window in overt confusion. Had I really crossed the length of the enormous room in a few blinks? I shook my head as if that would help me get a grip on reality.

The rings were emitting a strange buzzing that was extremely close to what a rip felt like, the static I had experienced during my dream and near the Boundary. They were all connected in some manner, they had to be!

My fist closed around the cold, cold handle of the lever.

Before I could pull it, a sudden bout of terror seized me and for a moment I couldn't move, transfixed with an otherworldly panic which paralyzed my entire body. Without thinking, I wrenched my hand from the bizarre machine and sprinted away as fast as I could, grabbing the key and slamming the door. Tears coursed down my cheeks and great sobs wracked my body.

Whatever was in that room, whatever made me turn back, I didn't know. As I cried with a passion in that dark wing, all the excitement of my discovery drained away and replaced by a consuming black hole of dread. Something was very, very wrong.

10

It took me a good ten minutes to control myself again. The feeling was similar to the effects of a punishment, but this time I was all alone and could tell nobody what was wrong, having forfeited all sympathy I might have been entitled to by lying.

I lay on the floor curled into a ball, tucked my chin into my chest, and wrapped my hands tightly around my head to try to calm my emotions. If I had felt overwhelmed when I had talked to Beatrix a few days ago, there were no words to describe what I was feeling now. Such a horrible, desolate emptiness...

With a choking gasp, I straightened out. I needed to pull myself together. Breaking down would accomplish nothing.

Slowly, I felt the distress drain away. The black hole, however, taking the form of a pit in my stomach stayed very much active.

I got up and dragged myself away from the area in such a fashion that an onlooker might have thought I weighed as much as the iron key.

As I put a good distance between the northern wing and myself, normalcy returned and my head cleared so I could properly mull over what I had experienced without distracting bouts of hysteria.

I would need to revisit the room again, that much was certain. The prospect terrified me, but I theorized that the terrible dread I had felt, that made me run from the room and collapse, could be emanating from the machine itself; what other explanation was there for how quickly it diminished. Perhaps the fear of the pulling the lever was something magical put there as a deterrent? The Master delighted in playing mind games with us, so it would make sense that whatever weapon was concealed upstairs should be protected with such a guard, designed to prevent intruders from staying long enough to cause damage.

However, I was tired from the little adventure and certainly not in the mood for a psychological battle.

"Here I come, ready or not!" I called, cupping my hands around my mouth and speaking with gathered enthusiasm. My voice bounced across the walls, spreading through the manor in a taunting echo, which would surely reach everyone hiding inside.

I tucked the key in my pocket, hitched up my skirts, and ran as fast as my bodice would allow to the grand foyer.

True, I hated seeking, but it was an excellent way to avert my thoughts what had just happened and pour all my condensed emotions into an act of playfulness rather than ponder on such a serious matter.

"I'm going to find you all!" I screeched in an imitation of a scary voice. I did a quick search of all the obvious places such as behind the drapes, behind furniture the common room, and nooks to no avail, so I decided to try the breakfast room.

I bent down on my hands and knees to check under the table. No. It was funny, barely a week ago we had sat in this room and worried about Evelyn's sickness and strange dreams minutes before I had learned the truth about – dare I think it? – Madon, Beatrix, and the machine locked away by a key.

No, I wouldn't think about it now. I was going to have a perfectly normal day before attempting a revolution again, which meant focusing entirely on finding my elusive friends.

I tried not to think about the wires, rings, and strange windows in the attic. Not until I was prepared to try again.

I threw open the French doors leading to the balcony, welcoming the fresh midmorning air with loving arms. After a few deep inhalations, I stepped out onto the area embracing the turret and leaned against the twisted metal banister to get a good look at the lawns.

No one was amongst the rhododendron bushes at the foot of the manor, nor were they crouched in the untamed grasses between the woods and garden. As I leaned my body further over the railing to try to catch a glimpse of movement in the trees, I heard the tiniest of sneezes.

Like a dog trained to a scent, I whipped around and set immediately about tracing the source of the sniffle.

I rounded the turret and triumphantly found a crouching Lucas backed into a crevice between the stone exterior and railing.

He wiped his nose sheepishly and struggled to pull his gangly limbs free.

"Am I the first one?" Lucas asked with a wry grimace as he wormed his way out from between the tight space.

"You sure are." I laughed. "Need a hand getting loose?"

"Please," he grunted, accepting my hand and heaving himself up.

"Goodness! That took you long enough! I was crammed in there for ages! Did you forget you were seeking and hide somewhere, or are you really this slow?"

I scowled at this, not impressed. My pride was so wounded I actually considered blurting out the truth for the mere reason of saving face.

"Actually, genius, I, erm, was…" My sassy back-comment lingered lamely as I groped for a feasible excuse. "I had to do a quick bathroom stop, but Beatrix caught me and reminded me I need to have some measurements done for my new dresses. It took longer than I thought…*I'm* longer than she thought!"

Lucas rolled his eyes, and I laughed uneasily, unsure whether he believed me or not. For all his introverted mannerisms, he was very clever and I was half expecting him to come out with the real reason gauged just from my facial expressions. After all, it was a pretty pathetic excuse.

"You better hurry up and find everyone else before luncheon," he said eventually, and I breathed a small sigh of relief. "I think Evelyn and Tressa headed towards the eastern woods, and Fred went down to the library. Avery could be anywhere so we better get cracking."

"Definitely," I agreed, praying that my face hadn't betrayed me and gone its signature shade of guilty red. "I'll nab Fred on the way out then go outside for the girls – and don't worry, I wouldn't dream of ratting out that you helped me!"

I had remembered that when in fear of displaying guilt, try to force the other into the same situation.

Lucas dipped his head, muttering, "I wasn't thinking, I just—"

"Never mind. Come on, let's go!"

I took his thin hand in mine and skipped in what I hoped was a merry way back into the breakfast room and down the remaining sector of the grand staircase to the library.

As I entered the dingy little room, a stale silence and thick dusty air greeted me in sly reminder of how it had all started right here. The empty bookcases seemed to obstruct everything else, and for a moment I just stood dumbly in the doorway letting the memories come rushing back to me.

"Whenever you've finished dramatically staring off into the middle distance, Penny."

I jerked and shook my head.

"Fred! I hadn't even found you yet!" I chuckled. "Sorry, my mind decided to go for a run."

"Don't worry about it," he chortled in the same tone. "I was getting really quite bored sitting in this depressing space. If I were you, I'd check outside for Tressa and Evelyn."

Obviously I had taken so long that everyone I met overrode the rules with no regrets at all just so we could finish the game.

Wincing at the dent in my self-esteem, I hastily left the library behind me and proceeded in my task to track down my remaining three friends.

Outside the air had risen to a noticeably warmer temperature, nearly humid but not quite. Though the ever-present mist still refused to relinquish its hold, the sun bravely shone through and the sparking dewdrops dusting the grass lit up like diamonds. It was beautiful, mystical, yet I could not feel any affection for my prison. Before Fred could tease me about zoning out again, I plunged into the dreamscape towards the woods at a steady gallop, with my frock still bunched in my fists for ease of movement. The boys easily kept pace with me, and I felt a familiar longing to be allowed to wear loose trousers and sensible shoes like them. I didn't see why I couldn't.

I slowed, puffing as I entered the outskirts of the woods. I dropped my skirts to the increasingly leaf covered ground and began to scan the area with critical precision for any signs of recent presence in the hardening mud. Then I remembered my cedar.

Only a few yards away, I exaggerated my footsteps in hopes of sparking a detectable movement. I highly doubted that Evelyn had climbed into the hollow herself; more likely she had led Tressa here and then hid somewhere nearby.

Out of the corner of my eye, I saw the swish of a burgundy dress disappearing behind the trunk of a nearby maple and the telltale black curls flitting in the warm breeze. Typical Evelyn.

"I found you!" I announced loudly.

"I wouldn't sound so proud if I were you, it felt like an eternity that I was standing there! My legs are aching from it," she complained, bending down to massage sore joints tenderly. "It wasn't as if I could even sit down, since the ground is so dirty with the fallen leaves that it would soil my gown something awful! Really, if you are going to show me hiding places, please make sure they are more comfortable for longer periods of time, or *do* make more haste seeking."

I patiently waited for Evelyn to finish ranting. When her downturned mouth ceased to speak, I calmly brushed past her to the foot of my cedar, taking hold of the big overhanging branch with practiced accuracy.

Not in the mood for hoisting myself around today, I just lifted my toes far enough off the ground to peak into the hollow, and sure enough my intuition proved correct; Tressa had flattened herself inside.

"I thought this would be the first place you would look!" she grumbled, pulling her numerous layers of garments free while getting as little debris on them as possible, quite the opposite of myself. "I wasn't even going to hide here, but it turns out that reverse psychology really does work."

I was starting to feel crushed about taking so long. It had ruined my reputation to perhaps an irreparable state. And for what, a sickening feeling and inexplicable…thing? I was going to have to have a big talk with Beatrix about her definition of useful.

"Luncheon!" Fred gasped, pointing at the overhead sun.

We all glanced up, shading our eyes with our hands and realized that it was shining directly above us, illuminating the silver enforcements of window panes in the rooftop dormer windows as it only did at midday.

On cue, my stomach rumbled with the thoughts of cucumber sandwiches and perhaps a cream cake if we were lucky.

"I still have to find Avery," I said reluctantly, twirling a stray auburn lock with a wistful expression. "Any idea where he is?"

"No." They all shrugged in unison.

I let the strand go in irritation. He could have gone anywhere, and I honestly could not be bothered to skip luncheon in search of him. This was precisely why I despised seeking.

"Can't we just leave him?" I begged. "Sooner or later he'll turn up."

"This is Avery, not a piece of jewelry," Tressa reminded me. "But tell you what, since I'm starving too, why don't we all head to luncheon and you can do another search of the manor for him. If you really can't find him, then you can come to eat luncheon with us so we can continue with you afterwards."

I gritted my teeth, promising to never ever volunteer for the position again.

"All right," I conceded grudgingly. "Save me some food."

"Will do." Fred patted my back cheerily. "Good luck finding that rascal!"

I cursed inwardly as Tressa, Fred, Evelyn, and Lucas sauntered back inside the manor with linked arms whilst I pondered where my missing 'friend' could have possibly run off to.

I had searched nearly everywhere I could think off the top of my head, but there were literally millions of possible nooks scattered some distance apart in which Avery could have disappeared, and if he didn't want to be found it could quite possibly take all day to track him down.

"Avery, you little…" I muttered scathingly as I made my way back into the house, glad Tressa was out of earshot.

I took one last precious breath of fresh air, and drank in some more of the autumnally colored trees as I hovered on the stone steps in front of the double doors. The splashes of bronze, russet, and gold, in contrast to the deep green leaves added a certain whimsical quality to the grounds, despite being duller than I remembered of previous seasons.

I half-heartedly began a casual search around the furniture of the foyer, even peeping down the dining-hall corridor and the servant's staircase. When this turned out to be fruitless, I went to check again upstairs, trying to keep my spirits up.

I will not slap Avery when I find him. I will not slap Avery when I find him. He doesn't mean to be such a bother, I chided myself.

My stomach whined in protest as I passed the breakfast room, and I patted it sympathetically. We lived on a very strict schedule, so when timing was altered even slightly, we felt the effects.

"Avery!" I shouted, wandering up and down the second floor. "You win! I admit it!"

He didn't answer. The bragging he was sure to do afterwards, didn't bear thinking about.

"Aver—"

If I hadn't been concentrating on every detail in the hope of finding Avery, then I probably would not have noticed the candle missing from its cove in the wall, a few yards down towards the north wing. Someone had moved the decorative ottoman from the common room so it now stood underneath it, no doubt put there to help a short person to reach higher.

My mouth suddenly felt very dry.

He wouldn't…would he?

Praying to whatever powers existed, I tried to keep my head as I strode down into the darkening wing, growing closer to the medieval-style door and the distressing secrets held behind it.

I had no reason to get so anxious. Normally such unsavory feelings did not belong to me, and after all, he had no reason to believe I had myself breached the rules and gone upstairs. If he confronted me, I would simply deny it and ask for evidence.

This was all worst-case scenario; most likely Avery had just thought the shrouded north wing to be a clever hiding spot, although I couldn't help but wonder how he has possibly reached there without me seeing him.

I approached the short door with my stomach butterflies going crazy.

Hardly daring to breath, I bent down to inspect the door. I let out a huge breath when I noticed the latch was still fixed over the bolt, untouched and still firmly blocking the staircase beyond.

Heaving a huge sigh of relief, I pivoted and nearly jumped out of my skin.

"What the…?!"

"I knew it!"

Avery and I both spoke at the same time, face to face with each other. He had been standing behind me the whole time, and now had his hands on hips with a triumphant smirk shaping his face into an infuriating leer.

"Knew what?" I asked, trying to look clueless.

"You went through that door." Avery gleefully took in my

struggling mask of innocence. "And before you try to slither out of trouble, I was following you the entire time instead of hiding, a few paces behind so you wouldn't see. I saw you go up and come down looking as though you'd encountered a ghost. Care to elaborate?"

I desperately racked my brains for a decent excuse, but none came to mind.

"It's none of your business." I frowned, my attempted forceful tone rendered weak and scrambling. "I was bored with trying to find you, so I decided to have a quick peek down this wing, that's all."

"Penny." Avery raised an eyebrow. "Don't insult my intelligence. You came here first, before you even attempted to find anyone else."

"All right. So what if I did go upstairs?"

"What made you so scared? Why the sudden rebellion? And most of all, what did you see that made you cry like a baby?"

I kept my mouth sealed, eyes shooting daggers at him and sincerely wishing a rather horrendous monster would materialize and devour him on the spot.

Avery waited for a few second for me to answer, but when I remained mute he suddenly darted past me with his candle in hand, unlatched the door, yanked it open and shot up the stairs.

I stood transfixed for a moment, not comprehending what was going on, and then felt the dawning shock bubble upwards.

"Avery no!" I screamed, tearing after him.

I stumbled up the staircase after him, blindly following the dim glow of his candle whilst hoarsely shrieking for him to stop.

My feet moved up the steps as fast as I'd ever seen them move, nerves threatening to implode with anxiety.

I banged into him as he stopped on the platform.

He stood, candle extinguished just as mine had been, fumbling around in the dark.

Avery turned to me. "A wall?"

"Congratulations," I hissed sarcastically, panting. "What on earth are you up to? Get back downstairs this instant!"

"You're turning into Tressa. Come on, show me what's inside! Prove to me the fun Penny still exists."

"No, you don't understand, I can't go in there until I've—"

"If you don't help me, I'll still find a way in. All the credit will go to me if we find anything inside, instead of you," Avery taunted.

"As will the punishment if we get caught," I added flatly.

"Punishment," he scoffed, arrogance overriding any rational fears he should have had. "We're all going to get annihilated eventually, and if that's going to happen, I'd rather it be for something like this. Besides, I'm an exceptional liar, and it's my word against yours. How favored are you feeling at the moment?"

I swayed, uncertain. Already my friends thought I was a fraud for failing them at seeking, and I didn't want to lose my reputation of being outgoing as well in the same day...not that it mattered, I chided myself, but losing credit for what might be our ticket to freedom to Avery? We had come this far...

"If you tell anyone else, I will kill you," I threatened, seriously meaning it at that moment.

I heard him tut to himself as I once again removed the key from my pocket and carefully edged it into the lock, pushing the loosened door open.

Excited, and pumped with adrenaline, Avery jumped into the darkness, dragging me along by the arm.

"What. Is. That?" he asked, his mouth dropping open.

I too found myself mesmerized by the intertwined rings and ornate lever, but was revolted to find bile rising in my throat from the mere memory of my artificial panic.

"Avery, let's go," I begged, feeling slightly sick.

In reply, he shook me away from him and approached the thing in a trance. Pulled against my better judgment towards it,

I followed him.

I saw a hand inspecting the many engravings on the old lever and was mildly surprised to see that it was mine.

"Penny!"

Avery had suddenly gone very white, face contorted no doubt by the same feelings I had encountered the first time. Now, though, I felt nothing.

"Pull it!"

"Pardon?" I stared at Avery, who was shaking uncontrollably and seemed seconds away from a total breakdown.

"Pull the stupid lever," he gasped urgently. "Then we can get out of here. Pull it!"

I hesitated. Then a determined frown set on my face and my fist tightened; I was going to get us out of here.

Not thinking too much, I closed my eyes and heaved a massive pull, with all my strength, anger, and frustration poured into that one movement. It bent easily.

For a minute, nothing happened. Then, in slow motion, something flashed on the screen and the rings began to move. Like dancers, they twisted hypnotically around each other whilst filling the room with the piercing buzz of a rip, and appearing to ripple as they moved faster and faster. A glow began to take shape in their center. Then the floor rushed up to greet the ceiling and I blanked out.

11

I came to, groggy, feeling as though I was being impaled to the ground by several spears and crushed under a ton of bricks. My limbs felt like lead, there was a crippling headache waging war with my skull, and my mouth was so dry I had to fight not to gag.

I just lay there, unaware of my surroundings and completely unsure of what had just happened.

"Urgh..." Avery groaned, retching on the floor beside me.

I tried to will myself into moving, but seemed to be glued to the floorboards and not capable of anything more than raising my pounding head a few inches from side to side.

A sliver of comprehension twisted into my subconscious as I realized the pressure holding me to the ground was slowly fading with the suffocating static. Somehow, when the rings had started moving, they had created a kind of rip so strong that Avery and I hadn't been able to stay conscious through it. I wondered what it had done.

Feeling crawled back into my toes and spread upwards through my legs until I found the strength to stand.

"Any idea what just happened?" I slurred, head spinning.

I stumbled, trying to figure out a way to stop the room from moving around me and to keep my vision from swimming. It was rather distracting.

"Not in the slightest..." Avery sounded just as awful as I felt. "That machine...did you see what happened?"

I spun dizzily around and noted that the contraption was once again lifeless, the circles stationary and the dials on the screen frozen, without the artificial light which had animated them before.

"Maybe it ripped the Master away permanently!" I guessed with a crooked smile. "Or tore down the Boundary! Come, let's go have a look and see!"

The possibilities welled up inside of me, shoving all the nasty sickness away with a beautifully refreshing tide of hope, something I had not experienced in a very long time.

"Blah…" Avery cringed. "I feel terrible. Give me a hand?"

I rolled my eyes and tried to ignore my own crippling symptoms. I took hold of a skinny arm and yanked his clammy body from the floor. Tucking it securely under the crook of my own arm, I haphazardly navigated us over to the doorway, taking care to lock the door behind me and collect the two discarded candles we had dropped on the landing.

One step at a time, we emerged into the corridor.

It had seemed disturbingly dark before, but now I had to pause to let my eyes adjust to the light.

"Now what?" Avery asked, taking a shuddering breath. "Do we tell everyone else or not? I know you weren't planning on it, but this seems like something that they should know about it. Just in case you really have just killed the Master or whatever."

"Ha, look who's suddenly telling me what's right and wrong!" I taunted, half-teasingly and trying to force our normal bickering back into the situation to make it seem less drastic. The serious expression on his face made my smile slide away, and I hung my head. "I don't know if we should. Tressa will only get angry with me, *also* I wouldn't want to get their hopes up if nothing has changed. And if the Master finds out, I don't want them to be involved."

"So be it," Avery said tonelessly, and I couldn't decipher whether he agreed with me or not.

An icy veil settled over us as we dragged ourselves over to the breakfast room for luncheon. Such a mundane activity seemed pointless and a complete waste of time compared to the monumental enterprise we had just been involved in, and I ached to bypass the entire thing to go find out what had been altered.

Still, the visions of thick cream custard sandwiched between delicate layers of sweet, sugary pastry beckoned me. I was surprised to see the breakfast-room door closed and no chatter coming from within.

"Hey, I found him!" I called.

Unwinding my arm from Avery's, I rushed forwards to burst in on their luncheon, only to see with a jolt that the room was empty.

Six stools were pushed neatly under the table, the stitched tablecloth was clean of crumbs, and the room void of food and people.

"Where is everyone?" Avery asked in a small voice.

I refused to panic, throwing open the balcony doors and craning my neck out into the crisp…evening air. Sure enough, it was evening; the golden sun had disappeared over the tops of the trees and a blanket of twilight had settled over the grounds.

I relaxed a bit. Clearly, Avery and I had simply been upstairs longer than we thought and everyone was now getting ready for dinner.

"We've missed luncheon," I stated, closing the balcony doors and turning back to Avery.

"My mind was just blown. Thank you for stating the obvious," Avery said dryly, his cynical old self returning with the color in his pinched cheeks.

"Shut up. Now, you go to the boys' chamber and I'll go to the girls', then we should *not* say anything about where we have been and try to have dinner as normal." When he raised an eyebrow challengingly, I explained further. "Do you want to tell them right before we face Him? When they haven't had a chance to absorb the information? You might as well commit us all to punishment and be done with it."

"All right, fine," Avery grumbled, shoving his hands into the belt loops of his trousers. "But tomorrow. I hate to deceive them."

I had to admit, I was shocked by his attitude. Due to his irritating and often antagonistic character, I'd never have guessed that he would be the one telling me *I* was being thoughtless when It came to our friends' feelings. Although I couldn't help but be impressed by his decency, it would cause me grief in the future if I decided to hide what I'd done due to it being a failure.

"Yes. Tomorrow," I agreed, somewhat grudgingly.

We bid farewell and headed to our separate wings once out of the breakfast room, with me still battling a massive headache. Perhaps I would trouble Beatrix for some medicine after dinner.

Fumbling with the handle, I massaged my temple as I entered the girls' chamber.

"Hey," I greeted them, trying to keep the dizziness at bay. "Sorry I took so long! I can't believe I missed luncheon, I'm absolutely starving right now!"

"That's okay. Things happen," Tressa replied from a chair with its back to me.

A chill crept down my spine. I didn't know why, but something about her voice was just...off. My headache began to worsen until I gasped out in pain and squeezed my eyes shut against the agonizing throbbing.

"Argh!" I winced. Still keeled over, I strained to see Tressa's face. "Where's Evelyn?"

"Over here!" Came a voice from around the L bend. Again, I felt the tingling sensation of extreme discomfort and my headache escalated again in ferocity.

"C-can you turn around?" I begged, vision starting to blur from the pain. "I can't see you!"

In perfect synchrony, Tressa and Evelyn emerged from where they had been hiding away and a horrified, bloodcurdling scream ripped through my lips.

Two pairs of solid black eyes stared at me. Dark, demonic voids set above skeletal cheekbones protruding unhealthily from waxen, almost translucent skin.

"Can you see us now?" They inquired angelically, both tilting their heads jerkily to the side. Their voices sounded so wrong, like there were several people speaking over them! *"Penny, Penny, Penny, what have you done, Penny, Penny, Penny? Who's laughing now, Penny, Penny, Penny?"*

As they sang, revealing pointy teeth leering vilely at me, a trickle of dark red leaked from the corner of their mouths. Blood!

I screamed and screamed until my lungs were bursting, and my throat so raw my voice was barely above a croak, and I could scream no longer. I tried to run but froze in terror – helpless as they advanced towards me, grinning, with blood now dripping from their lips…

*

"She's waking up! Penny, dearest, open your eyes! Quick, get some more water!"

Someone splashed my face with something very cold and very wet, and my eyes flew open in shock.

Tressa bent over me with an expression of intense worry written all over her perfectly normal face, hazel eyes alight with concern. Evelyn hurried over to peel off a damp cloth from my forehead and replace it with another, her white and straight teeth biting her blush-colored lips nervously.

"How are you feeling?" they asked at the same time.

Merely hearing their voices together was enough to make me start, but I reminded myself that they sounded as they always did, without the creepy overlay.

"Awful," I admitted, propping myself up on my elbows. They had set me down on my bed and loosened my bodice to help me breathe, which I took full advantage of. "I don't understand what happened…"

"Neither do I," Tressa said, handing me a dry towel. "You stumbled in with your head in your hands, mumbling something, and then you started screaming your lungs out! We rushed to see what the matter was, but you had collapsed before we got to you."

"It was rather noisy," Evelyn added, turning away to cough. "It startled me and I spilt water down the front of my chemise!"

"Oh dear," I muttered in monotone, and Tressa smirked. "My heart goes out to you."

"It was my best one!" Evelyn insisted indignantly. "You know, the one with the little daisies embroidered all over it?"

"Evelyn," Tressa said seriously, though I could see the ghost of a laugh being subsided. "I love you dearly, but it is only water, and I think we'd be better off worrying about what happened to Penny now."

She forced a smile. "Yes, I suppose you're right. Sorry."

"You best come and get ready for dinner." Tressa stood up to finish pinning her hair. "Skipping two days isn't a move I would pull if I were you. You probably just felt light-headed after missing luncheon, right?"

"Yes, that must be it!" I nodded wincing at the thudding. It was like my brain had become unattached from something and was now floating around inside my head, so that every move I made sent it slamming against my skull.

"I wonder what made you scream, though?" Evelyn said aloud as she began twisting my hair into an elaborate bun at the nape of my neck.

"I...erm." I searched around for a way to explain the monstrosities I had seen without seeming insane or insulting the girls. "I have no clue."

We didn't speak of my episode again, but it was clearly on all of our minds, especially mine.

I knew what I saw. Why I saw it was another question entirely, and its connection to our pulling the lever upstairs was pretty much a given. The whole sinister experience had unnerved me, for it was not at all what I had been expecting.

Still in routine, we met up with the boys in the foyer, going through the automatic polite complements of each other's outfits, though I noticed a sort of sickly undercurrent present.

"You look terrible, Avery!" Tressa noted, sounding much ruder than she'd intended. "Are you quite all right? Poor Penny passed out a few minutes ago; you look moments from doing the same!"

"Headache." He shrugged. "And I wouldn't be too worried; fainting's becoming a habit for you girls, isn't it?"

Evelyn coughed again, just to prove she was properly sick and not being pathetic.

No one said a word as we trudged into the dining hall with Beatrix and sat down on our seats. There was no squabbling, no fiddling whilst waiting for the food, and even the nervousness for the Master was somewhat dulled.

Well, until He actually came.

The rip made the toast I had eaten for breakfast almost make a grand entrance all over my brand-new dress, and I had to swallow down the bile. If there was a bright side, I had to focus so hard on not throwing up that I forgot to be intimidated when He strode behind me to His chair. In fact, I didn't even hear the "You may begin," as a fabulous lamb stew, vegetables, and cheese scones ripped onto the table. It didn't matter. I was utterly famished from going so long without food and took great care in scooping out the chunkiest bits of meat and plumpest scones from the arrangement.

I waited for everyone else to serve themselves before taking a grateful hunk out of the scone. I chewed it around in my mouth thoughtfully, trying to put my finger on a strange tang that was becoming more noticeable the more I ground it up. It was almost like…

Not caring about etiquette, I spat the ghastly morsel onto my plate and chugged down my entire cup of milk. I had never before experienced the taste, but I knew what it was.

Ashes. It tasted burnt, and of death and nothingness. Ashes, with the faint coppery hints of blood.

I wasn't the only one who had discovered the disturbing flavor, as my friends around me were following suit and gagging lumps of food onto their plates with bulging eyes widened with disgust. Even Beatrix seemed fazed, though she had supposedly cooked the foul things.

"Is there a problem?" came the cool voice from the head of the table. I groped around for words, but my vocal cords happened to be stubbornly refusing to speak.

He slowly and deliberately pushed back His chair, making no noise, and glided over to where we were all sitting.

I blanched, the old fear inside of me beginning to stir. This was all wrong; what was supposed to have been a glorious bid for freedom had gone so awfully wrong.

"Did you really think you could hide your actions from me?" He asked softly, almost pityingly. "I know all that goes on in this manor. *My* manor."

The last two words hardened, and I knew a storm was coming.

"I would have thought you were intelligent enough to follow such simple rules. I would have thought that by now you'd be able to understand that it's impossible to get away with breaking them. We can't have you all running rampant about this place like a bunch of wild things, and rules *have to be obeyed* if you want to keep living your lives in the security that I see you've now taken for granted. You may find I can revoke it just as easily as I have given it. Despite what you think, there are some things dwelling in this estate that are the stuff of nightmares, and thanks to one stupid girl, they're about to be awakened. For that, there must be consequences."

I froze, petrified. Beatrix gave a small gasp of alarm, sharing a fleeting glance with me before looking away. She would not stop Him, of course. She wouldn't even try.

"You." The Master directed the word entirely at me, and I felt my heart pound, then stop. I was numb, incapable of dread simply because the sheer amount of it would have driven me crazy had I let it take hold. "Come here."

His voice was so cold, so very cold...I couldn't move.

"Come. Here."

I set my chin, clenched my fists. I had broken the rules, I would no doubt suffer for it, but I would not show Him any regret.

Yet, anyway. I was a lot braver beforehand when it came to such manners.

I tried to keep my head held high as I approached Him, only thinking about controlling my breathing and nothing else.

"You went upstairs," He stated, not phrasing it as a question.

"I – I did," I said, thinking now about how hungry I was and staring at the detailing on the curtains behind His head, a trick I had learned from all those times Tressa had lectured me.

"You went deliberately into the room up there, where you touched a certain object I have been keeping in there. Against my orders."

Again, I nodded, bracing myself.

The pain came, but this time it was very different. He narrowed his eyes, and with a casual sweep of a slender hand and I felt myself slammed like a useless rag into the sharp edge where the window sank back into the wall.

I couldn't help but cry out, feeling my skin split on impact.

"I will not do more than this," He announced. "What you have done to yourself is far worse than a fleeting taste of agony. The true punishment is coming, and it is you who has brought it upon yourself."

My eyes widened, yet I felt no relief.

This could not mean anything good at all. He never let us off so easily, let alone for breaking such an important rule, and I psyched myself up for torture testing all the resolve I had.

"I understand." I bowed my head, cringing as I felt the wound sting. I was feeling many things, but in truth, understanding wasn't one of them.

As He whipped around, I could have sworn I heard Him hiss something about "family resemblance" to Himself, whatever that was supposed to mean.

"This dinner is over."

As He ripped away, a particularly forceful shudder rippled through the hall causing all the food to slide off the overturned table and splatter all over the floor where it promptly turned to dust, throwing everyone off their seats.

My head banged again against the corner again, but I didn't really feel it. I was too busy fearing the nightmares of the future to worry about flesh wounds of the now.

Beatrix shuffled over to me and helped me to my feet, trembling again as she surveyed the cut.

"Would you like me to heal it for you?" she offered. "Well, I can't properly heal it, but I can make the stinging go away if you—"

"No," I interrupted, a bit sharper than I had intended. A flash of hurt crossed her face, and I felt a twinge of guilt. "I just can't be doing with this supernatural insanity right now. I want normal."

"I meant with medicine. I'll get something made up."

I noticed Tressa, Evelyn, Fred, and Lucas were all goggling at me with identical expressions of confusion and betrayal, with Avery being sick under the tablecloth.

"I'm going back to the common room," Tressa said, her voice sounding forced as if unused for a long while. She cleared her throat before continuing. "Evelyn and I can quickly change out of our dinner dresses."

I hung my head as she clearly omitted my own name from her statement. Avery had come with me, why was he not being reprimanded, too?

I watched glumly as the five of them filed from the room in resolute silence, wondering what I had ever done to deserve such a downright rotten chance of luck.

The black night sky outside turned the windows into mirrors, and as I gazed into their depths I saw the full extent of the damage to my scalp: a nasty gash from the top of my right ear to the base of my neck steadily dripped blood. I suppose it had to count for something that all my bones were intact.

I couldn't help it. I was done with being brave, so I did what any other fifteen-year-old girl would do; I cried.

"What went wrong, Beatrix?" I sobbed, turning away from the windows and throwing myself into her arms. "What's wrong with me? All of my friends hate me now, He's madder than ever, and whatever that thing was upstairs only made everything worse! The food, the hallucinations, the dreams…I feel like I'm going crazy!|"

Beatrix didn't say anything, but I knew she was listening.

"Y-you t-told me to p-pull the lever!" I accused when my tears subsided into hiccups, wanting to find somebody else to blame.

"I did." Beatrix did not falter. "And you promised to accept the consequences. I swore not to tell you this, but since Madon clearly knows I'm involved now, there's no point in hiding anything I'm not bound to protect. What you did was trigger a series of…well, I suppose they're like tests. If you can stay strong throughout them, then I am certain the Boundary will fail and you will be granted your freedom."

"Really? Just like that?" The hope came bubbling back again at the prospect. "Were the hallucinations part of the trials?"

"I would assume so, a very minor starting point," Beatrix said ominously. "By the way, what was it you said about having dreams? I wasn't aware that you were troubled by nightmares."

"Oh, they're not nightmares, so to speak," I corrected, wiping my eyes with a palm. "More like really vivid daydreams. I've only had two, each the same, based on this scene where a man and a woman are murdered for this bundle thing. It's odd."

Beatrix's arms tensed around me, and I felt her steady

heartbeat quicken nervously.

"I am sure that is all they are," she said firmly. "Daydreams. I would not dwell on them if I were you, as there is much more you will need to focus on. You haven't told anyone else?"

"No," I replied, curious that if they were simply normal daydreams why it should matter that I had shared them.

There was a moment of almost awkwardness between us, until I untangled myself from her arms and got up.

"I should go clean this up." I gestured to my cut.

"Yes. And I should do the same with this," Beatrix swung her arm in the general area of dust and overturned furniture, the ruins of what had previously been a marvelous dinner.

With nothing else to say, we swiftly trudged our own ways.

I was almost at the exit when another question popped into my churning mind and I pivoted back to face Beatrix, who was ripping away the debris and manually picking up the chairs.

"Beatrix, what happens if we don't, or can't withstand these trials?"

"I don't know. But you can be certain it won't involve leaving the Boundary."

That was all I needed to know. Whatever it took, I wasn't going to let them beat me. Not for stakes like this.

Part Two

12

"One more time. Urgh, I still can't *believe* you would do all this without telling!"

I sighed and repeated my story from when I had first confronted Beatrix. We were all gathered in the common room in front of the fire, munching on some biscuits that Beatrix had left on the table.

Tressa set down her plate and listened to my story lividly, her face alternating between different shades of red as I spoke. She lived to be in charge of things, and for her to be left out of such an important turn of events was little less than a huge insult. Lucas, Fred, and Evelyn had not made a single comment since we had sat down more than two hours ago, not giving away more than a satisfied crunch of biscuit or slight adjustment of pillows on the sofa. Avery had also remained mute, and I supposed it was because most of my tale was news for him as well.

"Well, then," Tressa said icily, when I finished for the umpteenth time. "I'm charmed that you would think to ask before altering the course of our lives. Perhaps I'm just being harsh; maybe your adventures matter much more than our petty, simple little lives, which were clearly dragging you down enough to—"

"Don't be angry!" I pleaded. "You must understand that it could have meant the difference between freedom and a lifetime of imprisonment, and you would have stopped me! This could be good for us!"

"But it isn't, is it?" Fred volunteered hesitantly, speaking for the first time. "From what I've gathered, this is not good at all. In fact, it seems rather dangerous."

Tressa nodded in agreement, eyes flashing. "It wasn't your choice to make."

"Lucas?" I campaigned for support.

He was uncomfortable being put in the spotlight, fidgeting

and mumbling something about Tressa and Fred being right.

"I agree!" Evelyn announced, as if her words made all the difference.

I beamed at her support, but my smile faltered when I realized she wasn't agreeing with me, but with everyone else.

"Penny, how could you even call this imprisonment? Look at all we have, our clothes, our food, our jewels and furniture! Have you not read about poverty during lessons? It is restrictive, and sometimes oppressive, but it is not a bad life we lead."

I glowered at this. Why did their arguments all have to be so darn reasonable?

"Is this the price we have to pay?" I jabbed at the rag I'd been holding to the back of my head. "What do we have to lose? Come on; please stand with me on this! There's nothing you can do to change the past, so can't you just accept what I did and work with me to get through the future?"

Avery clapped his hands dryly from where he had been perched on the arm of the sofa, crowing, "Good speech, Penny. Now we can all slowly die knowing that—"

"Shut up, Avery, and stop pretending you didn't have a part in this. I haven't finished with you either," Tressa interrupted, and he fell immediately silent. She sighed, running her fingers through the few flaxen waves, which had escaped her plait. "I have a feeling that moving forward is all we *can* do now, since what you did seems pretty much irreversible."

"Exactly." I nodded, trying to contain my inner excitement. Together, united, we would work it out. We always had.

"Well, we should all get to bed now, it's getting late. See you all in the morning."

It was an excellent proposition, considering my head was fit to burst it hurt so badly, and my whole body felt drained from the chaotic events which had so rapidly befallen me in such a short space of time.

I snuggled under my duvet, feeling the soft pillows envelope my head and the mattress gently cradle my body in the same comfortable way it had done every night, closing my aching eyelids and trying to blank my mind. The candles were all out, so the smell was replaced by the sweet scent of fresh laundry. I imagined the black forest outside dipping into absolute silence, falling asleep and waiting for the sunrise...

And what should have been a peaceful night ended abruptly when I found myself bolt upright and shaking like a leaf, covered in goose bumps and breathing heavily. I had had the most horrendous dream, but for the life of me I couldn't remember it! It was nothing to do with my usual one, and the only recollection I had was a nightmarish jumble of...well, a nightmarish jumble.

Taking deep gulps of calming air, I glanced around for some sense of time, assuming that it was perhaps just past midnight or another wee hour of the morning. Contrarily, I was blasted with rays of sunshine seeping in from the translucent blinds across the room, indicating that despite my calculations I had indeed slept soundly through most of the night. Odd.

I winced as my head gave a cheerful pound to remind me of its existence. Surveying the room, I saw that Tressa's usually neat bed beside mine had been ruffled and unmade, the occupant no longer lying amidst the sea of pea-green covers. She must have gotten up early.

I slipped out, curling my toes at the cool wooden planks and hopping tentatively over to my cupboard to select a nice day dress out of a newly updated rack.

"Tressa?" I whispered, loudly enough for her to hear me yet softly enough so not to wake Evelyn.

"Yes?" She popped her head round, hair half-done, face wet from washing, and eyes...I did a double take as they changed from total black to their ordinary hazel. "Are you quite all right? How is your head feeling?"

"I – I...um, was just wondering...erm." I struggled to speak, bewildered by why I kept seeing her this way. "You're up early.

Did you have a bad dream too?"

"No." Tressa shrugged dismissively, offering no other explanation and disappearing back towards her changing area to finish her hair. "Wear something loose, Penny, it's a lovely day again and I thought we might play croquet outside to lighten the mood up a little bit before lessons."

If she hadn't had a nightmare, then what on earth had she been up to? I pushed any unsavory ideas out of my mind, firmly reminding myself that Tressa would never do anything stupid or against the rules, and that she had probably had trouble getting to sleep after the tumultuous events of the previous day.

I loathed croquet, even when I'd been young enough to still find games fresh, but I wasn't in a position to argue with Tressa.

"What an abominable night's sleep!" came the tired voice that signaled Evelyn's arrival to the awoken world.

"Beg your pardon?"

She shuffled over, bags under her eyes and plait so unruly it hardly seemed there. Scathingly, she reminded me, "It means despicable. Remember from handwriting?"

"Not really, I can't remember many of those long words when there are perfectly satisfactory shorter options which mean exactly the same thing," I said. "Did you have bad dreams also?"

"I did," she retorted. "Oh, and I like your new dress."

I thanked her for the forced compliment and continued weaving my way into the sleeves. If Evelyn had nightmares, then maybe Tressa had too, which left only one question – why would she lie?

We met up with the boys for breakfast, who spoke nothing of being disturbed by nasty nightmares but all looked tired and disheveled, especially Avery. We then gulped down the food as fast as possible so to get the longest amount of time playing croquet.

The equipment was stored in a small cupboard under the grand staircase.

"Oh!" I heard Lucas exclaim from the bottom of the stairs. He had gone ahead to open the door, having not wanted to talk. "I don't understand!"

I rushed to him, knowing full well what monstrosities could be confronting him thanks to the lever-induced 'trials', but was presented with nothing but an ordinary storage cupboard.

"What's the matter?" I asked, confused.

"The door's gone!" he gasped, thoroughly unnerved.

I squinted, tilted my head, but the door remained there.

"No," I contradicted. "Your eyesight must be failing. See?"

I demonstrated by opening the door myself and showing him the array of sporting equipment that lay waiting for us in the little room beyond. Lucas didn't grin or look relieved.

"Penny...there's nothing there. Just an empty wall."

"Are you blind?" I exploded, frustrated by the simplicity of the problem.

I turned on the others, who had just caught up. "Is there a door here or not?"

Tressa and Fred looked at me as if I were crazy, saying, "Yes...?"

At the same time, Evelyn and Avery looked stunned and gasped, "No!"

I ground my teeth, stomping forwards into the cupboard and retrieving a ball, brandishing it in front of their faces.

"But the door had disappeared!" Lucas protested. "I swear, Avery and Evelyn couldn't see it either, could you?"

"Don't be fools, you lot." Fred shook his head in a rare moment of contradiction. "There really isn't anything to argue about – clearly you're still tired, because it's as plain as the nose on my face that there's a cupboard here. Penny even went inside!"

"No, there most certainly isn't! See here," Avery snapped, rapping his knuckles against an imaginary panel of wood where the open doorway was positioned. "Solid oak."

"It's not funny!" I shouted, flustered, my headache crippling.

"Why would I joke?" Evelyn cried.

"QUIET!" Tressa yelled over the top of our bickering. "Don't you understand what's happening? It's trying to turn us against each other! Whatever force we're up against, it's trying to destroy us from the inside out, and darn nearly succeeding in the first day too!"

We stopped squabbling. To me, it seemed a bit silly that these tests, most likely orchestrated by the Master Himself, would begin a series of horrors by dividing us over the existence of the storage cupboard. But honestly, what other explanation was there?

A few nervous glances flicked back and forth between those who could see the door, and those who couldn't.

"I'll grab the other equipment then," I muttered, breaking the heavy silence.

"Yes. I'll give you a hand," Tressa offered. She and I dived into the room together, ducking around rickety shelves of racquets, balls, nets, and metal horseshoes. I heaved a long leather bag containing the mallets from a peg, stumbling out again with no idea what was in front of me.

"Oomph…" I grunted with effort, hoisting the bag across my back and nearly falling from the weight.

"Here." Fred chuckled, coming over to give me a hand. "Tressa, are you okay with the balls and goals? Avery, Lucas, why don't you be gentlemen and help her?"

"I'd love to, mate, really I would," Avery said in a mock-formal tone, clasping his hands together and wringing them humbly. I rolled my eyes; he was just being cheeky to calm his discomfort. "But I can't see the blasted door, so I can hardly — "

"I do beg your pardon?" Tressa scolded from inside.

Avery flinched, staring at what was to him an unremarkable panel of wood. She soon emerged with two more leather sacks flung over each shoulder, promptly handing each one off to the boys. "All right, let's play!"

"Hurray," Avery muttered. "I mean, it's not like we've being doing this every sunny day since we were six or anything..."

"That's why we pulled the lever," I reminded him under my breath. "And I'll thank you to remember that when the others are getting mad at me for it again."

Outside, the air was crisp and the woods more vibrant than ever, so the second we stepped out you could feel our moods improve considerably. Whatever dark presence had been lurking inside, was not out here.

I slung the strap off my shoulder, Fred did the same, and we overturned the bags to see properly the array of balls, mallets, and hoops we had collected.

"Do you want to play in teams, or individually?"

"Individually?" Lucas suggested. "Since we did teams last time?"

The others all agreed, and we set about pushing the hoops into a higgledy-piggledy course, which twisted its way for what seemed like miles across the lawns.

In fact, by the time Avery and Lucas jogged back to us after placing the last hoop, sweat had beaded on their foreheads and we were all panting slightly from the effort.

They rolled up their shirtsleeves absently, and I once again cursed my skin-tight dress sleeves. I would discuss with Beatrix about perhaps getting a gown made with short sleeves, no matter how improper it sounded. She would understand.

"This might be fun," I admitted. "But only if I get the mallet with the red handle."

Avery flicked me a devious glance, and we both dived for the red mallet at the same time.

"You two! Stop it!" Evelyn squeaked, jumping back from our scuffle having successfully retrieved one from the pile herself. "How old are you?"

"Dear goodness." Tressa rolled her eyes.

I yanked the handle, refusing to let down, until there was a sudden pop, and the hammer-like part at the bottom splintered free from the handle, sending Avery tumbling onto his back and the other part slamming into my head.

"Ouch! For the love of crumpets, Avery, that really hurt!"

For a second, I saw his eyes change from guilty to solid black. I shuddered involuntarily.

"Avery!" Tressa snapped, bending down to assess the damage. "You look fine, Penny. Nothing more than a—"

"Wake up, come on! You're fine!"

I blinked, confused. Why was I lying on the grass?

Five faces bent concernedly down over me, stars swimming in front of my eyes as my hearing fuzzily returned...I'd fainted again.

"It's her head," Tressa diagnosed. "It must be. Honestly, why do you both have to be so immature?"

"Sorry, Penny," Avery apologized, lending me a steady hand. "I forgot about you ladies and fainting, recently."

His apology did actually seem sincere, so I accepted and hauled myself to my feet. I felt very lightheaded, but otherwise all right. If anything, my strongest emotion was mortification that I had showed such an embarrassing display of weakness.

"Can I have the blue one, then?" I enquired hopefully.

Tressa shook her head. "I think it would be much better for you to sit this one out."

When I opened my mouth to protest, she held up a commanding finger and continued. "I'm not trying to be mean; I only think you shouldn't do anything too strenuous because of your head. I don't want anything to become...well...more serious."

"But what else am I supposed to do?"

The sun gleamed through the faint mist as if to remind me what I was missing, making the polished mallets seem suddenly desirable. Yet I knew Tressa was right.

"I can go for a walk with you?" Fred offered. "I could do with

Boundary

the exercise."

"Sounds wonderful." I forced a half hearted smile. "Thanks."

Tressa smiled at me encouragingly, turning back to her remaining players and drilling through the rules again.

Fred offered me his arm, which I took. With one last wistful gaze at the croquet equipment, I allowed myself to be guided across the lawns beside the house.

Fred launched into a characteristic rant on various, completely unrelated topics, and I did my characteristic zoning out. I bobbed my head, said the occasional "Oh, really?" and put on a pretty good show of being genuinely interested in the material of his favorite waistcoat.

"...finest cotton! So anyway, about this business involving starting some trials that will set us free; what exactly did you do again?"

"Lovely!" I murmured vaguely, unaware of what Fred was saying. Instead I focused on a vibrant chestnut tree with gorgeous autumnally shaded leaves and wondered what made them shift from green, to orange, and then fall.

"Penny, you're not listening to me."

"What? Sorry, I was listening, but my mind decided to go for a walk!" I defended myself sheepishly, well aware of how many times I had used that excuse of late.

"You should chain it up and give it a good telling off!" Fred chortled. "Never hangs around for very often, does it? Anyway, I asked you more about what you did with...well, whatever you did that aggravated Tressa so. I didn't really understand."

We drifted over towards the edge of the forest as a wooden ball came hurtling across the grounds following a loud *thwack* and hoots of laughter from Avery, deciding to play it safe and distance ourselves from the croquet course.

It was more peaceful here, shaded from the late morning sun.

"There isn't much more to say," I shrugged, wishing that everyone could stop treating it like my fault. "Beatrix gave me a

100

key, I went upstairs and unlocked a room with this bizarre thing in it, then Avery convinced me to pull the lever." I deliberately drew out those last few syllables before continuing. "And I think the circles created a rip, which prematurely started these trials. According to Beatrix, they test your mind, and if you are strong enough to endure them, then the Boundary will fall. If not, then…"

I didn't need to say. Fred kicked a tiny pebble playfully, watching it roll and bounce off the trunk of a tree with an expression deep in thought.

"I don't understand how that works. How long will we be subjected to tests before the Boundary falls? When were they *supposed* to start? What exactly are the trials, and how do we know if we've lost? Surely if it's all a mind game, you could go insane…but to d—" He broke off, refusing to say die.

"I'm no more certain than you, Fred," I admitted, titling my head to try to ease the ache. It was starting to throb again, but thanks to the antiseptic salve Beatrix had supposedly applied to my bandage, whatever that was, I could tell I would only be suffering from the wound for a small while longer.

"So far, it hasn't been that bad," Fred said cautiously. "The food, the nightmares, the door. I mean, they've not been pleasant but they've not been unbearable either."

"Don't jinx it!" I threatened, glancing over my shoulder to see Lucas running in an ungainly fashion after a runaway ball. Tressa was winning, of course, Avery having cheated his way into second place. I couldn't even see Evelyn, she was so far behind.

"Mm. Well, let's make the most of what we have now!"

I grinned, and jumped up to swing off an overhanging branch, letting my head hang back and the divine fresh air blow through my hair.

Penny! Come quickly, I need you! Hurry, hurry!

I stopped swinging and listened curiously. The voice was soft, barely noticeable, as if whispered from mile away and carried over on the wind.

"Fred, did you hear that?" I gasped.

"The voice? I did." He frowned.

We paused, craning to hear more, when the chilling sound once again materialized.

The Boundary, Penny, I'm trapped! Hurry, hurry, before they find me first! Hurry, Penny, they're coming!

"Who's coming?" I called back, certain they wouldn't answer. "Who are you?"

"We have to help them." Fred seized my shoulders, his face pale. "Whoever they are, outsiders maybe, we can't leave a plea for assistance unanswered."

It was all very sinister, in my opinion, but my conscience and curiosity propelled me to follow Fred's lead into the woods, alert for any more signs.

They are watching you, waiting for you to turn back! Don't listen to them, Penny, come to me and set me free. Penny, you must hurry to the Boundary!

"I'm coming!" I shouted desperately, caught up in their tidal emotions of panic. Fred and I began to run, dodging trees and hurdling roots, slapping the clawing branches out of our way impatiently, not caring about anything but the distress of unknown people trapped somewhere by the Boundary.

I skidded to a halt by the familiar buzzing creek, searching frantically for the people who had called out for help. There was nothing, nothing but fog, trees, the Boundary itself, and...shadows.

Yes, there were definitely shadows flitting around on the other side of the creek. I strained to catch a clear glimpse, but every time I became close to eyeing a visible human figure, the shadow would shudder and reappear somewhere else. It was almost as if someone was projecting puppets from the other side, which was obviously impossible.

"Where are you?" I growled, frustrated.

Fred was equally stumped, bending as close as he could to the Boundary without topping over.

Come to me, Penny, the Boundary will not hurt you. It is them who are the danger, do not be afraid and come forward. I need you. I need your help!

The voice was right. Why was I afraid of something I couldn't even see, when all the insanity was fully developed in the deadly realm behind me? I should be brave, step forward to help the mysterious shadow-people who were undeniably right...

As I approached it, the static made my hair buzz into floating strands, and I noticed that they weren't shadows at all. They had faces – faces which looked rather familiar – although I couldn't have seen them before... They didn't look like the people from my dreams, but that must be it.

"Look! Look! They're the people from my dream, they're real! Quickly, we have to save them!"

He nodded absently, eyes glazed over, staring beyond the creek.

My throat raw from the possibility of meeting them, I took a determined step over the Boundary...

"What in the blazes are you doing?" I heard Fred shout.

"Hey!" I cried.

Something grabbed me. A dark creature. In my haze I couldn't quite make out what it was. It wrapped its arms around me. I scratched out at it, scrambling hysterically to wrench free of its grasp, to get to the shadows before they went away!

The thing wasn't very strong and lashing out at its face, I managed to free myself. But it was persistent and threw itself at me, knocking me flat, seizing my ankle and dragging me backwards. Couldn't it see these people, the shadows, needed me? How important it was that I met them?

The creature abandoned me and headed for Fred. I could hear Fred fighting the creature a few feet away from me, but I didn't care; the only important thing in the world right now was to get across the Boundary to save the shadows. I struggled to my feet.

A sharp slap stung my cheeks, and I stumbled back onto the damp forest ground.

"Huh?" I blinked in confusion.

Suddenly, sight streamed back to me and I noticed that the creature who had barreled Fred and me away from the Boundary just before we crossed it to our doom, was, in fact, Evelyn.

Her cheek was covered in shallow claw marks where I had scratched her, her pretty, pale gold gown rather worse for wear and covered with mud and tears. Her eyes were wide with fright, and she was panting in disbelief. I glanced frantically towards to the Boundary. All was quiet; there was nothing there, no voices, just the low buzz of the static.

Fred was sitting beside me, horror dawning on his features. "Oh, goodness. We were about to cross the Boundary, and there was nothing there!" he gasped in shocked comprehension, gazing at Evelyn as if he had never seen her before. "Evelyn, if you hadn't been there we would be nothing but a pile of dust by now."

I let my head flop into my hands, overwhelmed by my own stupidity. What had I been expecting to find, two dead people from my dreams? What was wrong with me?

"I lost croquet, so Tressa said I had to go and find you two before lessons," Evelyn explained in a small voice. "You were both about to walk over the creek, so I didn't think, I just grabbed you both and tried to pull you away…you tried to fight me. I was terrified that if I gave up you'd run across the Boundary… Oh, dear, Penny, when you looked at me your eyes were all black! No whites, I was so afraid…" She collapsed into hiccupping sobs.

Now *I* had scary eyes? I shuddered. What could have happened didn't bear thinking about.

"I'm so sorry I hurt you," I apologized, gathering her into a hug. She hugged me back, holding on as if we were little again and hiding from a thunderstorm.

After a few minutes, we let go of each other and traipsed back to the house and the normalcy of lessons.

Wordlessly, Evelyn and I left Fred in the foyer while we quickly changed. I did my best to clean up Evelyn's face. She made no attempt at conversation, and I kept silent without protest.

All tidy, we rushed down to the library a few minutes late.

"Thank you, Evelyn," I said suddenly before we entered. "You're stronger than we give you credit for. I owe you my life."

"Thank *you*," she corrected with the ghost of a smile. "I'm jealous sometimes, you see; I'm not a natural leader like Tressa, not smart like Lucas, not as likeable as Fred, not as funny or clever as Avery, and certainly not as brave and energetic as you. I sometimes feel like the failure. Doing something like that reminds me that I'm worth something too."

"You are jealous of me?" I gasped. "B-but you're... well...beautiful!"

Evelyn tossed her curls vainly, smiling. "That's awfully nice of you, but what good are looks? Now I feel I have more confidence. Besides, did you see the way Fred looked at me? No one has ever directed that sort of – well, I suppose you could call it respect – at me before."

Despite the grimness of the situation we started laughing, then pushed open the library door with renewed strength.

We screamed.

The world swam in front of my eyes, and I felt my knees weaken beneath me. I think I was shouting, but all I could remember was a blur of pain and sorrow, refusing to believe what was before me. People around me were screaming too, but I was too numb with shock and pain to feel anything, not even Evelyn clutching onto my arm with her mouth open in a mute shriek of despair.

I sank to the floor, not even breathing. It had to be another trial. It had to be! This wasn't supposed to happen in real life... In plain view, lolling horribly on a table, was a body.

Someone I loved dearly, dead. Lost forever.

13

The estate died a little bit too that day. What had hours ago been a beautiful watercolor of trees in a lush forest turned against itself, curling into a deadened state that was normally never seen until after the first frost. It became barren of the vibrancy I'd grown to love; even the emerald lawns dulled to a pale yellowy shade, and the manor house itself appearing to darken. The sunshine left us and was replaced with a heavy fog with dreary drizzle, which never let up. No color, no laughter, no life. Only sadness.

I felt a single tear leak down my cheek. It streamed down my face and left a dark spot on the shoulder of my mourning gown. We were all dressed entirely in black, fitting perfectly into this new, melancholy mood.

The tombstone seemed awfully insignificant. It was meant to represent the entire life of a very dynamic, wonderful individual who had meant so much more to me than this piece of cold, hard granite.

How could a lifeless marker and blandly inscribed words be all that was left? It was cruel, really, a reminder of death in a place from which we could never escape. It would haunt me forever, and I would never be able to get away from the memories it held. Not ever.

We stood side by side in the rain, cheeks dampened by both tears of grief and the down-pouring spray, faces washed out by the stark black of our clothing.

Each of us held a single, withered rhododendron bloom in our hands, the only flowers that still appeared somewhat alive after the estate had begun to crumble.

Well, all of us except Him.

I had been surprised when He had appeared at our farewell. I suppose He must have been the one who had sanctioned the burial in the first place and created the headstone, but it was still shocking to see Him standing beside us in such a fashion, even if He seemed thoughtful instead of upset.

"Lay down the flowers," he instructed liltingly, as if He had almost forgotten and was amused by the notion.

I cupped the pale pink blossom tenderly, waiting for my turn to lay it down at the foot of the grave. Soft, simple, a fading beauty with potential to light up every aspect of the manor…it was a near perfect representation of her personality. I stroked the engraved name as I bent down, trying my very hardest not cry in front of Him.

IN MEMORY OF BEATRIX FARRINGTON

I had never known her last name, never even considered that she even had one. I knew about how they were used to identify different people with the same given names in real society, but assumed Beatrix would be exempt from this queer rule, having lived here for such a long time.

There were many things I had never asked her, and now I wouldn't get the chance.

"Thank you for everything," I whispered as if she could hear me. "And sorry for my prying…I hope wherever you are, you can forgive me."

I choked on the last few words, wiping my eyes as I stood back to let Lucas have his moment.

I was consumed by a heart-wrenching guilt that I had somehow caused Beatrix's death because I had coerced her into telling me forbidden secrets and left her at the mercy of the Master.

She hadn't been bluffing about her son's capacity for murdering as punishment. I was certain He had killed her; there was no other logical explanation. Beatrix's body hadn't been marked in any way, but the petrified grimace etched on her face had said everything.

"Why?" I found myself asking, my hands covering my face, my voice wavering with inconsolable sadness.

"You know why, Penny," He replied emotionlessly, and I jumped. "Because she was no more than a filthy traitor, breaking an oath she swore her life on. If I couldn't trust her, what use was she to me anymore?"

"She was your—" I began, too stricken to think about who I was talking too.

Before I could finish, I felt my body go rigid. I couldn't move a muscle! My eyes widened at Him, desperately wishing one of my friends would turn around and see my predicament, though they all seemed suspiciously preoccupied with staring at Beatrix's gravestone.

He turned deliberately towards me, face without a trace of feeling.

"Do you know what the rhododendron means?" He asked, almost casually. I couldn't even shake my head, completely paralyzed. "Every flower has a message, you see, almost like a language. These mean 'beware.' It's not a coincidence that they are the only flowers still alive on the estate, because they are here to deliver an important lesson to you all. I suggest you take heed, unless you want to be the next grave in my collection."

He turned back to face the tombstone, and I felt movement return as my friends suddenly lost interest in the stone.

My heart pounded, my head filled with a deep loathing for the Master. I wanted Him to suffer, to feel all the pain He had caused me the entire extent of my childhood, to be the one in fear of me for once.

It was a bitter dream, an impossible one.

For all I could do was stand in submissive silence and cry soundless tears for all I had lost and would never get back.

*

"It wasn't your fault, you know," Tressa said abruptly, glancing up from her sketchpad. "I can tell you blame yourself. Don't."

"How can I not?" I cried in despair. "If I hadn't pestered her into telling me all those secrets, then the Master wouldn't have killed her for breaking that oath. Beatrix would still be alive if it wasn't for me."

"When things like this happen, all people want is someone to blame. I'm the same; but it's the Master who dealt the fatal blow, not you."

"But he wouldn't have if she hadn't helped me," I argued. "And what for?"

We were sitting in the common room again, dressed still in our black clothes and trying fruitlessly to avert our minds from the tragedy at hand. The fire had spluttered out, and despite the heavy material of my shawl I felt chilly.

"Do you regret it?" Lucas asked abruptly, to everyone's surprise. He rarely ever entered our bickering, even when it got serious. "I don't mean her death, I mean being nosy and stumbling on all those secrets. Are you happier with the shot we have, or would you have preferred no danger but no chance?"

I knew the answer as soon as he said it, but felt selfish about it. What kind of terrible person was I, placing my own interests above the lives of others?

"No." I hung my head, ashamed. "I can't honestly say that I would take it back in normal circumstances. But if I'd have known somebody would *die* because of it, then of course I would have."

Lucas nodded as if that explained everything, and returned to gazing out of the paned window into the stormy sky outside.

It was lucky that the common room faced onto the opposite side of the gardens to where Beatrix's grave was located, or I would probably have been fixated to it wherever I went.

I rested my now nearly healed head on a pillow, thinking in the back of my mind I should find something to distract myself with, such as sketching pictures like Tressa, or at least talking like Evelyn and Fred. I just couldn't find the energy, though. I felt utterly drained.

"What do we do now?" Tressa inquired after a painful hour or so of silence. "I'm...beyond words about Beatrix, I never thought that she would ever... She seemed immortal somehow." She paused to wipe her eyes.

"We can't mourn forever," Avery said in monotone, looking up from where he had been dozing in his armchair with a gaunt face. "I agree with Tressa some actions need to be taken."

"Actions?" Fred raised an eyebrow warily.

"You expect us to let the Master get away with this?" Tressa snapped. I saw her fist tightly clenching her charcoal stick; her eyes alight with a fierce determination fired by the inconsolable sorrow that consumed us all.

"Um, yes?" Evelyn replied tentatively. "Like it or not, you cannot expect to challenge Him, Tressa, that's pure insanity! Tell me you're not serious?"

Tressa said nothing, setting her jaw and sharing a meaningful glance with Avery.

"Whatever happened to sticking together?" I frowned. "Let's not add any more drama to what's already happened. I assure you I could quite cheerfully lop His head off with a butter knife right now, but let's try to wait until mourning is over before doing anything brash. Out of respect to Beatrix, if nothing else."

It was one of the most reasonable things I had ever said, and despite my devastation, I felt a momentary flush of pride. Beatrix would have been pleased with my cool-headedness.

Tressa and Avery, however, appeared to disagree. Tressa refused to meet anyone's eyes but Avery's, moving her lips in silent speech, which I strained to understand to no avail. Avery nodded with a stony face, flicking me a deliberate glare.

Fred had noticed their suspicious, excluding charade with an unease which mirrored mine. Though he alone seemed to have picked up the duo's telepathic plot, I had a niggling feeling that it wouldn't stay underground for long. If there were two people I wouldn't bet against, it would be Tressa and Avery.

Then something else caught my eye. Evelyn, sitting beside Fred, gave a dainty sigh of weariness at the whole thing and moved so that her head rested on his shoulder. It shouldn't have been anything out of the ordinary, except that the way she did it seemed much too intimate, somehow, for friends. And that look of surprise and then silly happiness on Fred's face did nothing to alleviate my suspicion. *Did you see the way Fred looked at me?*

"Gross," I heard Avery hiss in disgust, plopping his tiny frame heavily down beside me. "With all that's going on right now, you'd think they would act more appropriately."

"I know," I rolled my eyes. "But it's all innocent. B-Beatrix always used to joke that this day was coming."

"What, that everybody would go crazy?" Avery shook his head scornfully. "Honestly, ever since He killed Beatrix all I've wanted is to *do* something instead of waiting for the next disaster, and suddenly they want to just sit back and enjoy the ride! I thought you were the one who wanted to fight for freedom?"

"Unless you have some brilliant idea that will both ensure our safety and beat the trials, I don't think anyone wants to hear it right now," I retorted. "If breaking the rules turns out like this, then maybe it isn't such a good idea after all."

I bit my lip, stopping. Deep down I hated sitting around too, but I was scared of what else the Master had in store for us. Losing Beatrix was crippling, and it didn't bear thinking about what might happen if one of my friends got hurt too. What was freedom worth, when we had everything to lose?

Fred then appeared to join our debate, a silly smile slapped onto his jovial face. Avery's face remained impassive, but I could feel the scorn radiating off him in waves.

"Hello, you lot! Cheerful, aren't we?" Fred greeted us happily.

"Considering Beatrix died three days ago, I would have to go

with not really," I said sullenly, flicking a glance over to where
Evelyn had fallen asleep on the window seat.

"Ah." Fred paled, bowing his head. "I'm so sorry, I'm not
thinking straight. I was just wondering what you were arguing
about?"

"Just discussing tactics," Avery cut in smoothly, every inch of
his body language indicating that Fred should go away and leave
us to squabble by ourselves.

"So you agree we should let time tell, Penny?" he inquired of
me, oblivious to Avery's antisocial mood.

"Not exactly," I replied awkwardly. "I think we should
certainly take action, just not now. Not violently."

"I'll drink to that." Fred sighed. "Lucas and Evelyn have
agreed with me that staying quite out of it is the best thing to do.
No action, no consequence, right?"

"When you all die, don't expect me to wear this stupid drab
black to every one of your funerals," Avery remarked darkly.

For a moment, I thought Fred was actually going to snap at
that comment, but then Tressa blessedly decided she was bored.

"I'm going outside for a walk! Evelyn, want to— Oh!" She was
interrupted by snoring. "Penny, then?"

"Sure." I jumped away from Avery and Fred without a
backwards glance.

We made a quick stop in the girls' chamber for black shawls,
mittens, bonnets, and a large black umbrella to shelter us from
the freezing downpour outside.

I hurried down the grand staircase a little ways behind Tressa,
fumbling with the thick satin ribbon underneath my chin. Then
we linked arms underneath the umbrella and waded out into the
spitting rain, ducking as it pounded the fabric like a dozen
drums.

Water saturated the brittle grass so that large puddles of
muddy rain had begun to form, and huge splashes from the
overhanging roof made walking near the house a veritable

hazard, so we opted for the higher grounds midway between manor and woods.

"Ghastly weather, is it not?" Tressa noted loudly over the sound of rain pitter-pattering overhead. "And everything else seems so bleak! Perhaps Beatrix was the one who maintained the prettiness here. Maybe that was what her powers were for."

"Maybe." I shrugged vaguely, not wanting to talk about her at the moment. "By the way, what's going on with you and Avery? Plotting, much?"

"Nothing at all. What an idea!" Tressa scoffed, absently pulling a tassel on her shawl straight. "We're both worried that if we do nothing, we're more at risk of the Master dominating us now Beatrix is...gone. Now, could we change the subject? How has your head been these past few days? I understand you haven't been given the salve since..."

"Healed," I said shortly, gazing at the flickering lights twinkling warmly from the upstairs common room.

I was beginning to regret coming outside into the miserable weather and awkward small talk. We lapsed into an uncertain silence, squelching along the muddy ground arm-in-arm.

"Have you seen Evelyn and Fred?" I gossiped, improvising. "Do you think they *like* each other? It came on very quickly, but I guess the death reinstated the live-for-today mindset..."

"Oh, come now," Tressa chided, and grinned. "I find it rather sweet! Evelyn has always been such a romantic, and Fred is ever such a gentleman with her – they complement each other perfectly, though I doubt they'd ever admit it to one another!"

I wrinkled my nose. The whole topic was very alien to me, and the old-fashioned values I had been taught still found it slightly improper. Still, it did give one something to discuss other than death.

"He is barely her height!" I criticized, half-enjoying the merriment and half actually putting them down.

"Ha, true! But Bea— I mean, I've heard that girls grow faster than boys up to a certain point, then he'll catch her up again!" Tressa laughed gaily. Then her face turned serious. "I'm sorry, I can't help but wonder… What are you planning to do now, Penny? Having been the one to start the tests in the first place, I assumed you knew precisely what you were doing and had the whole thing thought out. I know I'm being silly, but I have this feeling that if we leave these tests and the Master up to their own devices then none of us will succeed. I think maybe Avery is right and the offensive has to be taken."

"Urgh," was my genius response. It was all so complicated, and my most knowledgeable confidant was gone for good. What was my plan? Nada. Zilch. Nothing whatsoever. I would take the trials as they came at me, and hope for the best.

"I hate it when he's right," she muttered under her breath, abruptly turning away from me and storming off towards the manor. I didn't know what she meant, and at the moment, I didn't want to.

I didn't think that planning was a good idea at the present time. Yet something in Tressa's unimpressed expression had told me she thought otherwise.

14

Finally. It was over. Looking at the two dead bodies on the ground, he felt curiously empty. Relief at not having to chase anymore, and relief that nobody on his side had gotten hurt, but he saw none of the triumph on the others' faces. He was only eighteen, many years younger than the rest of them, yet he'd been allowed to come along due to his aptitude in such matters.

"Here, hold this," somebody said, thrusting the bundle of rags into his hands. "You deserve it. If you hadn't found this shack when you did, we'd still be on the road!"

He nodded mutely. He knew what was inside, but there was something more savage about what they'd done when you gave the thing a face. It was a baby, of course, only months old. He watched, transfixed with a sinking knot in his stomach as the baby wriggled in its sleep, jamming a fat fist shiny with drool into an untroubled place. It had no idea both its parents had just been murdered.

An older man materialized beside him and snatched the child away, and he felt a deep discomfort begin to well up inside of him. It was not a good thing; feeling like this would only get him removed from the position or even punished, but he couldn't help it. There was only one reason that the team would want this baby so badly, and it had nothing to do with love. He knew where the child's future lay and what it would become.

As he reminisced the dreaming infant, he realized the poor baby would never stand a chance.

"Against what?" I murmured, rolling over onto my side.

The sound of my voice woke me with a jolt, and I fell with a thud out of bed and onto the floor in a messy heap of pillows and duvet covers. Wearily, I hiked my bedclothes back onto the mattress, fingers crossed that I hadn't woken Evelyn or Tressa.

I lay on my back and stared wide-eyed at the distant ceiling, flexing my stiff limbs, now fully awake.

The bundle had been a baby! It hadn't come as an enormous surprise, since part of me had always thought that a child was probably one of the only things a woman would die for without question. Now all that remained was who each of the characters were.

That my dream somehow rang with truth was an absolute certainty. Never before had I felt so strongly connected one. It was not normal to see with the clarity I had three times, and therefore I knew I had seen an event in my sleep that had actually happened, or would happen.

Then another unsettling thought occurred; what if, just maybe, the child was…me? It would explain why I dreamt alone. That would make Elisabeth and Bernard my parents! I hadn't been able to see much of anyone's appearances, so unfortunately proving my theory through looks alone would not work, and now the only person who might have known was dead.

"Answers," I whispered softly into the night, closing my eyes and trying to relax my tense body. "That's all I want."

Somehow, sleep managed to claim me once again and I slipped out of awareness until…

My head snapped bolt upright in alarm as a shadowy figure closed the bedroom door as quietly as possible, then tiptoed across the floor towards where Tressa's bed was. In the moonlight, I saw her pale hair flying loose (unusual) and bruise-like shadows under her eyes (odd), as if she hadn't slept in ages. She glanced in my direction, but I had already hidden myself under the covers. What on earth was she up to? Maybe it was in my best interests to find out, but in the morning. I needed sleep.

I slept dreamlessly for the rest of the night, awakening to a dull light shining through my eyelids and causing me to stir once again.

I felt shaky and headachy again as I drearily pulled on my black day dress and splashed water onto my sleepy face.

It was almost as if the dream had been my reality and this life was nothing but a dull figment of my lively imagination. At the moment I wouldn't have minded the swap, my everyday existence had become so grey and cheerless in the two weeks since Beatrix was stolen from us that the hours blended into each other with agonizing speed, seeming to both take forever and fly by at the same time.

It wasn't just the weather that had decided to turn bitter. Cracks between us had begun to be more noticeable, and although we refused to admit it, it was only a matter of time before we crumbled entirely. The food was awful, the atmosphere was bleak, tempers were running high, health was running low, and the trials were taking their steady time to make any kind of drastic attempt on our lives. And so, we had settled into a monotone dance of waiting for something, anything, to happen. For better or for worse, I frankly didn't care.

That morning at breakfast, the kippers-on-toast tasted once again like they had been fried in ashes. As for the orange juice, it had the flavor of something vomited in and shaken. Funny how one's appetite declines.

"I had that dream again," I offered in a good attempt at perkiness.

"Oh?" Tressa feigned a tight smile of interest as she prodded her kippers disgustedly with a fork.

Should I ask? Risk provoking an argument that might shatter us altogether?

"I think...oh, I know it sounds ridiculous, but I think I'm the baby! That was what those people were killed over, and if it were me it would explain why I'm the only one dreaming about it! Don't you think?" I eagerly waited for their responses. This was more important right now, besides, there was nothing sinister about taking a walk to calm your thoughts at nighttime, which was surely what Tressa had been doing.

Instead of seeming excited about my dream, they sighed patiently and continued dissecting their fish.

"It would," Lucas said flatly. "Except for one teensy problem; it was just a dream. Beatrix told you that already, and besides, what sense would it make if you were actually some critically important child kidnapped by sinister forces who murdered your parents? How on earth would you have ended up here?"

"Thanks, Lucas," I muttered. "Your support is encouraging."

"Don't mention it," he replied in the same dry tone.

"Does anyone believe me? Anyone?" I inquired, surveying the miserable scene with a dull annoyance.

"It's not that we don't believe you, Penny, it's just that it seems a bit far-fetched that you would all of a sudden be dreaming about your distant past," Fred explained, sharing a reasonable glance with Evelyn.

Sourly, I slashed open the gut of my shriveled kipper and prodded the fleshy chunks into my soggy bread. Just for something to do which didn't involve making conversation, I cut a mouthful off and deliberately placed it onto my tongue.

It was revolting! I tried to remain collected, fighting an instinctive gag reflex. Reaching for my juice, I tried to wash down the foul food and only succeeded in adding yet another rotten taste into the toxic mixture.

"Just spit it out." Tressa sighed, watching me struggle with the barest trace of amusement.

Sheepishly, I turned to deposit the mouthful into a napkin with as much dignity as I could muster. The taste remained strong, though, and I dearly wished for a nice glass of refreshing water to gulp down and remove the nasty aftertaste.

"Pardon," I excused myself. "I don't understand what's being going on with the food these days, it's all so awful!"

"Tell me about it." Avery wrinkled his nose and pushed his plate away. "I don't know what idiot they think would possibly risk eating this. Kipper, Fred?"

Fred pulled a face at the offered dish and shook his head, oblivious to the insult, remarkably having eaten nothing himself either.

"Ugh, no thanks," he refused as politely as possible. "I prefer to live without food poisoning if I can help it."

In mutual agreement, we left the table and horrid breakfast behind us, opting instead to go and do what we had been doing every day – absolutely nothing in the common room.

Boring, dull, but the only option it seemed we had. Sometimes, I didn't blame Tressa and Avery for wanting a change.

As predicted, within minutes we had once again resumed positions in the common, Fred chatting bashfully with Evelyn, Lucas keeping himself up to date with a self-made numeracy worksheet, Avery and Tressa unconsciously perched close together on two poufs and talking seriously, leaving me twiddling my thumbs in a velvet armchair by the smoking, dying fire.

"Anyone want to talk more about my dream?" I asked again, already knowing what the answer was but I was out of other ideas.

"*Your* dream? We're all living one now. Welcome to the nightmare, Penny."

I jerked my head upwards to see all five of my friends staring at me with identical solid black eyes, skeletally protruding bones, and sharp leering yellow teeth grinning diabolically.

I squeezed my eyes shut frantically; trying to shut out the noise of their rhythmically thudding footsteps coming closer and closer, trying to convince myself that it wasn't real.

"Don't be afraid, embrace the darkness. You're one of us now, Penny, you who dreams and wonders…inside, we are all monsters." The voice didn't belong to them. It was several people talking at once, but not them.

"No!" I shouted, hands over my ears and eyes shut. "I'm nothing like you! I'm real and you're not! Leave me alone!"

Against the firm will of my bodice, I curled my legs protectively against my chest and waited for the footsteps to stop. After a few minutes, I heard nothing.

My breathing was coming very fast and my limbs were shaking in terror, but the comforting silence coaxed me into cautiously opening an eyelid to peer out.

I almost broke down as a flash of bloody teeth and soulless eyes hovered inches from my face. I wound myself into a tinier ball, singing loudly. I don't know why I bothered; letting my mind slip into insanity would probably be easier than trying to cope with it, I thought.

"Not real, not real, not real!" I chanted hysterically to myself, rocking in my chair. "Not real not real…"

"Penny!"

"Go away!" I shrieked into the pillow, clenching my fists and kicking desperately with my feet at the horrid monsters. "You're not real, I don't believe in you…"

"What are you blabbering about? Snap out of it, you're scaring us!" I refused to listen to their coy attempts to get me, stopping my chant but nonetheless tensed to react at the slightest approach. When I felt a cold hand seize my shoulder, I flinched and twisted away so violently that the armchair I was sitting in rocked once before tumbling over backwards, sending me crashing into a muddled heap on the floor.

I heaved myself up wildly, jumping back from the vision.

"You stay away from me!" I snarled viciously. I must have looked a fright: hair ruffled into a tangled bush, eyes flashing with fear and determination, and skirts torn from my fall.

Then I noticed how my friends appeared. Their eyes had color – irises, their skin flushed, not waxen, and their mouths normal if not extremely disconcerted. Breathing heavily, I collapsed once again onto the carpet and laid my head back to gape at the ceiling. Everything was fine – I was merely going mad.

"A-are you all right?" Tressa asked tentatively. Nervously. She was afraid of *me*.

"I don't know," I whispered. "I really don't know. I suppose no one else...erm..."

"Just you," she replied.

They were all staring at me as if I were an alien or something of the sort, as if waiting for me to break down and start yelling at them again. It was exactly like what had happened to Fred and me in the woods when Evelyn found us, although this time I alone had been affected, and thank goodness no one had come close enough for me to strike them.

"Want to talk about it?" Fred asked, the first to approach me. He came slowly, lightly, taking care not to startle me. I was going mad. Somehow, I was oddly at peace with the idea, but the thing that worried me was the effect it might have on the people who I cared about.

"I have to go," I said suddenly, causing Fred to stop in his tracks.

Five mouths opened to each object in their own ways, but by that time I was gone out of the common room and down the hallway, caring about nothing but putting as many steps between my insane self and my friends.

Beatrix had told me I was perfectly sane, that there was nothing to worry about; but Beatrix was dead. She could not convince me anymore. Down the corridor I strode, unsure of what to do next. Why me? The dreams, the monsters... If it really was the Master behind it all, I didn't see why He had gone to such pains to make only me miserable. And to what end? What were these things hoping to accomplish?

I felt like laughing, crying and screaming all at the same time, my mind a conflicted mess unsure of what I should be doing to make it better. The dreams weren't real, then. Darn.

My fingers curled into fists. I stopped in front of the staircase and gazed through the windows at the stormy gardens barely visible through the rain-splattered panes. If I craned my neck just so, then the stretched shadow of Beatrix's gravestone was distortedly apparent.

I stared at it with hollow eyes for a second, before shaking my head and hissing at myself to pull together.

Just because I was going round the bend, it didn't render me incapable of action. I knew what I had to do.

I hiked up my skirts determinedly and rushed down the dark north wing without so much as a flicker of trepidation. One of the positives of being crazy was that rational thoughts took much more effort to take hold, and my driving force was adrenaline and angst instead of reason.

I quickly lifted up the thick steel latch, and ducked swiftly through the tiny arched doorframe and up the long staircase. I hadn't brought a candle this time as I remembered how previously it had been extinguished, relying only on touch and memory to navigate my way.

I was going to push the lever back to the original position and reverse the trials. It was so simple, yet before it had never occurred to me! I stumbled a few times on the varying width of steps, checking consciously to see if the lumpy iron key was still floating around in the expansive realms of my pockets.

When I reached the pitch-black platform at the top, I confidently reached forwards to unlock the hidden door. I stepped into the cavernous room and glanced around for the bizarre machine. My stomach sank.

The room was empty. It was nothing but an unused attic, a vast area of dilapidated wooden bones and fogged dormer windows providing only minimal light from way up in the ceiling.

My knees decided to fall asleep right then, and I wobbled ungracefully to the floor.

"How...?" I croaked in shock. This was impossible. I swayed as I stood up; unsteadily rushing forward to check every corner of the barn-like attic just to make sure my mind wasn't playing tricks on me yet again. Nothing appeared.

Frustration piled up inside of me, threatening to explode.

Why did my genius plans all have to end so badly? What had I ever done to fate to deserve suck rotten luck?

I stomped my foot like a toddler in a tantrum, cursing loudly.

I stepped on a loose floorboard and it shot up at one end. Out of the corner of my eye I noticed something light and pale drift serenely to the ground having been propelled into the air.

Curiously I approached it and picked it up.

It was a letter, written in faded yet beautiful cursive letters on a stained and soggy piece of paper. I didn't recognize the hand; it was too neat and fancy for any of my friends and besides, how would it have gotten up here? There was no name or any indication of the writer except for an initial at the end.

I plonked myself down and began to try to read the blotched words with a mounting excitement that I had actually made a useful discovery.

If you are reading this letter, you've already activated a strange machine you found and as a result are living a lifeless and twisted routine. You are undoubtedly scared, unsure, and have come to try to reverse the effects only to find the lever has vanished. First of all, may I just say you're and idiot for messing around in the attic to begin with, but I understand exactly what propelled you into doing it. I have been in your position, and I know what you're going through, so don't for one second believe you're alone in this. Who am I? – you must be asking. To say that I'm a ghost isn't fitting, somehow, so I'd say more of a presence. And years ago, I was standing exactly where you are now, feeling utterly lost. Unfortunately, it did not end well for me, but I will do everything I can to ensure it does not go badly for you too. Write to me, I will respond. It is all I can do now...
Sincerely, D.

I read the letter over and over trying to make some sense of it.

Who was this D person? What did this mean, that someone else had been trapped here before us, faced the trials, and failed? How did the letter get here, and how could a long deceased person ever return my reply? Nothing fitted together, and it left me with more questions than answers.

Still, as I clutched the crumpled paper to my chest, I felt a bought of hope that this letter and the information it could hold would mean the difference between success and defeat for me. Just when I had thought my escalating struggle was futile, this sliver of promise had unexpectedly appeared. I left the attic feeling hesitantly happy, buoyed by this mysterious new ally.

Looking back, I wouldn't be able to help but see the irony. D had warned me about being too trusting and reckless when I'd pulled the lever, but never did I once question if the letter was telling the truth. For as odd as the content was, sometimes reality truly was stranger than fiction.

15

I think I left the key in the door, but that didn't worry me at all. The Master knew that I'd come up here, and I found I was becoming less and less afraid of what He would do to *me*.

Instead, I stowed the letter inside my pockets with the same care that I'd used with the key. Of course, it was wholly possibly that the letter might have been nothing more than another element of madness, but again, I couldn't bring myself to care. Hope was good, even if it was false.

Out of the north wing and back in the corridor, I delighted in the reactions my friends would have! Then my face darkened and I remembered their nervous flitters after my bout of hysteria and decided to give them just a little bit more time to forget the incident, though I had been gone perhaps over an hour already.

I could nip down to the library and get some stationary to write back to D! The sooner she answered my multitude of questions, the happier and more armed I would be to face the next ordeal. Then, once I had secured a response and confirmed D was real, I could tell my friends.

I descended the grand staircase with a new skip in my step, humming softly to myself an old lullaby Beatrix used to coo to us as toddlers. The gentle tune reminded me of happier times, and matched my newly optimistic mood perfectly.

In my expectant, merry daydream, I failed to hear the subdued hissing of whispers until I was about to round the corner to the library.

"…understand exactly what we're dealing with. All the lies, all the false security… Please don't pretend you're oblivious to what kind of 'test' this is turning out to be. I know they've spoken to you too, and convincing yourself that it won't blow out of proportion, like *really soon*, is just insanity."

I froze. It was Tressa.

Peeking my head warily around the corner, bubble of joy

evaporating on the spot, I took in the queer scene with a horrible feeling in the pit of my stomach. This could not mean anything pleasant.

She was standing in a rather defensive stance, eyes flicking nervously as if to check for eavesdroppers, yet still holding firm to a position that meant that whoever she had cornered in the space between a small decorative wardrobe and the library door could not escape. The fact her skirts were so voluminous also did not help her victim's case.

"I don't want anything to have to do with these ridiculous politics!" came another voice, sounding irritated but also slightly afraid. It was Lucas, funnily enough the only person taller than Tressa. I couldn't make out more than a cowering silhouette in the shadows of the corner, but the lanky shape definitely matched the voice.

"Do you honestly think that sitting back and watching the clouds will get you through this?" Tressa gave an odd, cynical laugh. "Come on, Lucas, you're supposed to be the smart one! We've all felt the physical effects, and poor Penny is a prime example of the mental tolls. It's only a matter of time before the next massive event happens, and if you want to stay strong you need to join us in fighting back. Beatrix is dead, for heaven's sake, how long do you think before it's one of us?"

"Not. Interested." Lucas repeated through obviously clenched teeth, voice wavering as she stared him down.

"Fine," Tressa muttered. She paced for a moment, brows furrowed, and Lucas hesitantly edged towards the open corridor. Before he could carry out his escape, Tressa pivoted back to face him and tried a new approach. "I won't force you; perhaps we each should try to play our own tactics. If you won't ally with Avery and me, at least give us what we want; if you plan to take a back seat, then surely you have no need for them anymore?"

"Ally? Since when did that term come into play?" Lucas retorted scathingly, vainly trying to mask panic. Her honeyed tone clearly not convincing him.

"Since you lot decided to do nothing." Tressa shrugged without missing a beat. "Stop avoiding the question. Give them to me."

"I don't know what you're talking about!" Lucas pleaded, trying now to dodge around her without much success.

I flattened myself against the wall, trying my hardest not to breathe or cough or step on a creaking floorboard and give away my position. What was all this about? What did Lucas have?

"You know full well what I'm talking about," Tressa argued, a note of impatience creeping in to the controlled sweetness. "You stole the—"

At that moment, I felt a sneeze begin to tingle at the end of my nose and my eyes began to water. I held my breath and scrunched my face, pleading with my senses to remain silent, but right on cue a snorting half-sneeze half-concealing cough made a loud entrance, sounding louder due to the echo.

Tressa whirled around and faced me in an instant, expression furious.

"What are you doing here?" she hissed, eyes flashing.

"I could ask you the same thing," I said, maintaining eye contact and a strong glower. "But last time I checked, the library wing was open to all of us. Oh, and before you ask if I was eavesdropping, yes I was, so care to elaborate on all that?"

Once again, her face softened into a more characteristic smile a mother might sport having found a darling child eating forbidden biscuits.

"It was nothing, don't bother about it," she explained lightly. "How are you feeling? Back to normal?"

"Save your damned excuses, Tressa," I snapped, sick of the lying. She nearly fainted with horror, aghast I would dare to even think of using such a vulgarity.

With a stunned silence, she marched away towards the stairs, skirts billowing, leaving Lucas and me alone. There was no retort strong enough that she could have used to answer back to *that*.

"Wow," Lucas said eventually after what seemed like an eternity. "Strong words."

"I don't know where that came from," I apologized, too irritated to be ashamed. "It kind of slipped out. Anyway, can *you* tell me what that was all about? What did you steal?"

He wrung his hands with a conflicted sigh, nervously glancing over my shoulder at Tressa's back as she strode away.

After some hesitation he said, "Do you remember when Beatrix got rid of all our books?" He waited until I nodded assent then continued. "Well...for some time before that, I had been...er, smuggling books back to our chamber for some out-of-lessons reading. I would hide one or two under my waistcoat each day and stow them under my mattress, then when I had finished I would bring them back. For some of the smaller paperbacks, I would conceal them in my sketchbook. I had...erm...*a lot* accumulated on the day she removed them, and when I got back to my bed I found the ones I had...borrowed...were still there, including a massive thick one with lots of really interesting information. It had a section on outside combat. Well...then recently Avery suspected I had them and told Tressa. I was on my way down to grab some more numeracy practice when she found me."

"Oh."

I was now the one awkwardly fiddling with my fingers. Even if Tressa and Avery got their hands on the book, they wouldn't do any harm to us, so I really didn't see what the big deal was. Right now, the greatest advantage we had was probably D, and all I wanted was Lucas to leave so I could get the stationary I had been after in the first place.

"I don't understand why she's being so nasty!" Lucas shuddered. "She and Avery are taking it way to seriously. It's bringing on more damage than the trials are at this rate."

"Yeah," I agreed. I had much to say on the subject – later – but right now I wanted him to drop it and go away.

"I don't suppose you'd consider backing Fred, Evelyn, and me?" Lucas inquired uncertainly. "Just to prove to the other two there is another way and we don't have to go all ninja to survive?"

I twirled my hair.

"No," I answered slowly. "I have my own views, and I think that I either want to work with everyone or as an individual. No in between."

I didn't want to admit it aloud, but to be brutally honest I did not want to place myself on the side that went against Tressa and Avery. They were just too dangerous as a team. What 'taking action' actually meant I didn't know, since unless they were planning to confront the Master there was nothing much they could do. More likely, if they'd discovered something like I just had, then I would want to be joining with them rather than ignoring it. I only wondered why they hadn't just shared their plans in the first place: maybe for reasons the same as mine? Even Lucas had suddenly become dubious about telling us of his own secret stash.

He echoed what Tressa had just said. "Fine. I won't force you. Watch out for yourself, Penny."

I nodded.

Lucas, blessedly forgetting his numeracy, turned and went straight back upstairs.

Heart in my mouth, I waited for him to go before hurrying into the library at long last, touching the pocketed letter just to make sure it was still there.

Drinking in the cold room like sour medicine, I made a beeline for my rickety wooden desk tucked in a lonely corner where it sat untouched and collecting piles of dust. Throwing aside nostalgia and firmly refusing to become lost in memories of fonder times with Beatrix, I threw open the top of the desk to reveal a yellowing pile of stale paper and curdled ink pens messily

130

arranged from their last use several weeks ago. I sat down on my stool and set out the writing tools. Licking the nib of the pen to start the flow of ink, I searched for the right words to communicate the excessive amount of things I wanted to say. Perhaps the best thing would be to start off small, then see if I even received a reply.

> *Dear D,*
>
> *My name is Penny, I'm fifteen years old and facing the exact situation you described in your letter. You cannot begin to understand the full extent of the questions I have for you! Finding your note was somewhat of a miracle for me – I don't know where to begin! Can you tell me your full name so I know how to properly address you? Did you really live here as well, and if so when and who with? Where are you now? What were some of the challenges presented to you when you faced the trials? Would it be possible to meet you? How, what, when, why, where, who...I want to know it all, nothing held back! Please answer, though I know it is a long shot. It would change my life, and perhaps even save it.*
>
> *Yours optimistically,*
>
> *Penny*

I reread my letter several times to make sure I had included all that was sufficient for my first reply. My hand had stayed mostly neat and clear, which was good, and I hadn't ranted like a madwoman, staying with the most pressing questions and leaving out all the extra.

Now what to do with it? I couldn't exactly hand it to D myself. I decided to keep it and wait for results.

I folded my letter neatly in half, put it safely in my pocket and placed the pen and rest of the paper back inside my desk. All I could do now was wait.

I ascended the staircase and prepared to rejoin my friends, pausing outside of the common room to tuck a stray hair behind my ears and smooth my ruffled dress.

"Hello everyone!" I greeted them all brightly. "Miss me?"

They looked up from their activities and gave me forced smiles, but there was no life to the gesture. They were all beaten and more strained than ever, without even a ray of sunshine such as the letter I had. Nobody mentioned why I'd left in the first place out of politeness, though I half wished they would. It was annoying, seeing them all sitting together like nothing was wrong, when in actuality they were all sneaking about behind each other's backs – myself included.

Today, though, the quiet did not last very long.

"That is the most disgusting thing I have ever seen," Avery drawled loudly, smirking at the area where Evelyn was sitting cross-legged with Fred and attempting to show him how to sew. Every so often he would make a silly mistake, resulting in jovial laughter from to two of them before a relapse of dreary silence.

Fred stiffened, but did not look up from his stitch. Instead, he stuck his tongue out in concentration and continued sewing a small tear in the leg of his trousers as if Avery hadn't spoken at all.

"Only just past fourteen, yet already acting like an old married couple! I tell you, it's wrong."

"Avery, shut up," I warned, surprised Tressa hadn't already intervened.

"Why?" he countered maddeningly, clearly wound up and ready for an argument. "It's not even as if they like each other! You'd have to be blind to not see Evelyn's only using his fat behind to hide from the trials!"

The cruel words seemed to reverberate around the room for a tantalizing moment whilst the meaning of them sunk in.

Then Fred threw down his needle and approached Avery in two big strides, expression perfectly calm, although he was shaking just a bit.

Tressa leaned casually against the mantelpiece as if faintly amused though unimpressed by the show, waiting patiently to see what would happen next, whilst Lucas and I hovered on the brink of intervention.

"Insult me all you want," Fred ordered. "But don't you dare bring her into it! What's she ever done?"

It showed just then exactly how much larger Fred was that Avery, not only in mass but also in height; he must have been a good half-foot taller, though still not quite my size. Fred didn't have an aggressive bone in his body, but this new loyalty to Evelyn brought on a whole new twist, one I didn't quite understand. For a split second I actually felt scared for Avery. Then I remembered what he had said and decided I would be pleased if Fred punched his stupid loud mouth.

"Now I'm terrified," Avery snapped. "And in answer to your question, she's done absolutely nothing. She never does anything, which is the point I'm trying to make: she's only latching onto the only person idiotic enough not to see that she's *using him*, because she doesn't know how to do anything herself."

"Hey!" Evelyn argued, just realizing what he was implying.

"Shut up, Avery, or I swear..." Fred growled. It was odd to hear him use such a deadly tone, and no one knew how to react.

"You what? Smile at me?" Avery tutted, shaking his head in a scolding manner. "Please. These threats coming from the person who's so wrapped up in a *girl* that he's refusing to see how shoddy everything else is getting around here."

"Shut up!" Fred yelled so loudly we all cringed. "SHUT UP!"

"I dare you." Avery opened his arms wide, nonplussed.

"Avery," Tressa cautioned in a mild tone, not overly worried. I couldn't believe her coolness, and it was very unusual for her to have not intervened as it was.

"Stop it," I interjected, unnerved. "Beatrix is only two weeks dead, and I know we're all feeling down, but really this is quite unnecessary."

Fred took a long, shuddering breath and gave Avery the filthiest look I had ever seen besmirch his usually kind face, then with enormous effort he turned around and went back to his comfortable spot on the carpet.

"Fine. Coward," Avery jeered.

He was being so horrible! When Fred refused to acknowledge him, Avery seemed to wonder for a moment whether to back out or throw another blow. "It's a shame this romance is going to be such a short one. If you weren't going to betray each other's lives when the day comes, I would be rather interested to see how it plays out! It's a pity you're both so vain and selfish reall—"

In a breadth of a second, Fred had pivoted from his graceful retreat and had punched Avery in the face so hard that the sound reverberated like a gong across the room.

Avery stood there, stunned for a moment, a look of anger and pain crossing his face along with an odd, hollow sadness.

Then it was gone and he leapt at Fred with a strangely pitched cry. In perfect synchrony, Lucas and I leapt into the fray and each seized hold of a boy, careful to avoid the increasingly vicious blows being dealt.

My arms wound tightly around Fred's middle, trying to drag him away from Avery, who was struggling against Lucas with equal fervor.

"Tressa!" I shouted desperately as I received a hard wallop in the face intended for Avery. "Do something!"

She smiled faintly, appearing to inspect her nails with complete calmness as if the heated duel was not happening right in front of her.

"Let go!" Avery yelled angrily, trying to both kick Fred and throw off Lucas at the same time, shaggy hair an awful mess and face alight with a deep rage.

"Tressa!" Lucas and I begged again.

"Oh, all right." Tressa sighed reluctantly, taking her time in slowly pushing away from the mantelpiece and entering the fight. She lightly stepped in between the two brawling boys, and after another deep sigh artfully took them both by the scruffs of their necks and clonked their heads together.

"Do stop it."

A trickle of red dribbled out of a shallow cut on Avery's lip where he had bitten into it. Fred was mostly unscathed, though his clothes were all untucked and his breathing heavy.

Avery threw one look of utter dislike at Fred, opening his mouth as if to start another quarrel, but decided against it, clenching his jaw shut instead and angrily storming from the common room, slamming the door behind him as he went.

"What did he mean, calling me 'a girl'?" Evelyn fumed. "He's known me his entire life! It would've been nice if he could've at least addressed me by my name."

Fred buried his face in his hands, mumbling, "I'm sorry. I just lost it… That was particularly low, even for him."

"How could you just stand there, Tressa?" I hissed. She was once again slumped nonchalantly by the fireplace inspecting the arrangement of her petticoats. "How could you do nothing?"

"They both deserved whatever they got, arguing so heatedly over nothing," she replied smoothly, not even looking up. "It wasn't my problem."

"Not your…?" I echoed in disbelief. Before, everything had been Tressa's problem, and now…now it was as if she didn't care. When everything was falling apart, she was leaving us.

"No. It was a bother, but quite honestly I felt it was nothing I had to concern myself with too much."

"I can't believe you. You disgust me," I snapped, searching around vainly for a decent word or two to describe the depth of feeling welling up inside of me.

For all I cared now, the cold-hearted figure staring mistily out of the window was as nasty as the Master Himself, and as much as a traitor as we had believed Beatrix to have been.

I couldn't stay there in the same room as her.

On impulse, I threw one last dirty look over my shoulder at Tressa before storming out of the common room and chasing along the corridor to find Avery.

I noticed as I searched that the door to one of the empty rooms was slightly ajar, so I popped my head in and sure enough was rewarded with the sight of Avery standing over by the fogged-up window, alone in the otherwise barren room.

There were only two other empty rooms in the manor, all on this floor, and as far as I could see they possessed no greater purpose than to fill up space. This one was covered in neutral striped wallpaper with a single off-white metal fireplace perched between once-magnificent plasterwork adjacent to the dirty paned windows.

"Avery?" I called uncertainly. "It's—"

"Penny," he interrupted briskly, not turning around. "I know. After fifteen years, I can actually tell who you are by the sound of your voice."

"I'll leave," I threatened, not impressed.

"Fine. Good. Splendid."

I paused, unsure whether to leave or not, irritated he had called my bluff.

"Or not," I decided, sweeping over to stand resolutely beside him, ignoring the rude grumbles that my actions caused. "Fancy telling me why you decided to have a go at poor Fred? I know we've all been under pressure, but it's unusual of even you to take it that far."

"Go away and stop trying to be Tressa!" Avery groaned, turning away from me to sulk over by the window. His choice of the empty room had clearly not worked to his advantage, as now there was nowhere for him to hide as I simply followed his footsteps.

Now it was my turn to be violent. Suddenly, I had had enough and seized him by his shaggy hair forcing him to face me, our equally startled eyes meeting reluctantly.

"Listen to me, Avery," I said in my best dangerous voice. "I don't know what the *heck* is going on between you and Tressa, I don't know why you're all being so nasty, and I don't know why you're taking it out on the ones who are trying to stay out of your way! But you better figure it out, or the trials won't be the one killing you, I will be. I'm sick and tired of all this nonsense!"

Finished with my monologue, I threw Avery down and looked away as the tears once again threatened to overflow. I waited for him to slash back at me, but the retort never came.

"It wasn't about Tressa, or the trials, or anything like that," Avery muttered, his flushed cheeks turning an even deeper red as he bowed his head, gingerly straightening his shirt. "If you must know, it was about who Evelyn and Fred *are*."

"I beg your pardon?" I asked, not quite understanding.

He laughed bitterly, kicking some nonexistent pebble and shoving his hands in waistcoat pockets.

"Taunt me all you like, I'm truly past caring. The thing is…I'm jealous."

"Of Evelyn?" I scoffed. "We can't all be gorgeous."

"No…" Avery hesitated, the bitter look still etched onto his features. "Not like that. I've never been *likeable*, not like they are, and it didn't bother me until…well, it doesn't matter. I made that perfect facade crack. I won. And it feels bloody awful. Tressa and I are like the bad guys now, but if that's what it takes to get out of here, then I'm willing to play the part. You don't know what we… There are some things you don't…" He broke off, unable to find the words.

I hesitated, not entirely sure what he was getting at.

"Look, just do us a favor." He sighed. "Don't judge us. We've got better reasons than you might think."

"*What?*"

"See you," Avery bid me as he retreated into the corridor, along with a smile that didn't quite meet his eyes.

My hands trailed into my pockets as I tried to process what he meant, when they brushed against my letter. Only, it wasn't mine; I had used much thicker paper than this.

D had replied to me.

16

Penny,

I am so delighted to hear from you as well! For years I have waited to communicate with the living inside the Boundary, as it has been eating away at me as time goes by that I can do nothing to help or guide you. Unfortunately, I cannot answer many of your questions and can merely offer advice. It is the way of the in-between world in which I am forced to reside. Listen to me when I tell you that you need to distance yourself from your friends as soon as possible. It sounds awful, I know, but the trials always take the same steps to turn you against each other; the only way to avoid the imminent destruction is to isolate yourself. I will not be surprised if your next letter tells of this. I grow tired, and must finish this regrettably short letter.

My wishes for good luck, D.

I repeatedly read the words until I was certain that it was not a figment of my imagination but a true, material letter. Besides my ecstatic happiness that D was real and replying to me, I felt disappointed that he had answered none of my questions and that his advice was less than pleasant. Still, if it was the only guidance he was giving me, then I supposed I had to take it.

Clutching it tightly, I took a shuddering breath and slowly lowered my fist into my pocket. I would write back as soon as possible to gain an equally speedy response.

I ran as fast as I could towards the library, throwing open my desk and beginning to scribble down words before the paper had even hit the top of the desk. I had only written a greeting before I stopped and tried to think again of how to phrase what I wanted to say. If only I could meet D and ask my questions to his or her face! It would be so much easier, considering my mouth worked much faster than my mind sometimes.

Dear D,

Oh my goodness, you have replied! I won't pretend that you didn't bring unpleasant news, but I'm delighted all the same! I don't relish the thought of abandoning my friends, but I understand what you mean…still, is there no way to protect everyone? Oh, another thought has just occurred to me! I think this is probably an unreasonable request to ask of you, but do you possibly know anything about the dreams I have been having? Am I the baby, as I believed? And another touchy question; is she – sorry, Beatrix – with you, wherever you are? Are you alone? If we fail, will we join you? I find myself with more questions than answers now, and so I shall leave my letter at this so not to swamp you.

Please reply with haste,

Penny

*

The next morning I woke up with a pounding headache, as usual, feeling slightly nauseous, as usual. By the looks of the minimal light escaping from behind our curtains, the weather was as dreary and bleak as it had been for the past few weeks.

Feeling truly done with life, I clambered into boring grey half-mourning dress and half-heartedly tried to tame my limp hair into a respectable shape again. Looking in my vanity mirror by my bed, I got a clear view of what the trials had done to me physically.

I had big purple bags under my eyes from the scant amount of sleep I had gotten, and I could have sworn that even to me they were slowly becoming blacker, like those of the demons that had been haunting us. My skin was pale and sickly, and I had lost weight due to the poor quality food.

I splashed water on my face, and then checked my pockets with a bit more enthusiasm for a new letter. I was let down; the only note was my own.

"Morning." I nodded stiffly to Tressa as she glided past, her scoop neckline showing her collarbones protruding unhealthily. She gave me a curt bob of the head to acknowledge me, but that was it.

"Urgh, I feel awful!" Evelyn whined crossly as she appeared, tearing at frizzy ringlets in desperation. Her dress hung off her like a sack, and even her soft heart-shaped face was gaining a sharp tone from the thinness. "Mental battles, I can handle, but as soon as my hair is compromised I'm finished!"

"You look fine," I said tonelessly, trying and failing to gather some emotion for life.

"Do I? Really? Fred said the same, but that's only because he's so eager to please." Evelyn frowned, bending in front of my mirror to double check. Her face fell when she saw herself close up, bottom lip sliding into a pout.

"We look hideous and ill, all of us," she announced in the same way a philosopher might proclaim a revolutionary discovery. "This has to stop before we waste away to our deaths."

"You and your looks," Tressa hissed in annoyance, pulling back her blond hair into a ponytail, which only enhanced the sharp bony angles of her face. "Honestly, if you had only listened to Avery and me about taking action before, we wouldn't be in this mess! We'd have made progress."

"You don't know that," Evelyn argued, trying to scoop some powder out of a tiny ceramic jar with the crook of her little finger. "It might have just ended up even worse. Besides, you could have acted without our consent and you didn't. We disagreed, but we never tried to stop you."

The two girls, who had mere months ago been the best of friends, glared at each other challengingly before Evelyn gave up and looked away first.

"Breakfast," Tressa suggested with all the warmth of an icicle.

"Yes," I agreed, rising to her commanding stance and tipping up my chin. "Let's go."

We all despised breakfast now. The food was guaranteed to taste ashy, and the only reason we choked it down was so we didn't starve.

Walking with several feet between us, we glided downstairs to the breakfast room like the living dead. The boys met us just outside as usual, also looking absolutely awful. Lucas was standing firmly in between Avery and Fred, though he couldn't block the venomous stares being shared between the two.

"Hello, all," he greeted us with relief, giving his two charges warning glances to be civil in front of us.

Fred beamed despite the circumstances when he saw Evelyn, breaking ranks to give her a warm hug, which she delicately returned.

I noted curiously that Avery made no conspicuous reaction to this, but retained his stony expression with darkening eyes. If he was jealous of their happiness, he was only half trying to hide it.

Tressa did not return pleasantries, forcing her was through the breakfast room door first and leaving us all to trail behind her.

My first reaction was shock. There was no food on the table! Only slender, shiny, pointy things I recalled from a while ago at dinner, that closer inspection made my breath catch in my mouth and my emotions change to ones of fear.

They were knives. Not harmless flat butter knives as we were accustomed too, but sharp things used only for slicing the thickest of meats. They were deadly, dangerous, and there were six of them: one for each of us. I did not know why they were there, only it could not be good.

"Where's the food?" Fred gasped in horror. "What's going on?"

Avery and Tressa shared a look then, and my throat went dry.

The mutual understanding that passed between them did nothing to boost my confidence in the situation, instead raising even more alarms that this was *bad*.

I took a closer inspection of the knives, taking in their razor sharp blades and wicked pointed tips. I noticed, they were emitting a low static pulse, rather like the contraption upstairs had but on a lesser scale.

We each reached forward in uncertain awe to touch the things, and all at once our hands closed around the buzzing metal.

It made my hand sting, but before I could register the feeling of touching the static, something even more bizarre happened.

There was an almighty rip in the room, and with a jerk, I felt myself and the others being ripped out of the manor and flung shrieking to the Boundary woods, to face the next event of the trials.

When the sickening spinning stopped and the blurred scenery came into focus, I felt more than a little ill and extremely nauseous.

We had been transported to the very edge of the estate, so close to the Boundary itself that I could hear the trickle of water as it made its seemingly harmless rounds about the perimeter.

The worst part was that we were trapped.

On one side there was the Boundary, and on the other sides there were enormous trees that had grown together into one massive trunk, forming a natural, solid wall at least five yards long that left us confined to the resulting clearing with no escape, holding nothing but our deadly knives.

"What the *bloody hell* was that?" Avery managed to gasp after we had all grounded ourselves and taken in the ominous surroundings.

For once, Tressa didn't correct him, seeming as shaken as the rest of us albeit slightly less terrified.

Fred dropped his knife to the ground as if it was something poisonous, a look of utter horror on his face, and Evelyn hastily did the same with the same disgusted expression at having to touch such a vulgar weapon. I, on the other hand, held on to mine grimly. We had been given them for a reason, and I wasn't about to discard my only means of defense without knowing why.

"A rip," Tressa answered flatly, evaluating the clearing critically. "We discussed this, Avery, remember?"

"I wasn't expecting it so soon," he grumbled, twirling the knife between his fingers with unsettling ease and digging a hole absently with his toes in the soft, earthy ground. "I thought we'd have longer to prepare."

"You knew this was going to happen?" I exclaimed incredulously. How much had they kept from us? I felt my anger boiling back up again at the stark impassiveness they showed to the situation, as well as a strong need to hit something rather hard. Preferably Avery.

"Not this precisely," Avery explained impatiently. "But—"

"Oh, go ahead!" Tressa interrupted in a slightly hysterical tone, fist white around the hilt of the knife. "Go and give them all the same advantages we have! I mean, if someone's going to die, it may as well be us right?"

"Die?" Lucas demanded, flicking them a furious glare that mirrored my own. "Advantage? I think some serious explanation is due from you two. We all understood that you wanted to take the offensive path, but we never knew you had actually discovered anything useful."

"*Au contraire*, Lucas old chap," Avery said with a huge smile, though the rest of his face seemed tired and worn. "We managed perfectly well without your precious books."

"Books?" Now it was Fred's turn to gape in betrayed amazement. "You had books all this time, and you didn't tell us? I thought we were supposed to be together on this!"

I snorted. "The 'let's work together' motto didn't last very long at all, did it?"

And then we were all yelling at each other like caged lions, letting loose all our accumulated anger and frustration in multiple rants and screaming, so that the clearing was suddenly deafening with the noise of our arguments.

I didn't know at whom exactly I was yelling, perhaps all of them, but I could feel the angry words spill out as my face flushed red with a tirade of accusations aimed at no one, everyone, and partially myself for letting it get this bad.

Through the haze of emotions I saw blows being dealt, curse words being bellowed, and eyes turn a solid, feral black. I did not stop myself at this though, only raising my voice louder over the racket so that it could be heard, and for the first time in weeks people would know exactly how I felt!

It must have been quite a sight for anyone watching. Then there was a high-pitched scream and I saw Tressa trip over a root. She was falling right towards the Boundary, hands plucking desperately in midair for a nonexistent handhold to break the impact.

Dimly, I was aware that I should be acting to save her, but my anger was still at too high a boiling point for me to care.

Lucas, on the other hand, still had his rational head intact. Without hesitation, he darted forward and seized her arm before she could tumble through the Boundary.

"That was close," he muttered to the floor.

"Good reflexes," Avery said in a drawling tone, though he too appeared shaken by such a narrow escape.

"Oh, Lucas!" Tressa gasped, face as white as her hair. "Thank goodness you thought to…when I wouldn't…I mean, thank you! I'm sorry…I've been so horrible and you still… But of course you don't know…"

"What are you blabbering about?" I rolled my eyes, dusting the dirt off my skirts discreetly all the while as if this new approachable Tressa was going to whirl around and scold me for it like the old days.

"I don't know," she whispered, eyes reddening – with tears? Was Tressa the Cold actually going to show regret? "Well, more like *you* don't know... Oh, Avery, what have we done?"

A muscle tensed in Avery's jaw as he regarded Tressa, and for the moment it seemed as if there was no one in the clearing but those two.

I found myself once again surrounded by secrets and lies, which I could not solve, but only watch and hope they unfolded in my favor.

How frustrating, but also interesting! A little near-death experience was all it took to make Tressa's harsh facade crumble.

"It was your idea," Avery reminded her in a low voice. "You said you were prepared to do it to win."

"But...how can we? They saved my life, when we would have just let them go...it's awful, Avery, and I can't stand it anymore," Tressa argued, her voice gaining strength towards the end. "This has been killing me on the inside for a long time now. Penny and Evelyn are more than my friends; they're my sisters. Fred, Lucas and you are like family too, and I always have felt like I'm their...guardian, I suppose...especially after Beatrix died. It kills me, Avery, and I'm surprised you don't feel the same."

"I do!" he contradicted, and with the tortured look in his eyes I actually believed him for a while. "I'm not heartless."

"As deep as this is, would anyone mind letting the rest of us know what you're on about?" Evelyn butted in crossly, folding her arms across her chest and pouting beautifully. "I hate being clueless in conversations."

"Hear! Hear!" I agreed crossly, feeling my hand tighten involuntarily around the hilt of my knife as a sliver of unease shivered its way down my spine. I had the peculiar feeling someone was watching me, although all eyes were trained on Tressa.

Avery and Tressa stared each other out for a few minutes, and it seemed there was a silent battle raging in the few feet between them. The rest of us stood quietly and watched, trying to keep our frustration contained.

To my surprise, it was actually Avery who first broke eye

contact.

"I'm sorry," he muttered to the ground, fists clenched. "To all of you."

I raised an eyebrow.

"Not good enough. You need to tell us what you've been up to."

"We…we did find something," Tressa began to explain, tears still rolling down her face in silent regret. "It was awful, and I half wish we hadn't found it at all; it made us realize exactly how dire the situation was and what needed to be sacrificed in order to beat the trials. We decided not to say anything because it would be better that way for you…you wouldn't have to live with the knowledge constantly weighing you down. Perhaps I still don't want to take that back. It's changed me, and not for the better; I've been simply horrible to all of you, because in some twisted perverse way that has helped me deal with the truth."

"What did you find?" I probed, perturbed by her cryptic apology, but pleased that it was an apology nonetheless. Avery was getting very agitated, twirling the knife with renewed ferocity, refusing to join in on the conversation. There was a shadow in his eyes, which I had never seen before, but I stubbornly told myself not to see it as a true threat. This was *Avery* after all, and what could he possibly do to us?

"I'd like to know why you were so nasty, Avery," Fred interrupted. "I can't hear any heartfelt apologies coming from you."

"You have something I don't. I got jealous." Avery shrugged carelessly. "Not that it really mattered; I just hated feeling outdone."

"Does this have anything to do with me?" Evelyn piped up hopefully, having forgotten about the argument already.

"Not anymore," Avery said under his breath, scuffing the toes of his boots against a prominent root.

I felt awkward, silly almost, as we plunged again into silence. There was not a sound but the wind whistling gently through the trees overhead, pulling the strands of the willow branches into a reluctant dance.

"How are we supposed to get—" I began, boredom working itself up in me.

When Evelyn and I walked in on Beatrix's body in the library, time had seemed to stop. What happened next was the complete opposite; it went so fast that I had trouble recalling the exact event even two weeks later.

Tressa, who had ceased crying, gave an odd sniffle and whispered something to Avery that sounded like "It can't be me..."

He nodded stiffly, a tear in his eye too...or maybe not as it was gone before I could look twice.

No one had time to react.

Avery flipped his knife so that the point was suddenly on the offensive, then he whirled around and stabbed out at Tressa.

I didn't see how badly he hurt her, only the mask of shock, pain, and a peculiar resoluteness as she clutched at her stomach, and stumbled backwards.

The knife was coated in blood, as were Tressa's hands as she numbly removed them from her wound, mouth an O of surprise.

It had all happened so fast none of us had time to call out, before Tressa's knees gave way and she fell awkwardly into the Boundary without anything to break the impact.

The Boundary gave an odd shudder – then Tressa was gone, the instant she touched it.

I realized the deafening noise was our screams at Avery, but I realized then that he too was gone, vanished as if he had never been.

There was a rip, lurching us back into the estate, but I didn't notice. All I could see was the knife.

17

"Urgh, that was an awful excuse for a night's sleep," I groaned, stretching and wiping the remnants of a dream from my aching eyes. They were red and puffy as if I had been crying, which wasn't surprising given the terrible nightmare I had experienced. "You wouldn't believe what I dreamt about; it was horrifying! So real…"

The vision of Tressa's pain and defeat as she fell limply towards the Boundary was still a fresh memory, as was my shock that it had been Avery who had caused it before he too had vanished. Thank goodness, it had just been a dream!

I poured some sludgy water into my washbasin in vain attempt to cleanse my mind from the plagues of the night. Splashing it onto my face, I caught a glimpse of myself as I reached for the towel to dry off.

It was not the sallow unhealthiness that nearly made my heart stop. It was the fact that I was still wearing my full day dress instead of my nightgown, and that it was coated with dust as if I had been outside recently wearing it.

"Impossible," I gasped, eyes dropping to my dirty hands with mounting panic.

It was only a dream! There was absolutely no possible way that it had been real. I was crazy.

I rushed to Tressa's bed to prove myself right, my breathing accelerating to hyperventilation.

The bed was perfectly made. The pillows plumped invitingly at the iron headboard. The duvet had been smoothed down to the last crease, just as Tressa routinely did every morning before breakfast, as she hated the sight of a crumpled bed.

The basin on her table lay parched of water, hairbrush untouched, and her powders undisturbed in their designated jars.

"Tressa?" I called, trying to stay calm. The curtains were

already open, and that was when I noticed the clouded sun was not low in the east, as it was every morning. It was setting towards the west, as if was evening time.

"Tressa!" I yelled, cupping my hands around my mouth so to enhance my cry even more.

"Penny!"

I started, glancing wildly around for the source of the voice. It came from the other side of the chamber, so I hitched up my skirts and ran towards it, realizing along the way that my shoes (why would I wear them to bed?) were trailing mud across the floor as I ran as if I had been in the woods.

"Penny..." Evelyn sobbed, embracing me into a tight hug as I rounded the L bend. She was wearing her daytime clothes as well, her eyes swollen. "Tressa isn't coming, Penny."

"No. This is just another trick. The Master's only playing with us again, and she's probably just downstairs with the others. Avery wouldn't..." I viciously shook away from her, tearing out of the chamber and slamming the door behind me as I went. The corridors blended into one as I sprinted, refusing to believe this nightmare was coming true.

"Tressa!" I screamed, throwing open the front doors into the dying evening light. "Tressa!"

I kept running into the dying gardens, not noticing the wilted plants or dull chipping bricks of the manor house, trying not to see the bizarrely thriving rhododendron bushes at its walls.

Out of the corner of my eyes, I saw Beatrix's tombstone silhouetted against the Boundary woods. It was not alone.

There was a tall black granite block there, smooth as ice and crafted into a pyramidal point at the top; much thinner than the gravestone but equally as tall, as if remembering someone who's name needed no mention.

I choked back a sob, lowering myself down to the yellowing grass in front of the monument. Only one; nothing for Avery, who was clearly still alive and well wherever he was.

In that colorless world of greys, blacks and dull browns, there was suddenly no emotion either.

There was a soft frost on the ground numbing my knees as I knelt, but I could feel nothing except the overwhelming pain inside my chest – the pain that threatened to destroy everything I had worked so hard to repair after we lost Beatrix. The strands of my grief had begun to heal, and now they had once again been frayed into pieces. Perhaps one of the reasons I felt so empty and desolate was that Tressa had not been killed by Him, like Beatrix; it had been one of our own. Avery. If I ever saw him again, I swore, I would – kill him? Did I really have that in me? Maybe not, but I'd make him sorry. All those things he'd said to me in the empty room, all that stuff about feeling regret for how he'd acted… What had that been, then? A cover up, so we wouldn't suspect his actual plan? And how on earth had he known what to plan for?

I reached out and stroked the glossy black granite with shaking hands, crying as I leant my forehead gently against the hard stone. Why was it that whenever someone had 'betrayed' us then made amends, they were brutally murdered? Why did Tressa not deserve the same remembrance as Beatrix?

Pushing myself away from the memorial, I let my head hang back so that the dark grey clouds of the infinite sky filled my eyes, then fell to the ground and closed my eyes.

Flashes of memories came to me as I lay there on the ground; Tressa's exasperated reminder of *Penny – no one can open the Boundary.* Beatrix's warning to me: *You are jeopardizing not only your life, but all your friends lives too.* The Master's monotone, amused predictions: *The true punishment is coming, and it is you who has brought it upon yourself. Do you know what rhododendrons represent? They mean 'beware.' It's not a coincidence that they are the only flowers still alive on the estate, they are here to deliver an important lesson to you children. I suggest you take heed, unless you want to be the next grave in my collection…*

Tressa standing in the clearing, a tear trickling down her face: *Oh, Avery, what have we done?*

My eyes jerked open, heart hammering. Drowning in my sorrow had done nothing last time except isolate me from my friends, and perhaps because of that we had lost Tressa. They had turned on each other, and I – I who had brought the trials upon them in the first place – had done nothing to fix it.

For Beatrix, I would stay strong. For Tressa, I would get us out of here. I slowly uncurled myself from the ground, admittedly feeling rather petty for acting so pathetic. Tressa would have been horrified! I imagined her with her sharp face, soft hair, and tall, elegant figure standing disapprovingly in front of me.

"You know, Penny, whining like a toddler is going to get you nowhere. You need to come up with a plan, and pull yourself together at the very least! I'm embarrassed for you, giving up so easily like that just because I'm not around anymore to tell you otherwise!"

I cracked a half-smile at the apparition, dusting myself off dutifully and even pulling an unpracticed curtsey at her memorial. It was then that I felt the crumple of paper against my leg, and realized that my note had been replaced by another, thicker piece of a quality paper: D!

My hands shook as I scrambled to pluck the letter from my pocket and unfold it enough to read; wondering all the while if D had been able to see the tragic events, which had so rapidly passed from wherever he or she was.

Dear Penny,

You must understand; these questions are very difficult for me to answer. I do not know what will happen to you if you fail, though I am alone, I suppose, though not entirely in the way you probably mean. Therefore, Beatrix is not with me. I will not address now the issue of your departed friend Avery, or indeed Tressa (who, incidentally, was not killed). What I said before about isolation is true; you need to listen to me this time, or else next time the fallen will include you. Also, forget the dreams. They will only bring you harm – whatever you do, DO NOT tell Madon.

D.

"All right, then," I muttered bleakly, put off by the impatient tone of the writing. It was almost as if D was getting frustrated with me, as if I was bringing catastrophe upon myself. The reference to the dreams did nothing to convince me of their redundancy, exactly what had happened when Beatrix tried to convince me of the same thing; instead, it only did more to make them seem important.

Yet there was a benefit in all of this, if D was correct. Somehow, after falling through the Boundary, Tressa was still alive! Where was she now, then? And where was Avery?

It started to drizzle, and I realized from the goose bumps appearing on my arms that I was cold. I gave one last longing look at Tressa's memorial with watering eyes before turning on my heel and heading back towards the manor, tucking D's letter back into my pocket before the rain made the ink run.

Once I had shut the doors, I debated between returning upstairs and going to the dining hall for the main reason of confronting Him at dinner, or to simply go to the library and write a reply as soon as possible. I instantly rejected the second choice, deciding that it was still too early for any face-to-face action between Him and myself yet, and then proceeded to eliminate the former in fear that their tears would only coax out my own.

"Penny?" called a voice from upstairs. I craned my neck to see Fred peering over the banister with hollow eyes, his clothes on the looser side rather than tighter for the first time in years. "Where were you?"

"I needed some fresh air," I replied, listening to my voice echoing in the vast foyer area, D's warning of isolation still reverberating in my mind.

"We were outside for over an hour," Fred contradicted, sounding very tired.

Fred waited for a moment for me to take back my answer, waiting for me to remind him that despite all that had happened we were still the same inseparable friends that had lived here together before the trails, sharing a common cause.

But were we? Were we all still friends like before?

Something snapped inside me then. I was sick of all the secrecy and scheming we had done to try and protect ourselves. We had been downright selfish, and contrary to what D might have said, I thought now that perhaps it had been the isolation that had lost us Tressa, and that it was certainly not the way to freedom. No one was perfect, and that included D. Perhaps he or she was wrong in that respect, and maybe the best thing to do was bind myself closer to my friends. After all, D hadn't succeeded, but failed. Maybe that was why.

"Fine," I sighed, glancing around as if D was going to dart out of the shadows to yell at me for talking to him. "I went to go and find Tressa…but all I found was a memorial next to where Beatrix is buried. It's true. She's gone."

"I know, I saw it out of the boys' chamber," Fred acknowledged hoarsely, though his mouth twitched into a contented half-smile that I was finally being open with him. "It's funny, but I felt more stricken when Beatrix died. Now I just feel empty. Is that wrong?"

I nodded to myself, understanding the feeling. I didn't feel empty though, not in the way Fred meant. In fact, a grim determination filled me like never before, desperate to show Him that He did not own us, and that we had the power to escape no matter what he threw our way. The loss had made the dangers more real, but had also given me something with which to fight.

"No, it's fine," I comforted him, just as a fuzzy static feeling shocked through my pocket; a rip. D had sent me another letter, and I had a feeling that it was not going to be a pleased tone. My correspondent was really watching me (an oddly disturbing thought) and hadn't bothered to wait for my reply before correcting my friendliness. "I – I don't think Tressa is actually dead. I don't know where she is, but I just have a niggling feeling that—"

"I know. Well, I don't know for certain, but I feel the same way. Normally things disintegrate when they touch the Boundary, not disappear. Lucas pointed it out, but...oh gosh, it's just too much at the moment. I'm going early to bed, see you in the morning." Fred yawned loudly, slinking away from the banister to retire.

What he said was true, and much more logical. It made the emptiness shrink a little bit, giving me the courage I needed to face D. I waited for him to leave, before tearing the letter from my pocket and unfolding it like a guilty child caught red-handed.

My eyes scanned the loopy handwriting with mounting surprise, then elation. It was not at all what I had been expecting; it was fantastic!

Penny,

Before you jump to conclusions, I am not writing again to yell at you for talking to that boy, Fred, whatever his name is, though I do strongly discourage your actions and once again implore you to stop talking with your friends. I have to strike a deal with you, which could play greatly to your advantage. 'Ripping' (as you have called it), Penny, is the key to Madon's power and is the entire bones of the Boundary. If you can master it, then you will be able to put your own stake in things and give the tables another dimension in terms of who is holding the monopoly. For yes, it is possible for anyone inside the Boundary to harness this ability, if they have proper instruction. Focus in on moving the very fabric of the air, see the magic in the in-between spaces and use it to move things. Concentrate. It seems simple, but it is not at all easy. You will not, for many reasons, be able

*to manifest or destroy, only move, but for now you will find that quite
enough. In return for this advantage and further teaching, you must
promise me to protect and isolate yourself.*
D.

"Ahh…" I gurgled, the words stuck in my throat before forming
coherent sounds. This was not possible. This could not be.

With few sentences, those few simple instructions, D was
suggesting that I could be like them – like Beatrix, and Him.

The possibilities were endless! All of us, we could protect
ourselves. I remembered D's condition dryly, mulling only for a
moment on whether I should actually listen; but I was born a
rebel, and when it came to my friends I was willing to risk the
anger of just about anything on earth to keep them safe. I had lost
Tressa, and essentially Avery, and I was not about to lose anyone
else.

My eyes fixated suddenly on a delicate vase filled to the brim
with the wilted brown remains of what were once daisies. It was
made of bone china, perched atop a simple wooden table beside
my favorite armchair.

I cocked my head at the vase, a curious grin lighting up my
face. Scrunching up my nose, clenching my palms, I focused in on
the edge of the vase until everything else disappeared into a hazy
blur and the silhouette became astonishingly clear. After a few
seconds, without blinking, everything began to swim as if the air
itself was moving – as if it could be broken or ripped.

"Here goes," I muttered to myself, unsure if it would work or
not.

I pictured the air splitting around the vase, pictured forcing it
into the air, but still nothing happened.

I cursed, eyes stinging from the strain, until finally I gave up
and looked away. "Darn it!"

The letter crumpled into my fist, disappointment
overwhelming me.

Of course, what was I expecting to happen? That I, ordinary little me, could match the Master's power? It was laughable!

Half-heartedly, I tried again, and my poor eyes watered and ached. Then a real rip resounded, causing me to stumble and retch from the force of it. I had, in my preoccupied stupor, nearly forgotten what a real rip was like for those who were close enough to experience it. My heart almost stopped beating. At the front doors, only a few yards away from where I was standing, He had appeared, casually unbuttoning His travelling coat and ripping it away with a lazy wave of a hand.

I looked away, using the old I-can't-see-you-can't-see-me theory, staring at the vase as if we might both rip away to safety.

"Penny!" came a calm, accusatory voice from behind me, and I heard the horrifying noise of boots crossing the marble with awful clapping sounds. I gave a little squeak of terror…and the vase smashed.

In my frozen guilt, I had subconsciously levitated it off the table a few inches, and then broken the bond when He had distracted me.

I had made a rip.

Slowly, I pivoted round; my face flushed a deep red from both excitement and fear. The Master's black eyes were boring in on me, and I could not read what He was thinking, but it didn't matter. I had ripped!

This adrenaline gave me the courage to do something I had never done before: turn my back on Him and run as fast as I could past Him up the stairs.

I nearly skidded over as I ran, panting with the rush, stopping at the top only to thrown a nervous look down at the Master to see His reaction. He had not moved, but His eyes remained trained on my sweaty face and a flash of anger crossed his features. Then, He whipped gracefully around, and ripped away.

I supposed that there would be no dinner tonight. What a shame.

18

There was a moment of static, then a dainty crash. A stunned silence, then a hesitant round of applause.

"Well. Um...I suppose this changes things," Fred managed to say in a shaky voice.

"Not really." I shrugged, keeping an outer impression of modesty. "I don't see how manipulating objects will come of use. But it is a pretty trick, isn't it?"

"Pretty?" Fred laughed without humor, still stunned by my sudden discovery of ripping. "No. Evelyn is pretty, but this is something else entirely! I don't understand how you can do it though, after all these years of nothing...it never even crossed my mind that we might be able to do some of the things He could do, it's absurd!"

"It isn't only objects you'll be able to move, though, is it?" Lucas added thoughtfully. "Would it not be possible to rip...people?"

We were in the common room, stomachs grumbling as usual, with my three remaining friends perched in awe on the sofa whilst I painstakingly showed them my new talent by levitating Tressa's old powdering pots and then trying to set them back down without breaking anything. So far I had only pulled this off twice.

"But who would I want to move?" I questioned, a smile twitching at my lips at the thought of forcing self-conscious Lucas to do pirouettes in midair.

"The Master," all three answered for me, Evelyn seeming rather pleased that she had come to the same conclusion as everybody else for once.

"In case none of you have noticed, He can sort of rip as well, only with added torturous side-effects. I quite honestly cannot see a showdown ending very well in our favor," I snorted, although with my savage anger over Beatrix I longed to be able to do exactly that. Imagine if He feared me, not the other way around!

"Avery and Tressa would have known what to do," Evelyn whispered sadly, her soulful brown eyes welling up with tears as she drifted into deep thought.

None of us spoke.

It was true. They had been much more cunning at playing with these advantages and turning them into true powers, and much more talented at coming up with a solution to our most puzzling problems. But look at where that had gotten them.

"No," I said harshly. "No. We can't just sit here and cry. I don't know where they are, but I do know that they're alive, and they wouldn't want us to do this mourning charade again. They'd want us to stick together and work this out."

"Avery wouldn't," Fred pointed out, face turning into a bitter frown. "He's still out there somewhere. You remember why? Because he slashed Tressa and made her fall through the Boundary. That doesn't sound very 'go get 'em' to me at all."

"I know!" I threw my hands in the air, exasperated. "But that's beside the point."

"What is the point, if you don't mind my asking?" Lucas asked with a sigh, sitting up and crossing his arms.

I was about to say something clever and snappy in retort, but nothing came to me.

Angrily, I whirled around and used my frustration to create my biggest rip yet, causing all three of the powder pots to fly in the air and shatter in a rainbow of colored china and powder into the fireplace. Evelyn applauded lightly again, easily distracted by the fantastic array of colors that flared out of the fire.

"Can you teach me how to do that?" she begged, pointing her skinny fingers at the calmed fire in delight.

I raised an eyebrow, since admittedly I had assumed this would be a talent that was mine alone. Still, I couldn't afford to be selfish when having four people with powers could turn out to be so great an advantage.

"Focus on the candle," I instructed, trying to keep the reluctance from my voice. "Don't blink; just keep staring at it until…"

I blabbed the exact instructions D had given me, and all three of them glued themselves to a large unlit candle with expressions of pure concentration on their faces.

"Draw upon a strong emotion to help you," I encouraged, deciding that it would be nice of me to show some enthusiasm. "Remember how much you want to be able to do it! Think about what Avery's face will look like when he sees what we can do!"

"It's not working!" Evelyn whined crossly, tearing away her concentration first. "My eyes sting, my head hurts, and I never even saw the swimming lines that you described! Dear, now I'm tired."

I gave her a pat on the back for her efforts, the selfish side of me secretly reveling in the fact I was still unique. Sure enough, Fred and Lucas soon gave up, rubbing their bleary eyes and flopping angrily down on the sofa.

"It's not that I don't want to do it, because trust me I *really* do, but apparently ticking off Avery just isn't a good enough prize," Lucas mumbled, irritated. "Which is odd, considering I can't think of anything I'd like better at the moment. Lucky thing, Penny! I'm jealous!"

"Are you?" I grinned, gloatingly. There was an awkward silence as they stared at me critically, put off by my attitude, so I quickly changed tactics. "I mean, don't feel like that. It'll only get me in trouble in the end, I'm sure."

They remained unconvinced, with the exception of Evelyn who had removed her short attention span from the conversation and had drifted over to the window to daydream, dragging Fred with her.

"Let's not fall out over this," I begged, anxious my actions had once again done more damage than intended. "Tell you what, why don't we make an…um…what's the word? Pact! Like a promise we won't turn against each other again, and won't keep important secrets hidden?"

I was aware that I was breaking my 'pact' as the words formed from my lying mouth, as I did not intend to tell them about D just yet, not whilst he or she was so set on my going against them.

It was almost possible to feel the furiousness coming from D, with me going against everything I he had instructed me to do. There was no pleasing everybody, and the choice I had to make was simply – who was more dangerous as an enemy, and who was more valuable as a friend?

"Seems like a decent idea," Lucas ventured, looking to Fred for agreement.

"Why not? Can't do any more harm than what's already been done, can it?" Fred chortled darkly, looking to his companion for her opinion. "Evelyn?"

"As long as nobody breaks it," she warned. "Because it'll mean nothing if even one person goes back on their word."

"Nobody will do that," I assured her, turning away all the same.

"So, how shall we go about this?" Fred joked, sitting back on the sofa and waiting. "Kiss your signet ring? Light a ritual fire and sacrifice Lucas as an offering to prove our commitment?"

"No," I snapped, using irritation to mask my uncertainty, admittedly having not expected them to agree so readily. "Just…promise. Swear on your honor that you'll never turn away from us, and that anything discovered must be shared. From now on we must be a team, no matter what. Agreed?"

What a terrible hypocrite I was! Guilt made me lower my eyes with shame as my friends bobbed their heads trustingly. But maybe it was all for the best…right?

"Okay, then. I swear on my honor that I shall never deceive any of you, and always tell the truth," Fred said seriously, his face perfectly straight as he raised a hand and placed the other over his heart. Only his eyes were laughing, betraying the fact he was still relaxed despite it all.

"Me too!" Evelyn cut in, holding her hand over the wrong side of her chest. Her jaw was set, though, determined as I had ever seen her. "I swear on my…on my set of real diamond jewels to be true to you all, if it kills me!"

I nodded, satisfied if not slightly amused by her choice of words.

"And me," Lucas sighed, stretching out on the sofa like a lanky cat. "I promise."

I felt a sense of relief wash over me as silence descended; we weren't going to hurt each other again. Then I realized they were all staring at me expectantly, waiting for something.

"I know I'm gorgeous and everything, but please try to control yourselves," I muttered uncomfortably, the guilt coming back for no reason with vengeance.

"Since this was your idea, I rather think it would be fitting for you to participate in our little oath," Lucas retorted dryly, his eyes boring into mine as if he could read my mind. Often, I wouldn't put it past him.

"Ah, of course!" I laughed hoarsely, aware of how false I sounded. "I forgot." I ended my laugh with a delaying cough. "I swear to always tell the truth when it, ah, could help our overall cause. I promise never to go against you."

Fred beamed at me, winking as if I would start laughing more sincerely and tell him how ridiculous and paranoid the oath sounded out loud, and how silly they were to take it so seriously. When I didn't, he shrugged airily and started talking to Evelyn about the weather.

"Interesting choice of words, Penny," Lucas whispered to be as he passed on the way to the bathroom.

"Was it?" I frowned, feigning confusion. "I wasn't trying to be clever."

"Clearly not," Lucas agreed with a smile that didn't quite

reach his eyes. "Otherwise you'd have been more discreet about altering your promise to fit whatever you're hiding."

My face flushed with a mixture of irritation, guilt, and embarrassment, at knowing how much he knew me. But I wouldn't tell him, put him in danger. No trust was worth a life.

"Watch yourself, Penny," Lucas warned with a wry smile before leaving, unintentionally making goose bumps stand erect on my arms.

Watch yourself, child, the Master had said to me.

I hadn't listened then either.

*

Don't question what you are told. Don't open the upstairs door. Don't attempt to cross the Boundary. And I will give you safety.

Don't tell anybody about me. Don't talk to your friends. Don't share what you know about the ripping and the dreams. And I will give you power.

What was the difference, then? Why was I so much more hesitant about breaking D's rules?

Pain, lots of pain…my eyes flew open with shock at the sudden burning against my leg. At first I had shrugged it off as part of a dream, but then it had become so intense that I was forced back into reality to try and locate the source as soon as possible.

I threw off my duvet and slapped out at my leg, cursing. It felt as though I had fallen asleep with a knife buried in the folds of my cotton nightgown, and now it was stabbing deep into my skin. This of course wasn't the case, but as the searing burn escalated I was forced to abandon any sense of decency – and the skirts of my nightgown.

Pale and thin in the dark night, only visible through the courtesy of a clouded full moon filtering through the mildewed curtains, I frantically scoured my legs for the source of the pain.

To my surprise, there was no sharp object lying against my patch of red, stinging skin; merely a crumpled piece of paper.

It fell softly to the ground as I shook it away, puzzling through my relief why such a harmless thing had caused so much hurt.

I bent to pick it up, but as my fingers brushed the paper I hastily withdraw them.

"Ow!" I yelped, biting back a louder wail of shock. Sucking on my sore fingers self-pityingly. I regarded the scrap with a new light.

It was a reply from D. Somehow, though, it had been charged with an odd energy that shocked who or whatever touched it.

I was obviously in deep trouble for throwing in my lot with Fred, Lucas, and Evelyn instead of fending only for myself.

Cursing D under my breath, I crept back under the covers and flopped against the pillow to wait for the sun to rise and give me my reading light.

Get ready for a telling-off, Penny, I warned myself with a sigh.

The sting ebbed away against the cool linen sheets, despite the fact they had remained unchanged since Beatrix's passing several weeks ago. Still, sleep refused to come back. No matter how I tossed and turned, my consciousness stayed fully alert so that every second ticked by with agonizing slowness.

Perhaps morning would never arrive, and I would never get to see the letter. Maybe the trials had somehow suspended time and would force me to stay in bed, waiting forever for a sunrise that would never come...

I brushed some hair from my sweaty forehead and groaned, pushing my face into the downy pillow in frustration.

Tick.

Guilt, that was what it was.

Tick.

Possibly I was just hungry. We hadn't eaten properly in days.

Tick

I mean, really, how much damage could D cause?

TOCK.

I sat bolt upright, suddenly realizing what thought was keeping me awake. I'd been having another of those dreams, and though nothing different had happened, there was one detail which was ringing like an alarm in my mind; the baby's hair color. Like the reddish fuzz on a peach, close examination had proved that the child would've grown up to be a redhead. I couldn't remember details about anybody else's appearance, but somehow this had stuck out.

There was no doubt left in my mind. I was the baby.

But that just left me more questions.

19

To put it mildly, D was furious. I awoke the next morning to the sure sound of thunder rumbling over the overcast grounds, with the occasional streak of lightning flashing through the windows, so strong that you had to blink a few times to regain your sight. Storms were rare, so I found Evelyn, Fred, and Lucas out on the balcony of the breakfast room watching excitedly.

"Look, look at that one over there! It was a proper fork, right down to the ground!" Fred gasped, leaning right over the railing to point out to the woods. "Gosh, I hope nothing catches on fire!"

"Start counting, that's supposed to tell you how far away it is— Ah, never mind." Lucas paused as a loud clap rang out, making the other two jump. "Though I suppose it doesn't matter here anyway, does it? It can't be more than a mile out."

"Penny!" Evelyn grinned, seeing me approaching. "You slept in! Come, have a look with us, it's amazing! The sky is purple, nearly orange in some places, and the lightning has been spectacular!"

I smiled at her fondly, thinking how much happier she looked with the pelting rain turning her dull curls back into a glossy ebony, laughing with the boys as if all the world was perfect again. Even they seemed to have forgotten, if only for a heartbeat, with Fred with his arm around Evelyn's shoulders, and Lucas's eye alight with intrigue at the mystery of the storm.

That was why I politely refused her offer, blaming a restless night (partially true) for my lack of enthusiasm, opting instead to sit quietly inside and eat breakfast (boiled eggs and bacon, which although appearing mouth-watering certainly tasted vile) whilst it was still warm.

"Suit yourself." Evelyn shrugged. Another boom of thunder, and she shuffled a little closer to Fred, still beaming.

I sat at a stool with my back to them, deciding to read the letter now so that I could enjoy the storm later. I unfolded the paper, wincing as it shocked my fingers, though the charge was somewhat dulled from last night.

My mouth turned from a thin smile to frown to downright miserable as I scanned the page-long rant.

You betrayed me, Penny, it began, the writing more scrawled and careless than usual. *I gave you power on a very simple condition, and you turned your back on it to share the power with the others! You think they are friends now, but arming people who could turn on you is the most imbecilic, lethal thing you could possibly have done! This isn't just a game of hide-and-seek, where the loser has to clean up – this is for keeps. I refuse to care anymore; in fact, I look forward to seeing you realize the consequences of your stupid actions. One by one they will fall, and you shall go last so that you can see their pain before your own. I could have propelled you to freedom. I can also ensure your failure. And I shall. You meddle around with party tricks and the petty matters of others, but you don't even begin to understand exactly what you're up against. Neither did I, before it was too late, but I have had ages to grow both savvy and bitter. Three weeks. Nobody said anything about having to have a winner.*

D.

Charming, I thought dryly. Just the sort of motivation you need to succeed. It was amazing how quickly D had turned from being a friend to a vicious nuisance, and I certainly wasn't happy about the switch.

Yes, I dearly wanted information that D could provide, such as how to rip, but I wasn't willing to sacrifice my friends in return.

Sacrifice. What if D hadn't just been writing to me? I thought suddenly, with panic. What if he had sent letters to the others, like Avery? Was that how he and Tressa had known so much? Had that spurred him to commit such a terrible crime?

I shuddered, not bearing to think about it. Then, deter-minedly, I took the paper in my hands and began to rip it into shreds. There was a faint pinch of static, but apart from that, it tore like ordinary paper.

Smiling in grim satisfaction, I kept the pieces in my hand as I walked out onto the balcony to join my friends.

"Penny! You recovered quickly!" Evelyn smiled, clapping her hands in delight at another bolt of lightning flashing just above the Boundary woods. "Are you going to watch with us?"

"Perhaps for a bit, if you insist." I grinned, feigning leaning far over the railing to catch a better glimpse, and discreetly throwing the scraps over the side to be scattered by the winds.

I let myself be caught up in the rare weather show, letting my hair loose as a flood of fear and awe at the power of the storm overcame us all.

I saw a small cyclone of dead leaves the winds from the woods whirled around, and out of curiosity tried to make them stand still.

"Why are you pulling faces?" Fred frowned as I scrunched up my nose comically, trying with all my might to create a rip so far away from me. I thought of how irritated I was with D, how angry I would be if it turned out Avery had been under his or her influence...and through my watering eyes saw the leaves stand perfectly still.

"Look, look!" I shouted, excited, but as soon as my concen-tration waned they started to move again, twirling and falling with the breeze.

Lucas rolled his eyes and gave a cough that sounded suspi-ciously like 'show off,' but I chose to ignore him. He then quickly gave a real cough so violent that we all jumped.

"Gracious, Lucas, are you all right?" Fred asked wide-eyed, patting him on the back in concern. "Couldn't tell if that was you or the thunder!"

"Very funny," Lucas wheezed, still coughing. "I just had a

tickle in my throat."

"Maybe we should go inside," Evelyn suggested with evident disappointment, "before we all catch a chill and fall sick."

With an unenthusiastic assent, we all traipsed inside and shut the balcony doors behind us. It was amazing how suddenly quiet everything seemed, after the pounding rain, thunder, and wind were locked out. In a way, it was comforting, but it also gave me the silly urge to run back outside and play in the elements like a wild thing, unrestrained and uncontained.

"What shall we do now?" I asked glumly, feeling the familiar boredom set in once again. Life before the trials had been tedious, but at least it had been structured and well supported. Now, we simply wandered around like ghosts, slowly starving and waiting for the next attack to come and maim us even more. I was beginning to question whether pulling that blasted lever had been worth it.

"Common room?" Lucas suggested flatly, flicking a wistful glance at the storm outside with the same expression I had. His voice sounded very hoarse, and I hoped he was okay.

"Good grief, what a suggestion!" Fred gasped sarcastically. "Why haven't we ever thought of going there before? Oh, wait a second. We *have* done that before! Nearly every…blasted…day."

I snickered, but fell silent at the sad looks Evelyn and Lucas sported.

"What other choice do we have?" Lucas sighed, turning and walking away. "If you ever come up with an alternative, please do let me know."

"Maybe we should have listened to Tressa and Avery," Fred muttered darkly to me. "At least they did something."

"What did you say?" Lucas hissed, freezing mid-step. Evelyn winced and began twisting her hair as she always did when anxious. "Are you actually supporting the biggest betrayal of our lives? Or am I just hearing things?"

"No, you heard me," Fred said stonily, standing his ground.

He didn't seem particularly defensive or contradictory, though; merely stating his opinion.

"Have you forgotten where that ended?" I snapped, peeved by his angle.

"How could I possibly forget? And believe me, I will be the first to kill Avery if we ever see him again. Well, maybe just permanently maim him, killing seems a little harsh for my tastes," Fred mused, drawing a sharp breath of irritation from Lucas and me. "All I'm saying is maybe we should try to figure out what's going on before it's too late, since clearly we're making no current progress."

Lucas seemed about to retort, but he only coughed again and said, "Good job Penny made us do that silly pact thing, because I'd really like to hit you now."

"Boys, please," Evelyn sniffed, and I could tell from her expression that she was bored already with the conversation.

"She was in it, too!" they both accused, pointing at me in annoyance.

"Makes no difference," she shrugged, tugging at their shirt-sleeves persuasively. "Let's just go to the common room anyway, and figure things out from there. My feet are aching from these ridiculously small shoes – it's been months since my last replacement – and I'm almost falling asleep."

Grudgingly, we followed her up the staircase, arguments forgotten for the moment. My shoes were small now too, so I could see what she meant, but I simply refused to let it worry me anymore.

In the common room, Evelyn and Fred went to sit on the window seat together. Lucas began to pore over his huge stack of stolen books while I flopped down on the sofa in front of the empty fire grate to puzzle over the unanswered questions.

I started with my parents. They had been murdered, and I had been kidnapped by 'sinister forces' and ended up here. Where exactly was here? And why with five other unrelated children?

Why was 'here' so isolated from everywhere else? What was so special about me that I had been taken in the first place? Who exactly were my parents, and why did they run?

Getting nowhere with that, I switched subjects to the Boundary and the trials. How long were they going to last? Where was Avery? Was Tressa okay? How did we beat them? What was that static?

Wait...static?

My eyes flew open in shock. Evelyn screamed.

We were all standing in a row about a foot away from the Boundary itself, so close that my hair stood on end and I could hear the crackly sound making my eardrums pop. If I so much as edged a toe forward, or wobbled and fell, I would have touched the dreaded wall and fallen through as surely as Tressa had.

The stream gurgled pleasantly under my feet, half submerged under layers of fallen leaves. Inviting, cajoling, and oh so deadly. The tips of my fingers burned unpleasantly in memory.

"What just happened?" Fred asked shakily, not trusting himself to move backwards.

"I must have drifted to sleep for a minute," Lucas mused, his eyes wide and white rimmed. "I was so tired...but only for a minute!"

He subsided into a fit of coughing, and stumbled backwards away from the borders into safety.

I was shaking so badly that I didn't have enough confidence to move, and merely tilted my head from side to side to see what Evelyn on my left and Fred on my right were doing.

Evelyn took a steadying breath and took a tiny step back towards Lucas, before whimpering and fleeing completely until she was several yards away.

Fred followed, looking at me in question, and I prepared to move back as well.

Then I felt a sneeze tickle my nose.

Eyes watering, I tried to hold it in desperately. If I bent over to sneeze, my head would touch the Boundary. And that would be it.

"Penny?" Fred called uncertainly, but I didn't turn to look at him. "A-are you coming? We have to leave!"

But I was too scared. I, Penny the Fearless-to-the-Point-of-Stupidity, was scared.

The Boundary swam in front of me as I tried to hold the sneeze in, and I began to see the blurry waves that created rips, form. They were different to those elsewhere, somehow thicker and overlapping so that I couldn't find a clear space to rip, but I wasn't really focusing on those layers. I should have done, of course.

"Achooo!" I sneezed, nose and eyes streaming. I peeked through one eye – alive!

The gladness did not last long. It was beyond unnerving how we had gotten here, because I was almost certain we hadn't been transported like before. Somehow, while in our separate little daydreams, the trial had guided us to the Boundary, perhaps in hope that we would step forward when we came to.

"That was sort of scary," Fred admitted, not blinking as though closing his eyes would lead to another lapse in awareness. "I'll not sleep very well tonight. Perhaps we should lock our dormitory doors."

"If you'd like. But I don't see that it should be an issue, since these tests have never repeated before." Lucas shrugged, beginning to pick his way back through the undergrowth towards the manor. "Unless next time, they send something to shove us in..."

"Wait for me!" Evelyn cried, giving a rare burst of speed to catch up with him and Fred. "Coming, Penny?"

"In a minute," I said distantly, and she didn't protest. As they left, I stared at the Boundary in deep thought. The dense trees beyond didn't look any different to the ones on our side of the wall, besides the fact that they were cloaked in heavy mist. I wondered how far a person would have to travel to get to civilization in the real world.

The Boundary flickered, like a gentle ripple in a puddle to remind me of its existence. What would happen if I stepped through? What if it only shocked you if you merely touched it, and physically going through it let you pass? No one had ever tried it before...

I shook my head to clear out those thoughts. The darn thing had a compelling way of making me want to touch it, even though I knew what would happen.

My eyes scanned it with a mixture of hatred and reluctant respect. For I had to give the Boundary credit – it had terrified all of us and kept us prisoner for fifteen years, without faltering or showing weakness once.

I glanced up at the spindly trees. Perhaps that was why they grew thinner and less substantial here, so that we could not ever attempt to use them to get over the Boundary. If this were even possible.

A soft breeze blew, and I was suddenly cold. Making to turn back after the others, whose departing backs were still visible, I nearly missed the slip of crumpled paper blowing around with the dead leaves.

Coughing slightly, I stepped cautiously though the crunching brown soil, making sure to stay well away from the unassuming telltale stream, to retrieve the note.

It was, of course, from D. And, as expected, it shocked my hand slightly as I picked it up.

I think we both overreacted, but I'm not going to apologize. You are a fool to think you do not need me. I know more about the Boundary than you could ever imagine, including all the people in it. Not convinced? Well, I know who the baby in your dreams is. And it isn't you.

"Liar," I hissed, tearing the paper to shreds and throwing it to the ground. It was pathetic, that D felt he or she had to play these silly little mind games with me when I had clearly stated I wanted nothing more to do with them. Besides, wasn't it them saying they'd happily watch me die from the sidelines? Taunting and teasing would do nothing. I had made up my mind, and no amount of blackmail could change that.

I ignored the chill that made the hairs on the back of my neck stand up in fright, chalking it up to nerves after the small trial. There was no truth in the letter. It didn't make sense that the baby wasn't me.

I saw a shape moving up ahead, so I picked up my pace to catch them. Though I tried to shake off the feeling, there was an anxiety around me that was not at all pleasant, and I longed for the comforting presence of my friends.

"Lucas!" I shouted, recognizing his height. He was quite far ahead, partially obscured by the barren trees, but he paused and waited at the sound of his name. I ran to catch up. "Sorry I took so long, I was just looking at—"

The words caught and froze in my mouth. Lucas turned around to face me, but it wasn't Lucas. It wasn't his monster either.

"Do continue, Penny. I am very much intrigued as to why you are hovering in the woods alone at such a time." The Master spoke softly, as if genuinely interested. His black eyes betrayed Him, though.

He was wearing a rich, long travelling coat with a high collar, the color of old ashes. His hat was different, more rounded, perhaps the latest style in the other world. But the dangerous calm mask covering a barely contained fury remained the same, as did my consuming fear of Him.

"I was, um, just..." I gestured around wildly, looking for a plausible excuse. "Stretching my legs."

"Were you now?" He nodded, tone still light, but cold as a frost. "Why not with your friends, though? I was watching them up ahead."

Always watching, always waiting. I shuddered.

"You weren't looking for these, by any chance?" He asked politely, producing a stack of…I squinted to see that he was holding…

The color drained from my face so fast, it was unbelievable. I swear that my very heart stopped beating.

"Letters," I whispered, feeling very weak.

Every one, which I had ripped up and thrown over the balcony into the storm, was once again whole and in His pale hands.

"Very clever. Letters." He nodded liltingly. That musical, almost inviting tone He used before a punishment. "Who are they from, Penny?"

"I don't know," I said truthfully, wondering if He had read all of them. *Of course He's read them*, I reprimanded myself.

The Master nodded thoughtfully, a slight frown creasing His face.

"Are you going to punish me?" I asked, resigned. If He was, then there was nothing much I could do about it.

"I think not," He declined airily, as if refusing a cup of tea. "There are more important things to attend to. These letters are indeed a very strange find, and I'm dying to know every detail."

A faint boom of thunder echoed in the distance, but the rain withheld for the moment. The air was thick with the humidity that always comes before a storm, thick with a chilly moisture – and my fear.

"They just started appearing," I explained in a rush, sweating at the prospect of what He could do. "And I replied, but I have no idea who D is – I promise! I was only trying to make sense of things."

"Do not lie to me, please." He sighed, taking off His hat with an elegant sweep of His arms. "If there's one thing I just can stand, it's when people lie."

"I ripped them up," I blurted hysterically.

"And I ripped them back together again," He retorted simply. "Come now, Penny, you of all people should understand what those like us are capable of." He leant in close and I shivered, wanting nothing more than to run away as fast as I could in the opposite direction. "If I were you, I'd have burned them. Ashes are harder to repair than fragments."

I nodded numbly, unsure of why I had heard a hidden threat amongst those seemingly harmless words.

"Now, get out of here. And don't ever speak of these letters again, understand?"

"Yes, sir," I muttered timidly, ashamed of how pathetic I sounded.

As I ran, I dimly wondered why He had not punished me, for surely, if speaking out of turn warranted such an ordeal, then this treasonous act was even more suited to it.

It hit me as I jogged up in front of the doors with a wicked stitch in my side. Whatever the Master had read in those letters, it had brought up a strong emotion in Him that He had tried to hide from me. One that I had never seen before: fear.

Madon was scared of D.

Part Three

20

"Oh, please, not again!" I whined as soon as my eyes opened the next morning. My voice sounded scratchy and my nose was bunged up. The sweat on my brow and my aching bones indicated a fever. That wasn't why I was complaining though. Well, perhaps partially.

We were all standing at the Boundary again, inches away from it like before, so that the static pulse radiated through my body, feeling both alien and natural, as if it were supposed to be part of me.

At this hour in the morning, I was clothed only in my long white nightgown, hair a bushy mess, and bare feet flinching at the cold, wet ground. I was freezing, miserable, and tired. Not a good combination.

"Goodness!" Evelyn shrieked, officially having woken up enough to realize where she was and what she was wearing. Her black hair was still curled around strips of wet cloth to keep her limp ringlets visible, nightgown hanging like a sail off her skinny body. I had to catch onto her arm to stop her from flinging herself forward into the Boundary out of embarrassment. "Don't look at me! Oh dear, how improper this is!"

Fred and Lucas turned bright red at our situation and hastily looked away, they themselves only wearing button-up shirts and loose trousers without shoes.

"This is really quite ridiculous," Evelyn exclaimed, unintentionally causing more attention to fall on her. "Do these people have no concept of propriety? Hmm?"

"Who on earth are you talking to?" I laughed, almost amused by her flustered behavior.

"Whoever's fault this is!" she snapped, stepping easily away from the Boundary and running into the safety of the woods, calling out, "Don't follow me; give me a chance to get dressed!"

"Poor thing," Fred said sympathetically, but too frozen to

move after her. "She's so concerned about this sort of thing. I wonder if this trial was aimed specifically at her?"

"No." Lucas shook his head. "Evelyn's actually the only one who's moved away to safety. If anything, her obsessive modesty is actually her protection."

"It isn't obsessive!" Fred rolled his eyes. "Just…particular."

I shivered, admittedly feeling rather exposed myself in such a thin dress so early in the morning.

After the storm yesterday, the sky was black, but somehow a tiny bit of sun managed to get through and light everything up, so that the raindrops hanging off the trees glistened like a million diamonds. It was indeed beautiful, but only until they splashed down my back. Then they were just plain irritating.

"Shall we go back for some tasteless sludge?" I suggested dryly, referring to our guaranteed awful breakfast.

Just as we were about to turn and go, out of the corner of my eye a shadow moved over the Boundary.

"*Hey, Penny,*" came a familiar voice, gentle and inviting.

"Tressa?" I gasped, feeling slightly lightheaded.

Fred and Lucas clearly heard her too, stopping in their tracks and staring at her.

And there she was. Tall, straight, sharp. Tressa. Alive.

"What are you doing over there?" Fred spluttered, his eyes wide and mesmerized by the apparition.

"*I fell, remember?*" She laughed bitterly. "*But I'm okay. It hurts a bit, falling through, but after that it isn't so bad. The woods on this side are so much bigger. I've been exploring them for weeks! They probably go on forever, since I've never found a boundary apart from this one.*"

"Can you cross back over?" I whispered, wanting so dearly to rush to her, make sure she was real. To hold on and never let her go again.

"*I'm too scared,*" Tressa said, a tad reproachful. She paced up and down in front of the Boundary, wearing the same gown with the lacy collar she had on last time we saw her – no blood, thank goodness.

"Don't be, we'll be here for you!" Fred encouraged, extending his hand as if to pull her through.

"Why did you not show yourself before?" Lucas added sharply before she could reply. There was a deep mistrust in his blue eyes, and he was staring at Tressa as if she was about to bite him.

"You never came back," she explained wistfully, winding a white curl around her thin fingers. *"Not until yesterday, at least. I waited for days, until I got bored and decided to look around a bit. I think you'd all like it over this side, there's so much to see! No trials, no sickness, no worries. You could join me, and we'd all be together again! We'll walk all the way to the edge of the forest together, you'll see!"*

Her face had lit up with excitement, and I couldn't help but feel a rush of excitement for the prospect of running away all together again through a limitless forest. Yet I had my doubts that any of what she was saying was even real, so I kept my feet firmly planted on the familiar side of the creek.

"I'll go and get Evelyn?" Fred offered, looking at Lucas questioningly.

"No," he muttered, and Tressa leaned closer to hear him. "This isn't right. We saw her fall, but we never saw her reappear again. This has got to be a ruse to get us over the other side, to meet the same fate she did."

Fred pouted, torn between Lucas's advice and his friendship and concern for Tressa. "She must be so lonely."

"Oh, I'm not alone!" Tressa giggled, and suddenly I wanted to leave. My feet stayed firmly where they were, though, and I felt a deep panic begin to rise. *"See? There are lots of us over here, all the people who made the right choice and came to the right side. Come on out!"*

The situation turned worse when Avery stepped out from behind a tree with a curious, albeit a little bit nervous, expression.

He was looking at me as if I might wring his neck regardless of the Boundary, which I as definitely trying very hard not to do.

"*Hello,*" he greeted us meekly, not meeting our eyes.

Fred took a step forwards, an unfathomable expression of hate written all over his normally jovial face, and a hissing sounded from the Boundary sizzled through the tension in the air. He jumped back, cursing, and I saw with revulsion that the tip of his nose and his whole left hand were burned a sickly greyish color.

"That supposed to convince us to join you?" I snarled at Avery, throwing as much anger as I could into every word.

"*No.*" He shrugged. "*But this might.*"

"It can't be," Fred murmured, sporting his injured hand as dead weight and gazing transfixed at the Boundary.

"Beatrix," I said in amazement.

"*I'm so sorry, my darlings,*" she apologized emotionally, wiping away a tear. "*I'm so sorry I had to leave you like this.*"

I felt as though I hadn't seen her in years. The lined face, messy grey bun, and big heart had been sorely missed, so Avery had been right in guessing she of all people had almost convinced me to cross over. But I held firm.

"You filthy liars," Lucas snapped, making Fred and I flinch. "Beatrix is dead. We buried her. Are you telling me that the other side is some kind of afterlife? Because I don't fancy dying just yet, no matter how perfect death is."

"*Won't you join us, please?*" Tressa begged, and my heart cried out for her. She looked so forlorn and helpless – so very unlike the Tressa I knew.

That was when they began to change.

Like the mind monsters that had haunted me before, their eyes turned completely black and demonic, as their teeth elongated to sharp deadly points stained with crimson. A dribble of blood leaked out of the corner of their mouths, and their features became skeletal against translucent skin.

"Please? I've missed you so much," Beatrix pleaded in a grating voice like a badly played violin. It sounded so very wrong coming out of her mouth, but I still couldn't move.

"What's happening?" Fred shouted, alarmed. "I can't move backwards!"

"Well, we sure as hell aren't going forwards," Lucas exclaimed, clenching his fists and wrenching himself away from the nightmarish scene. At once, his face cleared of the pain, so I guessed that the visions had faded with his escape. "Penny, Fred, just turn away!"

"I can't," I choked, feeling the truth hit me. I physically couldn't turn away. My legs just wouldn't move backwards, even as a demon Tressa began to jerkily ascend upon me. "Fred…"

"Me neither!" he panicked, hair standing on end at his proximity to the static Boundary. Beatrix was only a few feet away from him, and reaching out a distorted hand to pull him through.

"Not yet," another voice spoke, and I froze. It was neither male nor female, not even really human, and I could see no one else standing behind the three monsters. Fred hadn't so much as flinched, so only I had heard the strange voice. *"You and I, we aren't finished. I have a promise to upkeep, and you won't get out of it this easily."*

Just like that, Tressa disappeared seconds before she was about to grab me. Avery and Beatrix vanished too, and I felt sadness as if I had lost them all over again.

I stepped away from the Boundary with a shudder, an inkling of who had spoken in my mind but too afraid to speak it aloud.

Fred still stood transfixed at something I couldn't see, reaching out to touch an apparition with an expression of internal conflict. Standing there in his pajamas, feet turning blue against the cold and burned hand starting to blister painfully, I realized what the trials were doing. It might not have been my time, but apparently they thought it was his.

"Fred, no!" I shouted desperately, grabbing hold of his arm and trying in vain to pull him away from the monsters. Reflexively, he pulled away from me and moved dangerously close to the creek, which was gurgling a lot more eagerly than usual. "Lucas, help me! He can't hear me anymore!"

There was nothing I could do, and we both knew it. It was down to how strong Fred was against the will of those controlling the vision.

"It's all right, I'm decent again!" someone called merrily from behind me. "You can all look now."

Evelyn sauntered near, her hair back in free curls and a pretty blush color dress on. She stopped when she saw Fred, her smile dropping faster than a pebble in the water.

"Fred!" she screamed, running forward to him before I could stop her. "Fred, what are you doing?"

"Evelyn, stop, it'll only make it worse—" I began, also rushing forwards. Yet Fred didn't shy away from her. In fact, a look of relief replaced the blank expression on his face. Then he wrenched himself away and fell heavily to the ground, sweat beading on his now flushed face.

"You utter fool, what were you thinking?" Evelyn sobbed, pulling him into a brief hug before wiping her eyes with a soiled hankie. "Why would you even consider leaving us like that, I'd be dead in an instant without you!"

"I'm sorry," Fred whispered, slightly dazed.

He sat there, shivering in his nightclothes on the damp muddy ground, staring with hollowed eyes at the once again serene Boundary, as if waiting for the monsters to appear once again and drag him to the other side.

"We should go," Evelyn whispered in a high-pitched tone. "This place is giving me the shivers."

I fought down a loud cough, nodding as my chest racked with the need to expel whatever was causing the discomfort.

After the leaves fell we always felt a little under the weather, but usually Beatrix gave us some of her medications to quash them within a few days, just as she had with Evelyn's cold. I had no idea how long they lasted if they were unattended, and for all I knew they could be fatal.

"Dear me, Penny, stop sniffing or I shall personally chop your nose off!" Fred chuckled, only half-joking.

I threw him a poisonous look, snapping back, "You wouldn't dare, considering that the number of unharmed living people seem to be becoming a rare species! Besides, Lucas has been sniffling all day and you haven't told *him* off!"

"This is true," Fred acknowledged reasonably, and Lucas guiltily removed his nose from his shirtsleeve.

"Maybe we could go and get some medicine from the kitchens," Evelyn suggested vaguely, sliding over to take hold of Fred's burned hand protectively. "Fred needs something for his hands, and you two could do with some cold remedies. I myself have a slight sore throat, and I'm near certain the lower quarters are left unlocked since…"

"Good idea!" Fred smiled, gently pulling his hand away. A flash of pain crossed his face, but was quickly replaced by a typical warm grin. "Sorry, Evelyn, it's a little bit tender."

"I shouldn't have left you all." She frowned, pouting so prettily I felt a familiar flash of envy that I tried to subdue. "It was terribly selfish of me. To think of what might have happened had I not come back!"

"Don't worry," Fred comforted. "Gosh, you've already saved Penny and I from crossing over once before, remember? You owe us absolutely nothing!"

Evelyn blushed a deep pink that matched her gown, and I looked away. I had a feeling the conversation wasn't supposed to include Lucas and I anymore, so I zoned out to allow them privacy.

Irritatingly, we had sleepwalked to the far side of the Boundary, and there was absolutely no recognizable path leading back to the lawns. I also knew we would have to pass by Beatrix's grave and Tressa's memorial, which would not be pleasant considering which state we had just seen them in.

My nightgown snagged on a bramble, my arms scraping against a gnarled tree trunk. I tripped over a network of roots covered by a layer of shriveled leaves. By the time we reached the spot where the trees became less dense, I was in a foul mood and sporting an array of bruises. And it was only before breakfast; some days were simply destined to be awful.

I threw out my hands to stop my friends.

"What's wrong?" Lucas asked in confusion, rubbing the spot on his face where my outstretched arm had slapped him.

"Where's Evelyn?" I replied, spotting Fred beside me. He must have heard the panic in my tone, as he whipped his head around to find her so fast that I heard his neck snap.

"Ouch!" he hissed, stumbling into the overhanging branches of a dead willow. "She's right here."

"I never went anywhere," Evelyn informed me, puzzled as the rest of them.

"Oh no," Lucas said, deathly quiet.

I followed his line of sight and saw him looking at the same thing as me, his face quite pale. "That cannot be good news."

For just visible amid the rolling mist over the lawns were a couple of familiar shapes outlined in black granite against another dead tree, eerie and melancholy at the same time. Beatrix's grave was the largest, the writing still perfectly legible on the smooth speckled surface. Tressa's tall, thin monument equally was polished but plain as ever, standing a few feet away but just as prominent.

That wasn't what had stopped my heart.

There was a third stone.

It was the same size and shape as Tressa's but without writing. A memorial for those who had failed to withstand the trials, by their hand or another. A sign of what was to come, and the fate that awaited one of us.

"Perhaps it was meant for me," Fred suggested shakily. "You know, as if I was meant to step over the Boundary and disappear a few minutes ago. Evelyn probably wasn't fixed into the equation, so He didn't count on me surviving and planned ahead."

"You still think He is behind all this – the trials?" Evelyn pressed curiously, wincing at the dread any reference to Him brought.

I briefly thought back to the barely concealed fear He had sported whilst reading D's letters, then focused in again on the situation at hand.

"It doesn't matter," I said dismissively. "I don't think this was meant for Fred – at least, not at the moment. Look what's at its foot."

Lucas stepped forward and picked up a crunchy brown ball of something from below the pillar, showing it to Fred and Evelyn solemnly.

"A rhododendron blossom," Evelyn gasped, covering her mouth with a wavering hand.

Beware.

"It's meant as a warning," Lucas explained darkly, dropping the flower to the ground as if it was unlucky. "But it might only be to scare us into doing something stupid, so let's not lose our heads just yet. Besides, if it is a legitimate foreshadowing, there is probably nothing we can do to stop it from happening, so why worry?"

His words hung in the air like the low storm clouds, but instead of bringing comfort they just set a mood of anxiousness and dread.

I looked at each of my dear friends, thinking about which one of them it would be. Perhaps it was gentle, positive Fred, who had already experienced one too many narrow escapes. Shallow, sweet Evelyn, never one to think about her actions. Dependable, clever Lucas, who like me could be hiding secrets of his own. Or me, grimly certain of my immunity.

I couldn't stand losing anyone, but Lucas was right, there was nothing we could do.

"We should go," I suggested flatly, my voice lower than usual. "If we're going to get some medicine before breakfast, we'd better get moving, or else all the food will disappear."

"Shame," Fred muttered sarcastically. "I rather enjoy the taste of dirt in the morning."

Evelyn giggled, drawing a pleased beam from Fred, and I found myself looking away again. What was wrong with them being happy? I chided myself.

The third tombstone vanished as the thick silver mist enveloped it, only the pointed top visible through the dense blanket, like the point of a shark's fin in the foggy ocean.

I was only too glad to finally turn the corner towards the front doors, away from the graveyard. The slightly higher elevation also meant that the ground was clear of fog, and the brittle grass was once again visible under my blue, bare toes. It was positively freezing, sharp bits of twigs and a thick layer of caked mud covered the souls of my feet. What I wouldn't give for a nice, hot, steamy bath!

The first thing we did when we were back inside was rush upstairs and put on proper clothes. I pulled on my favorite, most comfortable navy dress and accidentally 'forgot' my chemise, not even bothering to comb my hair yet taking extra time to select my thickest stockings. Evelyn patiently waited on a chair whilst I made myself decent, applying some power to her pale face to make it seem rosier.

We met the boys in the breakfast room, deciding to get medicine afterwards, and choked down some disgusting substance that resembled colorless vomit. Whoever was in charge of food had clearly decided that disguising foul tastes with appetizing-looking dishes was not worth the bother, for now the food seemed to resemble how it tasted.

I ate because I didn't fancy starvation, and my stomach was grumbling meekly inside my rapidly shrinking tummy.

"That was probably the worst meal yet," Lucas exclaimed, looking somewhat greenish. "Nothing edible should have that consistency."

"Urgh..." Fred moaned, rushing out to the balcony and leaning over to be sick. Evelyn hadn't even eaten anything at all!

Then we went to what had been Beatrix's quarters. Down the few steps, along the passageway, and through the unlocked door straight ahead to the kitchen.

The kitchen was a tiny room of simple whitewashed cabinets, with slabs of varnished wood for countertops. I could see no oven or any sort of stovetop, and when I peeked my head into the little pantry, there were only a few loaves of bread, tins of flour, and a couple of jars lined up along the back. It wasn't functional at all, which of course meant our food was coming from outside the Boundary. Which meant there had to be a way out.

We found all the cabinets to be empty of food, only containing the dinner service and cutlery that we used during our meals. In one end drawer, though, we found Beatrix's old first-aid kit, complete with bandages and a few containers of odd substances.

"Do you know which ones are which?" Fred asked me, as if I was suddenly the expert. "They all look exactly the same."

"No idea. Maybe we should just try all of them and see which ones make us feel better," I suggested, picking up a little white bottle and sniffing the contents testily. They were utterly odorless – so perhaps harmless.

"Don't be stupid." Lucas rolled his eyes scathingly. "These things can be poisonous if taken the wrong way, I read about them in a book. Besides, they might not even be medicine."

"Do you have a better idea?" I replied in the same tone. "Evelyn, do you remember what Beatrix gave you for your cold?"

She shook her head. We stared at the twenty or so bottles in blank confusion, until my eyes started to become unfocused and I saw the little wavering rips in between the air. Offhandedly, I levitated one about an inch off the ground before I was forced to blink and drop it.

"Do you know what?" Evelyn announced into the silence, and we wearily turned to look at her. "I think we should abandon this. It's just a cold we all have, not serious at all, and since we don't know what these medicines do it really would be silly to experiment with them. They might just make us worse, and for all we know they could be part of the trials!"

"Beatrix's medical stash part of the trials?" I said scornfully. "It's been here forever."

"But what if the sickness is a test!" Evelyn explained vigorously, throwing her arms around to try to get her meaning out clear. "What if taking the medicine counts as failing and we lose? Disappear like Avery did!"

It was quite peculiar being lectured on a deep, cryptic subject by Evelyn, yet what she said made sense. Were we willing to take such a risk for the sake of a stuffy nose or sore throat?

"Thank you for scaring me!" I shuddered lightly, taking a step away from the jars as if one might force itself down my throat.

So we left. It had been a hectic morning to say the least, with so many events in quick succession happening like hops over a pond. It seemed like everything was happening – yet nothing had happened.

I visualized the bottles in the drawer as tiny tombstones, with demonic clones of their owners appearing from behind in the mist. Was there anything I could do to stop that last grave having an owner?

21

I had a peculiar dream. It hadn't anything to do with the baby or strange, realistic scenes, and was in fact just like every other normal dream. I was walking through the gardens by myself, admiring the freshly blooming flowers (it must have been springtime) and wandering about in an exceptionally good mood. The graveyard was silhouetted in the distance, but I paid it no mind. Until I smelled something odd.

Smoke rose from behind the granite like a great billowing cloud, but unlike normal smoke it was forming hideous monstrous faces which tried to bite me as I walked. In my subconscious, I was both afraid and steadfast, facing the smoke with unsure interest.

Then the flames exploded and I backed away, feeling the heat singe my hair. The faces remained, though, leering down at me as I ran painstakingly slowly towards the safety of the house.

Evelyn, Lucas, and Fred stood at the door to let me in. I smiled at them gratefully, but to my surprise they wouldn't let me in. Panicking now, I noticed the fire spreading behind me and begged them to move aside for me. Evelyn shook her head sadly and pointed at my dress.

It was made from crumpled paper, the notes D and I had once shared. As I reached out to touch it, my hands left a smudge of red behind, and upon glancing at them I realized my palms were coated with sticky, hot blood.

My head snapped up to ask my friends what was wrong, but in their place was the Master, smiling cruelly at my horrified confusion.

"*Everything is crumbling because of you, Penny. You see the secrets you have kept? Winners don't play fair, but that was why you cheated in the first place, isn't it?*"

I shook my head frantically, trying to wipe off the stains but only creating more. The smoke faces loomed closer, choking me, calling out my name as the advanced, *Penny, Penny, Penny...*

"Penny!"

The last name was a scream that tore me from my nightmare. Evelyn was shaking me awake, her eyes wide with an inhuman fear. I rubbed my own eyes awake, trying to clear the haze of sleep from my sight...until I realized exactly what was making my vision so blurry.

The manor was burning.

I couldn't see the flames, but there was no other explanation for why the bedroom was suddenly filled with a thick, suffocating plume of smoke.

"What do we do?" Evelyn sobbed, coughing so violently I jumped out of bed to pat her back. The toxic air filled my own lungs with the first breath, and for a terrifying few moments I was paralyzed by a fit of gagging that made me feel quite light-headed.

"Go!" I managed to wheeze, gulping desperately for some untainted oxygen. "Get outside!"

If we stayed here, we would certainly choke to death before the flames got to us. Evelyn was too breathless to cry now, running to the window and trying to open the catch. She shook it with every ounce of strength she possessed, but to no avail.

"It's not opening, Penny! I don't want to go. What if there are actual flames out there? Where's Fred?" she blabbed hysterically, alternating between gasping sobs and coughs.

"Let's find them," I croaked, seizing her wrist and steering her out of the room.

I soon figured out that the air seemed to be purer closer to the floor, so we both crouched awkwardly whilst moving. Already our white nightgowns were stained a yellow-gray, and I knew the smell would stay on them forever – assuming that we managed to live to wear them again.

I couldn't see more than a foot in front of me. On my hands and knees with Evelyn following close behind me, I crawled like a baby down the corridor, squinting my stinging eyes against the burning smoke, every now and then bumping into piece of furniture or the wall.

If I were you, I'd have burned them. Ashes are harder to repair than fragments.

The Master hadn't been talking only about the letters, I realized suddenly. He had been referring to us. Dividing us was now a useless attempt, so the trials were going to burn us; ashes cannot be repaired.

I seethed with anger at the whole thing, specifically Beatrix for making it sound as if we had a chance at getting through alive. If I had known that the stupid trials were going to plough us down one by one, then I would never have touched that lever in the first place! This wasn't even a test, it was attempted murder!

"Are you all right, Evelyn?" I coughed, trying to see through the smoke. I couldn't make out her shape beside me anymore.

I turned struggling to see her. My brain was beginning to become fuzzy, and I could barely breathe at all now, so I lay flat on the floor to catch my breath and wait for her to catch up. It seemed like time had slowed down, as all my concentration focused on trying to inhale and exhale what little air remained close to the floor, and to keep my eyes open long enough to see Evelyn when she finally caught up.

I thought I could hear distant pounding footsteps ahead of me. I strained to listen then heard a faint call from behind me. "Penny, where are you! I think I need help!"

I could hear the crackling of flames now. I knew I had to get to Evelyn, but there was not enough strength left in my lungs to get my legs to work.

My mind had solely concentrated on survival, and I was unable to do anything else but lay there and wait for my own help to come.

"Please!" Evelyn whimpered, and I forced myself to turn around and crawl back the way I had come.

I was panting like a dog, completely blinded by the heavy atmosphere, but intent on getting to my friend before I passed out.

Behind me the footsteps were closer, as well as a cacophony of hacking coughs, but I refused to let it distract me.

"Ev-ee-lyn..." I called feebly, using my hands to feel the way.

Then something heavy tripped over me, and what little breath I had in me was forced out in one big choke.

"Penny?" came a confused voice. It was Lucas! Lucas would help me! He landed on the floor next to me. "What on earth...?"

He grabbed me trying to pull me backwards. My eyes stung excruciatingly when I opened them, so I kept them firmly shut.

"Evelyn," I managed to squeak, which sparked off a bout of coughing. "She's—"

"Do you know where she is?"

"No..." I began another bout of coughing. By now I couldn't think straight. Lucas mumbled something else. I didn't understand him, perhaps asking if I was all right. I nodded. He tugged hard at me. At first, I struggled against his grip, but my strength was failing and I couldn't breathe. Reluctantly I allowed him to yank me back in the right direction.

At last the smoke cleared somewhat and Lucas pulled me to my feet. All I could do was hang onto his arm for dear life and let him guide me down the stairs and out of the door. Then at last I gulped in some fresh air, and it was like the breath of life. Blinking furiously, ignoring the pain, I began to see again.

Even tainted by the smell of fire, the air was cool, clean, and pure. I hungrily sucked it in, feeling my light-headedness clearing with each lungful.

I had seen fire before, naturally, but only the tame ones inside our mantelpieces. This was another beast entirely. Massive orange tongues were consuming the beautiful historic annex of the house, which contained the dining hall. It hadn't yet reached the rest of the manor but smoke billowed from the windows, many of which had shattered due to the heat.

"The curtains caught fire for some reason," Lucas explained as we helplessly watched, "and that spread to the rafters. Fred and I only got out because he was awake and smelled the smoke."

Before, being in my nightgown had felt awfully exposing. Now I was glad to be clad in such a light material, for had I been dressed in my usual heavy gowns I surely would have melted!

Lucas had clearly had time to pull on a jacket and trousers, though, and had his boots loose on his feet. He caught me staring and without meeting my eyes, kicked them off.

"Go on, take them," he muttered, as if wanting to avoid seeing me in my nightgown. "I'm wearing socks."

I shrugged and pulled the black, shiny things on, feeling rather like a croquet mallet. They were several sizes too big. Still, it was better that standing barefoot!

Fred was standing off to the side, watching our home burn with a dazed expression. He suddenly turned and looked around, comprehension dawning. "Evelyn...I thought she was with you!" He turned on Lucas, eyes flashing with accusations. "You promised to get them both!" he snapped. "You heard them yelling, and told me to wait outside whilst you did your heroics! *You left Evelyn behind in a burning building!*"

Evelyn! Somehow I had forgotten about her.

There was something behind Fred's anger, something petrified. I had never seen him so scared in my life; not one of the trials had affected poor Fred more than the idea of losing Evelyn to a lonely, preventable demise.

"Penny said she was all right!" Lucas reassured him gently, not wanting to argue. "Didn't you, Penny?"

"I – I," I stuttered, trying to remember what had happened.

"I asked if she was safe, and you nodded," Lucas pushed, suddenly pale.

"I – I was confused...didn't really hear you," I admitted,

starting to panic.

"Where is she?" Fred yelled. I thought I would vomit as he searched my face for any sign of hope.

"She was calling for help," I remembered miserably, sinking to my knees and hiding my face in my hands. "I tried to reach her but then Lucas came. I…"

I hadn't even finished my sentence before Fred sprinted towards the burning manor, not even looking back to see if we were following.

"Fred! Don't be an idiot!" Lucas shouted, but it was too late.

"We have to follow him!" I exclaimed shakily, the unclaimed grave fresh in my mind.

There was then a creaking groan, and I screamed in shock as the entire roof of the dining hall collapsed in on itself. A burst of sparks and smoke billowed up into the air, and hit us with a rush of heat. As the sparks touched the dry, brittle grass, infernos began erupting all around us.

"The building's not safe," Lucas managed to choke out through the surprise. "Evelyn was in the other wing…Fred still has time to get there before it comes down."

"Where are we going to go?" I shouted over the terrible crashing sound of more walls breaking.

The grassfires had spread much faster than those in the manor, with nothing to stop them and acres of land for fuel. There was now only one way to go; into the woods, towards the Boundary.

"We have no choice," he said.

"Would it be selfish?" I asked, holding up a hand to shield myself from the blaze.

"I'm not going to think about that," Lucas replied, turning towards the woods and without waiting for me set off running, still in his socks.

I followed, hoping that the flames would burn out before they reached the trees – else there would be no feasible way to escape.

A fire exploded by my side, only a few inches away, causing me to tumble shrieking to the ground. A mouthful of dirt greeted me, but I forced myself to get up and keep moving. Then I was in the confines of the woods. The branches flashed by, occasionally whipping my face, but I ignored them. All that mattered right now was to get as far away from the fire as possible.

As the trees became denser, and I could hear the Boundary buzzing, I made a decision.

"Give me your hand!" I called, grabbing hold of an overhanging limb and kicking off Lucas's boots I hoisted myself up as if playing hide-and-seek.

"Are you crazy?" Lucas replied, looking away as he found his head directly under me, and my nightgown. "Why would going up there be any help?"

I rolled my eyes and reoffered my hand. "This way we can see everything. Come on!"

Biting his lip, Lucas grabbed hold of my wrist and pulled his gangly self into the branches with me. He was wobbly and awkward, clinging onto the trunk as if seconds away from falling. I was much more comfortable, so I climbed through the layers of dead foliage until I could see a panoramic view of the burning manor.

There hadn't been so much color in days, the vivid reds, oranges, yellows and blues consuming foot after foot of soft brown stone. The beautiful, ancient hall was now nothing more than a smoldering bonfire, with all those intricate and unique details gone forever. What had not been destroyed was rapidly disappearing into a storm of smoke and fire, so thick that it was impossible to tell what was left unscathed. The small lawn fires were burning out quickly, only for an array of sparks to reignite them instantly. Somewhere in that deadly blaze was Fred and Evelyn...

It was the most horrible moment of my existence. Waiting in much discomfort for my friends to appear, with the agonizing knowledge one was prophesized to fall. Unable to do anything but watch, ready to help when they emerged. If they indeed both did. Fred without Evelyn, Evelyn without Fred...it didn't seem to work somehow. I envisioned lanky Lucas falling from the branches...

"Stop!" I snarled at myself. "You're letting them get to you. Nothing is going to happen. Everyone is going to be okay. The grave was just something to scare you."

"Are you talking to yourself? Sign of madness, you know."

"Shut up, Lucas," I hissed through clenched teeth. "Like you never used to recite arithmetic in your head when—"

"*Penny!*" Two voices called, laughing.

I nearly fell out of the tree, such was my relief! They had both made it out! I scrambled down and slid onto the thick limb next to Lucas, and together we pulled Evelyn up with us.

She was nearly unrecognizable; her face masked so completely with soot, hair burnt singed, nightgown filthy. As her chest rose and fell with each breath, I could hear an unhealthy wheezing sound – she had gotten out just in time.

"Fred? Come over here and we'll pull you up too," I called, scanning the smoky ground for him.

"Is Fred not here with you?" Evelyn asked in confusion.

"He went in to get you," Lucas said. His relief at seeing Evelyn turning to concern.

"No," she shook her head feebly, tears spilling down her cheeks causing white streaks in the soot. "I had to crawl out by myself through the breakfast room balcony. No one was around to help. I assumed he was with you?"

"He's in the manor looking," I whispered, hoping with every fiber within me that he had realized Evelyn was safe and found shelter. "He wouldn't know you're all right."

"Then we have to go and save him!" Evelyn shouted, preparing to jump straight out of the tree. She lost her nerve and straightened back up, looking to me for instruction.

"Hang on," I commanded, scurrying back up to my vantage point in the canopy.

The woods were now on fire. The front line of huge, old trees transformed into massive fireballs, their once-impressive girth holding back the encroaching flames from taking told of the smaller plants. The lawns were now nothing but black, ashy space, a few red-hot embers glittering in several spots

Through the smoke I caught a glimpse of the breakfast room, which still looked pretty much intact along with the boys bedchamber above it. If Fred had made it that far, he could still be okay; after all, Evelyn had manage to escape.

Evelyn was screaming at Lucas below me. "Please, we have to go! I don't care how dangerous it is, this is *Fred*!" She jumped down.

"Wait for...oh, gosh." Lucas sighed, shakily craning his neck up to where I was sitting. "What now?"

"Not hanging around today, are they?" I groaned, easily bending my knees and jumping down for a soft landing. Lucas made to follow me, but I held up a hand. "You stay here. I'm the fastest, I can catch her in no time. Let's not lose anyone else."

"Shouldn't we stay together?" He frowned anxiously, though still apprehensive about jumping the five-foot drop.

"At least this way one of us will be safe," I answered grimly. "I'll borrow your boots again." I retrieved them and slipped my feet in, before hurrying after Evelyn.

It was so very frustrating. If only Lucas had come a bit later, and Evelyn had been rescued alongside me. If only Fred had kept his head and waited for her to emerge. If only Evelyn wasn't so fast when she was scared.

I ran short of breath a lot faster than usual, but luckily so did Evelyn. I saw her leaning against a bare trunk for support, gasping in exhaustion.

"I can't...can't...lose..." Her face was filled with anguish. "P-Penny...he...is—"

"Probably safe somewhere," I interrupted quickly, wishing I believed myself. "And you stumbling into a collapsing house is not going to do anything but worry us all more."

She fell to the ground crying more deeply than when Beatrix died. I awkwardly fell beside her, and watched my life burn to the ground.

A shadow moved out of the corner of my eye. I snapped my head up hopefully, but straight away I knew from the tall physique that it wasn't Fred.

It was the Master.

His face was pale, but his expression still stone cold. He raised a hand, wavering slightly, and made a complicated gesture.

A huge rip shuddered through the estate, knocking me out for a few moments due to sheer powerfulness.

When I came to, blinking in confusion, I saw that He had gone again. The crackling sound of flames had ceased. The rip must have extinguished the fire. I looked up, the hall was nothing but a pile of blackened rubble, as was about half of the manor. A great gaping hole was visible where the roof had caved in, taking with it Beatrix's quarters, the common room, and the girls' bedchamber in the east wing. Suffocating smoke still thickened the air.

"Fred? Lucas?" Evelyn whimpered, propping herself up feverishly.

I waited. Waited for a miracle.

Lucas appeared from behind us, and I found myself crying too, pulling him into a hug. He then joined us on the floor, waiting. Waiting.

Fred never came out of the ruins.

After a few desperate hours, we scoured the entire lawn and woods, finding nothing so much as a footprint.

I had failed yet again.

Fred was gone.

22

Evelyn screamed. It was a feral, animal sound, and I winced at all the emotion welling up behind it. So much sadness, so forlorn, so heartbreaking.

"Evelyn…" I began, trying my best not to cry and completely failing.

"No!" she shouted viciously, tearing away from my outreached arm. "He's not dead! I'd know, I'd feel it, but he's still alive! It'd bet my own life on it!"

"Then where is he?" Lucas asked bluntly, face so expressionless it was impossible to tell what he was thinking. "It's nearly nightfall."

"I don't know!" she yelled back, face red and tear-stained. She strode around like a caged lion, shaking. Her expression wild with disbelief. "I d-don't know." Her voice broke, and I ached for her, wishing I could understand and say it would be all right. The truth was, I didn't know anymore.

I patted her shoulder, not knowing what to do.

Evelyn pulled away. "Why are Tressa's and…and…the other t-tombst…memorials unmarked? Beatrix is the only person we know for sure is dead, and she's the only one with a proper grave! For all w-we know, they all might actually b-be on the other side of the Boundary!" she blabbed, struggling over some of the words and hiccupping. "W-what if to win is to c-conquer our fears and s-step over? What if the t-trials are helping us? P-pushing us towards s-success?"

"Don't be daft," I said hesitantly. It was simply too easy. "Fred burned himself, remember? When he got too close to the Boundary?"

"Don't say his name as if he's gone," Evelyn growled fiercely.

"Look, nobody's saying he's dead. He's was probably forced over the Boundary, like Tressa," Lucas decided, gesturing around to the barren landscape. Evelyn hiccupped again and started crying, but Lucas ignored her. "In under two months, half of us have disappeared, we don't know where they are, we don't know who's next, we don't know how to stop this madness. Something has to change here, because I for one don't plan on losing. I'm getting out of here."

"Me too," I agreed. "We've lost everything, and—"

"How many times have we said this?" Evelyn interrupted bitterly, kicking a smoldering tree trunk so that chunks of ashes exploded into the air. "To be honest, I don't care anymore. I'd rather be where Fr...*he* is than have to deal with these ridiculous ordeals. Like you said, no one knows how the Boundary works, and therefore nothing can ever be accomplished."

"Or do they?" Lucas gasped, his eyes lighting up all of a sudden. He turned to me, grinning in a scared anticipation. "Why haven't we thought of it before?"

"Because it's suicide," I snapped, suddenly realizing what he was suggesting and the magnitude of it. "Gosh, Lucas, don't be an idiot!"

"I'm not, I'm not!" he insisted, turning to Evelyn for support. "Granted it's dangerous, but then what isn't nowadays?"

"I'm not following," Evelyn admitted, but her interest was roused and she stopped crying.

"He wants to interrogate the Master," I explained, waiting for her reaction.

"Go ahead then," she replied, and my jaw dropped. "No, really, I'm done with caring. Do what you feel is right. Nothing matters now."

"Penny, don't you see?" Lucas turned once again, his face imploring me to understand. "You can rip, for a start, which has got to count for something. We as a trio can give up and cross the Boundary to...wherever it is people go. That would leave Him with nothing to rule over, which I'm guessing he would hate. We can bargain for information."

"Lucas," I retorted in amazement. "You moron. You realize

that He'd probably just call our bluff? Then punish us for even asking?"

"Tressa and Avery found something," he insisted, his smile slipping into a frown of irritation. "I intend to find it too, one way or another."

I gestured to the crumbling ruins of the manor, still flabbergasted that a clever boy such as he would even dream of doing such a silly thing.

"Assuming it isn't a pile of ashes?"

"I think it's information." Lucas shrugged stonily, crossing his arms. "And they got it from somewhere, or someone. Before you say Beatrix, she was dead long before they started getting all secretive."

D. It was the only explanation.

"Lucas," I began, accidentally taking a deep breath of smoky air. "There's something I need to tell you. I should have said it long ago, but—"

I broke off in alarm as a great creaking sound echoed behind me. We whipped around, and Evelyn shrieked as a massive tree, burnt to black, began to fall straight towards us. I tried to run after the other two to safety, but realized my nightgown was snagged on a stake of wood buried deep into the ground. I yanked and tugged, but it was stuck fast.

I closed my eyes and threw my hands up over my head, waiting.

A moment later and nothing had happened, it should have hit by now. Tentatively opening one eye, I noted with shock the tree was hovering a few inches above my head, moving so slowly that it appeared to be floating.

I don't care what promises I made you. Tell anyone, and you will *be disposed of.*

It was that voice again, the one that could be any age, any gender, or any number of people.

And now I had no doubt who it was.

The tree moved again, crashing down within a foot of my head and sending hot sparks spraying onto my bare arms. The pain meant nothing, and I was frankly just glad to be alive.

"Are you all right?" Evelyn and Lucas asked in unison, rushing back over.

"Fine," I muttered, pulling my nightgown free with absolute ease.

"That was lucky. I was prepared to go into mourning for another person!" Lucas remarked cynically, and Evelyn gasped.

"Don't joke!" she squealed, tears welling up again. "And besides, we don't have to 'go into mourning' as you so put it. He. Isn't. Dead."

"I know, I'm only teasing, however inappropriately timed it may be. Penny, what was that you were going to say?"

A pile of deadly looking debris was picked up by a faint breeze just to my left, swirling around warningly. Bits of splintered wood, chunks of rubble; things much too heavy to be carried by a regular wind.

"Ah, nothing. I was just going to suggest that we take a look inside, now, and see what can be salvaged," I shrugged lightly, and the air stilled again. "I think it should be cool enough now. That rip was powerful enough."

"I suppose we should, better sooner rather than later." Lucas shrugged. "Besides, He might be there and—"

"You're not going to talk to Him." I clenched my fists in irritation. "I'm not going to let you do something that imbecilic, especially when we need every life that's left."

"If you really want to, I could do the talking?" Evelyn offered gloomily, her puffy red eyes refusing to meet mine. "I don't mind, because if it ends badly I might get reunited with Fred, whilst you two might have a shot at freedom. If such a thing even exists, of course."

"Of course it exists!" I snapped, chilled by the idea. "Good grief, I shall have to lock the both of you in a padded room, you seem so bent on your own destruction!"

"It isn't giving up," Lucas argued, affronted. "It's the exact opposite! Now stop finding fault in everything I say, and let's go inside."

I grumbled under my breath, but relented. Evelyn, still sniffing, followed us into the ruins.

It was tricky even getting near the front door – or, at least, where it had been. We gingerly climbed over the rubble, some of which was still smoking.

Lucas was only wearing socks and Evelyn was barefoot, and they both kept wincing as they trod on odd warm embers. The front doors lay on the ground like a drawbridge, carvings filled with dirt and tinged black in many places. A massive open archway was exposed, showing the dust-coated interior and cracked marble floor littered with pieces of stone, melted glass, and broken furniture. Chunks of blackened beams were reminders of what had once been the spectacular rafters, and I supposed that great hunk of melted metal was the chandelier. Plasterwork was gone entirely, as was most of the furniture, and the velvet drapes contributed to the largest pile of ash. The walls themselves were charred up to halfway down, the remainder dusted grey and rather unstable.

"Why would He burn down this place?" Evelyn breathed in a hushed tone, awed by the sheer extent of the damage. "It's so sad. It feels as if the manor itself is sad."

"I don't think He did," I whispered, wading through a carpet of ashes to the stairs, which were thankfully intact. "He came and stopped the fire." I pondered on this for a moment. "But then if He isn't controlling the trials, who is?"

"This is precisely why we need to question Him," Lucas repeated in a sickening know-it-all tone. "Who knows, perhaps He's angry at them for burning down His castle and might tell."

I chose not to answer, grinding my teeth and pushing forwards up the stairs. Gosh, why couldn't Lucas have disappeared instead of Fred?

There was a chill coming in from where the hall used to be, carrying dust from the forest of ruins. Oh, how I longed for those days when lessons were the worst things. Well, them and the Master.

Now we were thinking of actually approaching Him for help against something even bigger.

"At least the breakfast room is okay," I quipped, nodding towards the turret to our right. "And perhaps the boys' bedchamber."

"My dresses!" Evelyn screamed in horror, forgetting her sorrow for one moment. "Do you really mean I shall have to wear my nightie all day, with no change of clothing?"

"Quite possibly," I nodded, feeling buoyed by the prospect of having never to wear a corset again. "Of course, Lucas will be able to lend us some of the boys' old outfits. If they've survived that is. And even if they're smoke damaged, they would still be better than what we have now."

"Wear Fred's old clothes...?" Evelyn whimpered faintly, and fell with a thud on the landing, passed out cold.

"Dear lord." Lucas rolled his eyes. "There's not even anyone left to impress."

"Try telling her that." I sighed. "Wherever there's a mirror, there's a need to look good. It's her motto."

"I think I bumped my head," Evelyn piped up in wonder, heaving herself off the floor and touching the spot tenderly. "It hurts."

Then she burst into tears again, genuine, heartfelt tears. Her whole body shook, and we knelt next to her in alarm.

"Evelyn, it's okay," I lied soothingly. "You'll be fine."

"How do you know?" she wailed, getting up and shaking us away forcefully. "We promised if we stuck together it would be okay. If we didn't do anything brash it would be okay. If we waited long enough, it would be okay. But it isn't, is it? We're all going to die."

Before I could object – or agree – she had run away from us, crying at the top of her lungs.

"Let her go," Lucas ordered gently as I made to chase after her. "She needs time to process what's happened."

"She can't shut out on us now, though! Dear me, if we followed traditional mourning each time we lost someone, I'd be wearing black to the grave!" I chuckled a tad hysterically. "You said so yourself!"

"I think Fred meant a little bit more to her than just a friend, though," Lucas reminded me, his tone becoming less confident at the subject of affections. "And like she said, there still might be reason to believe…"

He trailed off, eyes glazing over, and went completely still.

"Lucas? Lucas?" I waved my arm in front of his face, trying to see what he was looking at to no avail. There was nothing but a mangled mess of ruins to one side, and the same old (if not dirtied) manor to the other. "Am I missing something?"

"I might be going round the bend," Lucas said frowning, raising a shaky finger to point at something amongst the splintered beams, "but see if you can notice something odd in that pile of wood."

I squinted until my eyes watered, searching for the elusive detail, but alas could see nothing. Delicately, I stepped a little ways into the ruins and took a closer peak at the area he was pointing to. When I finally saw it, I was actually rather peeved at how mundane the issue was.

"An 'R'?" I questioned, not bothering to keep the disappointment from my voice. Nothing special, nothing that could help us unwind the web – only a miniscule scratch in the largest beam that distinctly resembled an R. "You have better eyes than I thought. Now, shall we go upstairs and try to salvage something to uphold the collection of Evelyn's wardrobe?"

"You don't think it's a little odd?" Lucas pressed, still staring at the letter as if it were a fascinating specimen, instead of a blemish the height of my hand. "To have a scratch that perfect? I mean, it's so clearly an R, and how could it possibly be formed by something as wild as a fire?"

"So are you saying one of us quickly ran into the blaze and carved a random letter into a chunk of wood, just for fun?" I joked scornfully. "Please, Lucas. Stop over-analyzing things."

"I will analyze whatever I want, however I want, thanks very much." Lucas frowned in irritation. "And I have a gut feeling that it's important, so I shall commit it to memory."

"That gut feeling," I remarked with a snort. "It couldn't be caused by under-eating, could it? Something nasty in the gruel?"

"Shut up. Those are my boots you're wearing, don't forget, and it was me who saved your unworthy backside in the fire."

"What, these are boots?" I gasped in mock surprise. "I thought they were clues. I was going to wear them, because committing to memory is old-fashioned."

"I surrender." Lucas sighed, not even looking at me but pushing ahead up the creaking staircase. "Because that is the worst taunt I have ever heard anyone say. It's embarrassing to even be involved with an argument that infantile."

I smirked to myself, not at all offended, and rather pleased to be acting like a young teenager again.

Our suspicions were confirmed; though the breakfast room remained intact, along with the boys' chamber and two empty rooms, the girls' chamber had been completely obliterated as we thought. It was now nothing more than a pile of smoking rubble, hidden under the splintered remains of what had once been the roof and the attic.

"Heavens," I breathed, thinking only that this wouldn't help Evelyn's mood whatsoever. "I fear we'll have to be borrowing from you, Lucas, after all – this doesn't look good for our wardrobes."

"There's a pile of clothing just over there," he replied quietly, pointing to where a lonely sleeve was fluttering in a slight breeze.

"Tressa," I remembered sadly. "They must belong to her."

Deciding that it would be better than forcing Evelyn into a shirt and trousers, I ducked under a beam and crawled through the jungle, occasionally hissing in pain as my flesh made contact with a still-burning ember or particularly sharp splinter of wood or glass. My nightie snagged on a nail and ripped up to my thigh, exposing the most skin I had ever seen, but I kept going.

Underneath the bricks and shingles, it was possible to see the shattered remains of our life. The blackened duvet of someone's bed, an ornate chunk of a vanity, porcelain remnants of a washbowl. And, miraculously untouched by the flames, a couple of Tressa's old day dresses.

I quickly cleared the rubble aside and sifted through to find as many as I could which were still wearable. It turned out that only a few fitted that criteria, as many had their sleeves burned off, torn, or were trapped underneath bricks. I didn't understand why this was so, and was at first suspicious. But on closer examination there wasn't anything untoward apart from the fact they were undamaged. This must have been D's doing. I was thankful as we at least had something to wear.

"Three," I announced when I was safely back in the corridor with Lucas again. "We can make do with that until…"

Until what? Until we got out, or died?

"Two," he corrected upon further inspection. "This one is burned on the back, see?"

Lucas held the soft yellow dress up so that I could see the strange black mark that someone had branded onto the bodice.

D.

"It says 'D' on it!" I shouted, panicked, before I could think.

"I suppose it does," Lucas affirmed wryly, a small smile creeping up the sides of his mouth. "But please don't show favoritism towards letters. If you refuse to acknowledge R, then what makes D so special?"

"Because…" I stuttered. *Because my crazy, vindictive, possibly psychic ex-pen pal is called D!*

"Exactly. Two letters in five minutes, there's got to be a pattern here." Lucas frowned, excited by the prospect of a puzzle he might actually be able to solve. "Keep an eye out; they've not been obvious, and if we miss one, it might not solve." I rolled my eyes and threw the faulty gown into the mess, folding the other two over my arm.

We made our way to the boys' bedchamber.

I stood for a moment looking around the room and thinking. "So for sleeping arrangements, shall we drag two spare bedding sets into one of the unused rooms?" I suggested, deciding that someone had to take care of domestics before we got too carried away with puzzles.

Lucas agreed, clearly having not thought of such matters. I dumped the dresses in the corner, and we spent the next few minutes gathering the duvets and pillows from Fred and Avery's abandoned beds to take into the closest empty room, not trusting ourselves to speak.

I had never been in the boys' chamber, and even after all that had happened it still felt terribly scandalous. I had once wondered what kinds of interesting, new things it held, and now I was inside it looked disappointingly ordinary.

The layout was exactly the same as ours had been, despite the room being slightly smaller and a different shape, with the vanity tables being replaced by small desks and the color scheme more neutral than pastel.

We heaved the linen down the hallway into the first undamaged room, halfway between the chamber and the partially burnt common room.

Evelyn was inside, curled up next to a moldy lace curtain and letting the open window blow in a cold air, as if to blow her problems away. It was the same room Avery had complained about her and Fred in, and my stomach twisted uncomfortably.

"Hey," I called, but she didn't look up. "I've found some extra dresses we can change into! And we're setting up temporary beds here until we figure something else out."

"Super," she shrugged flatly, not seeming to care as much as I had expected.

"Come on, Evelyn, don't be a sourpuss," I teased. "Come and help."

She didn't react at all, save for heaving her skinny self over with a sigh, and adjusting the sheets next to the peeling wallpaper so that they were far enough away from the little iron fireplace.

"Shut the window?" Lucas asked, his hands full of pillows. "It's raining again, and we don't want the room to rot any more than it already has."

I got up to do so, when a loud voice made me jump and stop.

"What do you mean you *meant* to?" Someone was shouting furiously, and I flinched as I recognized the tone. Madon. Oddly enough, He had lost His temper quite often, but scarcely yelled as He was doing now. "God, this whole place was already crumbling to pieces, why the hell did you have to go and *burn* it?"

He must have had an answer we couldn't hear, because a few seconds later He spat back, "You don't need to remind me, I'm no fool. But I'm getting fed up of waiting, and having these ridiculous, childish whims damper my own plans...yes, I know. That's no excuse! And I don't see why we have to talk here, when it would be so much easier to..."

His voice slowly lowered until I couldn't hear anything else.

Lucas dropped the linen, pleading, "Penny, this is our chance! We have to confront Him."

"Did you not catch any of that?" I hissed. "Someone else burned the manor, not Him. You're not going to find out anything, you're just going to get yourself killed! He clearly isn't in the best of moods right now!"

Lucas glared back at me, not moving, and I matched his stare.

Then Evelyn gave a little huff of frustration and ran out towards where the Master had been shouting.

"Evelyn!" I gasped, but she was already gone.

We ran after her, skidding to a stop as she slowed down herself. Just around the corner, the Master was standing wearing His travel clothes. I couldn't quite see who He was speaking to, and wasn't about to wander closer to have a look.

"Everything is going according to plan; we're nearly finished and they still haven't come close to guessing. Relax."

I froze, realizing who it must be. What was D doing here?

A cold chuckle sounded, raising the hairs on the back of my neck.

"We have visitors. I must go. Remember what I have told you."

A shadow swept across the hallway, filling me with an icy paralysis as it passed, and then it was gone.

"What are you doing?" The Master said expressionlessly, turning towards us.

"I want to know why you let Fred lose!" Evelyn shouted, and I winced. I didn't see that kind of anger coming, not from her! "You cold-hearted, selfish, horrible, evil, murdering *devil*!"

He raised his eyebrows and laughed coolly.

"Charming praise. Now get out. I'm not in the mood for these games."

"Tell me!" Evelyn shrieked stamping her foot on the ground. "Why are we here, and why can't we get out? Why? Why are we the only ones left?"

His smile vanished, replaced by a scowl. "Let me give you a hint, hmm? Being dead and being lost isn't always the same thing; and getting out doesn't mean you've won. Besides, I think you've gathered that I'm not alone in this…which reminds me, eavesdropping is rather a nasty habit."

And just like that, a rip tore through just like the shadow.

We all cried out in pain as it hit us, but instead of falling to the ground in utter agony, I merely clenched my fists and rocked on the spot. Yes, it hurt, yes, I wanted to scream, but no, it wasn't excruciating. I wasn't on the verge of madness, only on the verge of tears.

Push back. Go on, I dare you, D whispered in my mind, but the tone was amused rather than helpful.

Who are you? Why are you talking in my head now? I snapped back, perturbed by the sensation.

I'm D. You're not responding to my letters. I made alternate arrangements. Now push back!

So against my better judgment, I did.

I let the air swim until I could see the gaping rips He had created, wrapping around all of us and causing the pain. Struggling to stand as it increased in intensity, I created my own rips around His, and slowly let them expand so that they pushed His away. The pain lessened, and I saw His eyes widened in shock.

I bit my lip until I tasted blood, eyes screaming in protest as I pushed; the torture second now to my intense concentration. I felt my knees buckle and I collapsed, but refused to relinquish my struggle.

Then it finished entirely. I closed my eyes and slumped to the ground, so that I didn't see the anguish on His face as He ripped away.

Normally that act alone would have caused nausea, but now it was only a faint buzz.

Interesting, D remarked, sounding somewhat bemused and more than a little disappointed. *I suppose I shall have to reward you for that...try the letters 'O' and 'U'. Not that it will help you much, but apparently your friends think it important, being as misguided as they are. If you want to actually succeed, then go find the place where it all began.*

And then the voice faded, just like that. More importantly, though, there was the increasingly outstanding fact that for some reason, whilst His power was in decline, mine was increasing.

23

"What did you think was going to happen?" I was aware of Lucas snapping at Evelyn. His voice sounded distant and unclear, like I was underwater. "'Yes, dear children, I shall quite happily tell you exactly what you must do to defeat me and live happily ever after'? It doesn't work like that in real life!"

"I know, I'm not stupid!" Evelyn retorted impatiently, fists clenched and face pale. "It was your idea to confront Him, might I remind you, but I did it because—"

"Of Fred?" Lucas suggested tersely. "Stop living the past, Evelyn, we need to focus on now! And that charade ended in torture, what if it had been worse? What if He now goes to whoever is controlling this thing, and gets them to ramp it up a little bit?"

"Fred disappeared yesterday!" Evelyn shouted, and I could hear tears in her voice now. "That isn't the distant past! Please, let's stop bickering."

I shook my head as everything slowly crept back into focus. It seemed that the more I practiced ripping, and the more difficult a trick I tried to perform, the longer it took to get back into an ordinary state of mind.

"I'm okay," I announced, wobbling as I stood up.

"Did you make that punishment go away?" Evelyn gasped.

"I think so." I nodded, faintly pleased with myself.

"This is fantastic!" Lucas grinned, patting me on the back and receiving a proud beam in return. "Gosh, you must be getting stronger to be able to contend with Him, soon you'll be able to— Oh my goodness, what if you managed to rip out of the Boundary, like He can?"

I was stunned, having honestly never thought of that. The question was, if ever that became possible, would I do it? Would I leave my friends behind for my own freedom?

"That's not the half of it," I blurted, not wanting to think about it too much, not trusting myself to pick the right choice. "Did you interpret what He said like I did? Our friends aren't dead! 'Being dead and being lost isn't always the same thing.' What else could that mean?"

"It could mean that not all of them are okay." Lucas shrugged, ever the bringer of regrettable logic. "That wording sounds too fishy. Besides, we knew that already. But I did not understand that last bit whatsoever."

"Me neither," Evelyn piped up, as if to remind us that she was present.

"I have some other information though," I brought up hesitantly, my mind churning for a way to present it without giving D away. "The letters O and U. Oh, and I think our friends are setting up the letters to help us."

"Where did you…?" Lucas began, but he must have seen my pleading expression, begging for him to not go there, as he trailed off his question. "Never mind. This is probably the best sequence of events that have ever happened to us! Most or all of our missing friends are still alive, we have two more letters in a puzzle *they* have set up to help us, and Penny is beginning to rival the Master Himself in terms of ripping power! There's only one thing for it!"

"Lucas, you don't have champagne in your room?" I laughed, remembering a piece I read during lessons.

"Hardy har har. I have something better."

He sprinted away down the corridor, running into his chamber without stopping for us.

"We aren't going in the boys' chamber, are we?" Evelyn asked anxiously, chewing her lower lip and giving a nervous grimace as we followed him.

"If you do, I shall give you a proper dress," I coaxed, smiling.

As I knew she would, Evelyn relented and followed me through the doors, relaxing a bit as she saw nothing out of the ordinary inside.

Lucas was sifting through something on his desk, so I led her over to where I had safely stashed the two undamaged gowns in the empty corner. I dearly hoped the attraction of proper clothing would keep her from realizing what Lucas was doing.

One was a soft lavender dress with thick petticoats and paisley embroidery sewn delicately over the bodice and skirts, possibly a dinner gown, and the other was a simpler item of navy blue, made of a heavy material we wore in chillier weather. It was an easy decision who got which dress. We took them to the chamber we were now to use.

It felt extremely odd putting on a gown without anything underneath, but I rather liked it. We didn't need sucking in as much as we did whilst still well-fed, and considering they had belonged to Tressa, I found mine rather tight anyhow.

Evelyn hated changing in front of me, so I left her to go and see what Lucas was up to.

"It fits?" He glanced up as I entered the chamber, oddly surprised.

"Well of course it does!" I defended myself, hurt. "I wasn't that much larger than Tressa, just slightly stockier, and… shorter."

It was indeed strange, I admitted, that the dress of a girl a good few inches taller than me fitted almost perfectly, and was exactly the style I loved to wear. Almost as strange as finding two dresses unharmed in a room that had otherwise been destroyed. It must have been D then.

"Anyway, on a lighter note, I was thinking that maybe we should write down what clues we have already and see if we can make any sense out of them?" Lucas suggested eagerly, like a child on his birthday. "It's like a mystery now, much better to deal with than trials."

"I don't think the fire was the end of it," I muttered ominously, but sat down at the desk anyway.

Evelyn breezed in, looking much happier now, and perched

delicately beside me with an expectant expression.

RDOU, Lucas wrote. *Being dead and being lost isn't always the same thing. Getting out doesn't mean you've won. Master not alone in this. Penny's power increasing.*

Lucas finished the page off with a flourish, brow furrowed in confusion. "I don't get it. I wonder if we unscrambled the letters...dour? That's a word, right? But it means gloomy and severe, I don't see how that helps at all."

"Can I add something to this?" I asked, hoping to not be questioned. Lucas handed me the pen, and I scribbled, *If you want to actually succeed, go to the place where it all began*

"Don't ask. Just interpret," I ordered.

"That's easy," Evelyn exclaimed, and we turned to her in alarm. "I mean, it's the library, right? Where the books first disappeared, and we began to question Beatrix? That chain of events led to Penny pulling the lever, and here we are today."

"She's right," Lucas acknowledged, winning a proud blush from Evelyn. "But the only problem is that the library doesn't exist anymore. It burned down."

"Books?" I suggested, trying to win my way back into the conversation. "Are any of those left?"

"A whole bucket load, actually," he admitted. "Want me to bring them out?"

"No, I'd rather we sat here and contemplated life for a couple of years. What do you think, genius?"

Lucas flashed me an irritated look before sighing. "All right, all right. I'll go grab them. Want to give me a hand, because there are literally tons of them!"

He wasn't exaggerating. I had been expecting three or four books, certainly not the massive library of more than a dozen thick volumes he had somehow managed to keep hidden in the cove between his bed frame and floor, on everything from geography to fairy tales.

Seeing the information up close, I once again felt that familiar rush at the prospect of knowledge of the outside world, and feeling the wonderful worn leather covers under my hands…until they were stacked a mile high in my malnourished arms.

"Good grief!" I panted, and Lucas scooped a last 900-plus-paged book and plopped it onto my wobbling pile. "When did you get all of these? I was under the impression you only took a couple!"

"Well…" he started, slightly guilty. "I did take a couple. Then a couple more after that. But I was petrified one day Beatrix would claim it to be too dangerous and take them away – which, incidentally, she did – so I didn't give any of them back. It isn't technically stealing, I do live here!"

"Don't apologize." I laughed, straining to walk. "It might just save our lives!"

We plunked them down on Lucas's desk, and then sat down to inspect our new pile of clues with thoughtful expressions.

"*A Study of Sociiety,*" Evelyn read, picking up a slender old book on top. "How odd, I never knew society was spelled with two Is, did you?"

"It isn't," Lucas uttered immediately, snapping the suspect book up and scanning the title, which sure enough was misspelled. "Another letter. It looks like somebody scratched it in there. Subtly hidden, but I'd have noticed that if it were there before. I suppose the hidden word isn't 'dour', then! *R-D-O-U-I.*"

"Do we just read them, then?" Evelyn asked, pleased that she had spotted the abnormality.

Lucas affirmed that yes, it was necessary, and we quickly dived for the least intimidating and more interesting books.

I seized one about a dwelling in the outside called *London* with lots of illustrations showing magnificent buildings and a massive creek that looked much wider than was possible. Seeing the way it encircled part of the city, I wondered whether they had Boundaries too; it was probably more bearable if there were thousands of you, though.

"I wonder what it's like," I mused aloud, enraptured by the sketches of people – women in beautiful bonnets, men in splendid top hats, and merry children skipping down cobbled streets full of horses and carriages. "Outside, I mean. Where were we from? Who were our parents? When we get out, what will we do? Coming so close to freedom rather makes you wonder if you're actually prepared, doesn't it? What if there is nothing…what if the Boundary is the only world, and these books are about fantasy?"

"The only way to find out is to get out," Lucas answered briskly. "No point in worrying. It'll only scare you."

"I'm not scared, I was only wondering!" I argued, but when no one answered, I glumly fell back into reading. I didn't blame them, since thinking about all the possibilities gave me the chills.

So we settled into an easy rhythm, reading every page of as many books as we could, glad to have something to do for once which might have some significance. We left nothing unread, fearing to leave the vital clue undiscovered, although by nightfall my eyes were starting to ache and water.

"We need sleep," I announced, slamming down a book on animals. "I simply cannot focus anymore."

"Hear, hear!" Evelyn agreed tiredly, slumping in her chair. "I'm so hungry I can't think, and now my eyes are betraying me. Goodnight, Lucas."

"Night, girls." He nodded, still buried in a thick textbook. "I'll finish the last two hundred pages on this before turning in, I think."

Lucas's eyesight was already terrible due to such conditions, but in his mind, the end justified the means, and I couldn't argue with him.

Evelyn and I slipped into the chilly room and pulled on our sooty nightgowns, gagging at the stench of smoke still deep within the fabric. Our makeshift beds were much less comfortable than what we were used to, and having never slept in a different room my entire life, it felt extremely odd.

I stared long and hard at the ceiling, first trying to unscramble the letters, then giving up and thinking about how much better the room would be with new wallpaper.

"Penny?" Evelyn called softly from over in her own pile of sheets. "Are you awake?"

"Yeah," I affirmed with a yawn.

"Do you think Fred really is okay?" she asked hesitantly. "I can't seem to stop thinking about it. I know I should be trying to help you and Lucas figure things out, but quite frankly, I don't want a future without him. I'd rather things stay as they are with us all together."

"I wonder if it would have been better too sometimes," I admitted, suddenly feeling very selfish. We had lost Tressa, Avery, Fred, and Beatrix due to a quest started by me, and there was a possibility we'd lose more. Was it worth it? Probably not. Was I able to change the past? Nope. "But as for Fred, and the others, I think they're fine. Honestly."

Evelyn didn't reply, but sighed contentedly.

Perhaps there was hope left after all.

24

The next morning we got dressed and went for breakfast with our hair uncombed and faces unwashed, nibbled at as much gruel as possible before nearly being sick. I found some old shoes near the kitchen and although too small for Evelyn and me, they would have to do. I gave Lucas back his boots. We returned to the boys' chamber and resumed reading books until our heads began aching again.

"I swear," Evelyn whined, planting her head down in the middle of two pages, "I shan't last much longer. I'm so hungry I could faint, and my poor eyes are nearly falling out, and I must look a frightful mess – I haven't bathed in days!"

"That makes three of us," I sighed. "I've read most of these already in lessons, and to be honest I'm not absorbing it any more than I did then. My mind is slowly being eaten by my stomach."

Lucas wrinkled his nose. "Gross, that is not a pleasant mental image! I know it's hard, but we need to keep going. There has to be something here, and it's the only lead we've got. Failure isn't an option whenever success is!"

We fell back into reading again for about five minutes, before Evelyn slammed her book shut and pushed her stool back in frustration.

"This is ridiculous!" she snapped, viciously twirling a limp curl around her finger. "Could we have a break now, please? I cannot endure this torture for another second!"

"It isn't torture," Lucas defended lamely. "But if you really need to…"

"I've found something!" I gasped.

"Really?" The both shouted in unison, standing up so fast that a stack of seven books fell onto the floor with a dusty *plunk*, scattering loose pages everywhere, and their stools toppled backwards and rolled halfway across the room.

"No," I laughed, trying and failing to keep a straight face.

"Just trying to liven things up. You should have seen your faces!"

"Penny, that's not funny!" Evelyn complained, though I could see laughter in her eyes. "You nearly gave me a heart attack!"

Lucas shot me a dirty glare, tromping over the pile of fallen books to go and fetch his stool. I was laughing so hard there was a stitch in my side, and goodness, did it ever make me feel better! I hadn't really laughed properly in such a long time.

"I found something!" Lucas shouted from across the room, straining to pick up his stool.

"You can't get us that soon after I just did!" I giggled, trying to relax and get back to reading. "Silly Lucas."

"No, seriously! Come and have a look!"

I shared a quick glance with Evelyn, unsure whether to go and risk being made the victim of a lame prank for the sake of a possible clue. With the alternative being more reading, we both decided to play dangerously and see what he was on about.

There was a book lying open on the floor, clearly from the pile they had accidentally knocked over. At closer inspection, it seemed to be on folk tales, with full-page drawings of colorful characters and a narrative tone to the writing. Beautifully bound in faded chocolate leather with thick ivory pages, it was pleasant to look at and probably entertaining to read, but I couldn't see what the big deal was about it.

"Um…" I searched for words.

"Look closer," Lucas ordered sternly, and Evelyn bent so far forward that her head nearly touched the paper and completely blocked my view.

"There's a few pages missing," she analyzed carefully. "But that's all I can see which is odd. They probably fell out when we knocked them off, I wouldn't panic too much."

"No," I checked, peering over my shoulder to see if there were any pages which were the right size and quality for the book. "Nothing that matches."

Lucas carried the volume to the desk and set it down so we

could all have a look, him kneeling on the floor. Sure enough, if you looked closely at the spine, there were telltale jagged edged which signaled the forceful removal of probably three or more pages. It skipped between two fables seamlessly, but clearly one had been taken out. What was more, there were three letters written on the skimpy remainders of each stolen paper.

We now had R-D-O-U-I-A-E-S.

We updated our notes, but for once we didn't dwell on them.

Lucas flicked a quick interpretation at us. "So dare u?" Still makes no sense, there's probably more letters to go. I'm more interested about where these papers are, hmm?"

A sudden thought came to me. "I know! This has to be what Tressa and Avery found, and they ripped it out and hid it somewhere! Maybe this was why they wanted Lucas's other books, so that they could see if there was anything else!"

"They must have taken this one from me whilst I was reading it, then they couldn't find my other ones," Lucas theorized mildly. "I wondered where it had gotten to."

Half of me was relieved that it wasn't D who had given them information, and the other half felt strangely sad. Why had D isolated me, then? Why was I so special, besides the dreams and the fact I could rip? What did it all mean?

"Now we just have to find the story." Evelyn sighed, flopping back onto the bed behind her in exhaustion. "Why can't things ever be easy?"

"It's pretty obvious where they are." Lucas shrugged. "The only place we ever hid things – under the bed. Tressa's bed it nothing but ashes now, so I'm hoping Avery had them, else we're finished."

Hardly daring to look, Lucas lifted up the coverings and clutter to peer under where Avery had once slept, grabbing blindly into the darkness in hope of catching hold of a clue.

"Got it!" he shouted triumphantly, and I nearly knocked him down again trying to see the writing. "Get away, Penny, I'll read it out."

Once upon a time, there were three little girls and three little boys. They lived with their caregivers in a cottage on the edge of a dark forest, and they were very happy. As they grew older, however, things started to change. The children were no longer content with what could be found in the confines of their house, and so one day, a girl wandered away from the garden and into the forest. Far from the horrors she had been told to expect, the girl found nothing less than the entrance to Faeryland itself, concealed in an old log surrounded by toadstools! Even though she had been told to beware of the creatures that lurked in the woods, she was entranced by the faery's sweet music and strange magic, so every day she would escape from her lessons to listen. The faeries didn't mind, saying that she could sit and listen to their music as long as she didn't bring her other friends along. They were gentle creatures, but their word was their law, and they could not stand for it to be broken.

The girl was too blind to see this. So enraptured was she with the sounds of Faeryland, that she could not imagine a punishment harsh enough to prevent her from bringing her friends too. And so she brought her friends along the next day.

The faeries were furious. The six children unwittingly trampled the clearing, their excited chatter nearly blocking out the fae songs, but that was not what angered them the most. The girl had lied to them. And so, as punishment, the court faeries trapped all six children in a realm that was neither Reality nor Faeryland, but a dreamscape that reflected all the darkest parts of their personalities. Before, they had been defined by their good traits: leadership, wit, kindness, curiosity, intelligence, and love. Now, there was nothing left but their vices: jealousy, hatred, bitterness, greed, fear, and deception. They were stripped of everything but their flaws, and those who had once been great friends turned into vicious enemies.

The court faeries took pity on them. Whoever proved to be the strongest and managed to stay good through the trials would be allowed to leave the prison and return to Reality, but the rest would have to stay forever. Using their magic, they watched how the children reacted to steadily worsening nightmares. One by one they succumbed to their inner weaknesses, until only two were left.

As it happened, the faeries from an opposing court discovered what was going on, and began favoring one of the children. They offered him one wish, and he asked to know what his opponent's biggest weakness was. The answer surprised him: it was friendship. They were each the other's biggest weakness. Armed with this knowledge, when the next nightmare attacked them, the boy did not help his friend, but coaxed her into putting herself in danger for him. True to their promise, after her fall, the faeries let the boy back into Reality.

Friendship can be either your greatest strength or deadliest liability.

"Is that it?" Evelyn leaned back, frowning. "How is that relevant in any way at all? Are they saying this entire place is being controlled by fairies? What?"

I read it again, ignoring her. A pit seemed to be growing in my stomach as I realized what the legend was saying, and what it would mean for us. Everything Tressa and Avery had done made sense – mostly, and half of me wished I hadn't seen it myself. Designed so that only one could escape.

"It's dated to 1899," Lucas whispered hoarsely, pointing at a date below a charcoal sketch of a winged creature watching two children from behind a tree, a thoroughly unreadable expression on its pointed little face. "All the other books were dated at least fifty years earlier! We don't know a thing about what's out there anymore. If this is true, we're not even part of that world, we're in some kind of other pocket that can be controlled from the outside. I mean, obviously it's just a fairy tale, but there're just too many similarities for it to be unrelated. Somebody, maybe Beatrix, planted it here to hint about—"

"Dear lord, that's what bothers you?" I snapped, feeling strangely angry. "Lucas, this is basically saying only one of us is ever going to get out, and everyone else will be stuck here forever!"

"For all we know this might have been put here to divide us,'" he argued, sounding unconvinced. "It certainly worked with Tressa and Avery, didn't it? He disposed of her thinking that they couldn't both make it. Got rid of the competition, didn't he? Perfect if someone wanted her gone, or wanted our numbers to dwindle faster."

"It doesn't change anything." Evelyn shrugged, eyes distant and glassy. "Let's try our hardest to crack the secrets. If only one succeeds, fine, but it won't be because we stabbed each other, it will be because of who figured things out first. Which would have happened anyway. So stop worrying."

"Damn it," Lucas swore bitterly, pushing back from the desk and pacing the room. "Yes, you get to be with your precious Fred, but what does this mean for Penny and me? She already knows something I don't, I can tell, and neither of us are likely to give up cracking this darn code."

"You're smarter than me," I retorted, not denying anything. "You have the books, the brains, and I have nothing but a piece of information that's a pain in the backside rather than of any help!"

We stared each other down, and my heart beat unevenly inside my chest. For whoever won, they would face a whole new set of challenges outside the Boundary, alone and unsure of what would be found. The rest would be together again, back to everyday life in what was left of the manor. Which was the better option?

"You've forgotten Avery," Evelyn added thoughtfully. "He got a free pass to the finals by slashing Tressa, and I'll bet he won't get down easy."

Lucas and I both swore colorfully again at the same time, making Evelyn squeak in protest like the old days.

"It sounds like some sick game now. Finals, winner, loser,

prize. I wonder if Beatrix knew."

"Of course she did. I wouldn't have been surprised if she'd started training favorites, since we all know she liked Fred and Evelyn best. Typical they ended up together, eh?"

"I'm still here," Evelyn snapped. "And don't turn me down so easily. If there's even the slightest possibility that we could get out and still be together, well that's a future I'd fight to the death for."

"Let's hope there isn't that chance," I said without thinking. "I'd hate to fight you – your nails are much longer and I bet you don't play fair."

"Don't, Penny," Lucas cautioned tiredly. "It won't come to a fight. Our strategy would simply be to dispose of the beast known as Avery, then take everything else as it came. May the best person win after that."

25

We found the remaining letters scrawled on the walls of the room we now occupied the following morning. It gave me the goose bumps to think that they had been written whilst I had been sleeping in the same room, but it was comforting at the same time to know it was our friends doing it from wherever they were.

"Why don't they just write the whole thing out?" Evelyn frowned, rubbing the sleep from her eyes and quickly pulling on her lavender dress.

They had been penned in some kind of black chalk, messily and much larger than the other, more subtle predecessors, pointing to us having perhaps missed some hidden letters before. It seemed rushed – our friends thought we didn't have that much time left to figure it out.

"I don't know," I answered vaguely, doing a quick scan to make sure I hadn't missed anything. "We'll just have to ask them if and when we see them again."

I was about to go and get Lucas when something stopped me. It would be so easy to write them out and rub the chalk from the walls. He would never know, never solve the puzzle. I would have a better chance of getting out.

"Penny?" Evelyn pushed hesitantly, her wide brown eyes telling me she knew exactly what I was thinking. "Don't be like Avery. It isn't worth it. Please."

I sighed, hating myself for the doubt. "I'm sorry. Let's go now before I change my mind."

She nodded, relieved, and we pattered down the sooty corridor towards Lucas's room, reciting the letters under our breath so that we would not forget them in the ten seconds the journey took.

Lucas was still asleep in bed, snoring slightly, covers pulled sideways so that they heaped over his torso and left his feet bare.

An evil grin crept onto my face.

His washbasin was filled with a murky water that hadn't been changed for days, left to sit in a china bowl and saturate in ashes, leaving it ice cold. It really was petty of me, but I couldn't resist.

"DEAR LORD WHAT ON EARTH!?" Lucas yelped, jumping out of bed at a speed I had never before seen him accomplish. His hair was plastered to his head, dripping onto his pajamas and onto the floor in a freezing puddle.

Evelyn turned away, unable to look at a boy improperly dressed in clothing made see-through by the water, but I could tell she was hiding giggles from behind her hands.

"Time to get up, sunshine," I said tonelessly, arms folded across my chest. Goodness, I wanted to laugh! "We found the rest of the letters."

"Penny," he hissed through chattering teeth. "That wasn't funny at all, all right, *at all*. I'm cold now, my bed will be soaking for days, and I haven't got any more water left! What's *wrong* with you?"

"Oh, Lucas," I snorted, composure breaking as I regarded his furious face dripping with the contents of the basin. "You should have seen the look on your face."

For a moment, his eyes flashed black, and I took a step back in alarm.

"What is it?" He frowned miserably, shivering with blue lips.

"Nothing…" I shook my head. "Get dressed and I'll make it up to you; I think we can finally solve the letter puzzle."

"That was terrible of you," Evelyn chided as we hurried back into the room. "Truly appalling."

"You were trying not to laugh," I accused, opening the door and going back inside. "Don't act so innocent!"

"I know!" she gasped, a mixture between a wail and a chuckle. "That's why it's so terrible, I shouldn't have found that funny!"

Lucas strode in with as much dignity as he could muster a couple of minutes later, fully dressed and hair drying off to look rather on the fluffy side of things.

"What have we got here?" he muttered to himself, whipping out a pencil and scribbling down the letters. "All right, so we have R-D-O-U-I-A-E-S-T-W now. Are you absolutely certain this is it, Penny?"

"Yep," I nodded. "See over there, by the 'T', there's a full stop? Kind of like telling us they're done, I thought."

Lucas went over to inspect the little chalk dot and turned back to us with an odd expression on his face.

"It's not a full stop," he began, fixing Evelyn with that strange look of mixed pity and concern. "Don't freak out, but that looks like an, ah, kiss. An X. Like what people use on cards to—"

He didn't have time to finish. Evelyn had barreled past him and stared at the marking for a few long seconds, before whispering, "It's in his handwriting."

She backed away slowly, eyes welling up and shaking her head. Before I could say anything, she had let out a small sob and ran from the room at full speed, tripping over the threshold but not stopping.

"Evelyn!" I shouted. "Come back! We need to figure this out!"

"Her eyes had gone black," Lucas told me fearfully. "When she turned…"

I wiped that image from my mind, not wanting those mind monsters to ever come back in full form again.

We had to go after her before she did something stupid, that much was for certain.

We ran after her, dodging past the debris and through the ruins to the gardens, desperately trying to keep our eyes on the steadily retreating form. It was a veritable minefield out there, charred grass making balance impossible and scattered rubble sticking up in all the most unavoidable places. Around the border of the woods, massive black tree trunks had fallen all over the lawns, and for a moment I was overcome with regret for the once-beautiful forest I had loved so much. Even the manor looked forlorn, with its stone walls crushed by a collapsed roof.

"Keep going," Lucas urged softly, seeing my expression. "It's all we can do now."

"I know. It just seems like such a shame…I never realized how lovely it could be before, and now it's destroyed…" I shook my head, trying to focus. "But it doesn't matter. We'll get out, and it won't matter what state it's in."

"Exactly," Lucas agreed. Neither of us mentioned the fairy tale.

Even the rhododendrons had finally died, I noticed. This detail I was actually glad of, as the constant 'beware' symbol had given me the shudders whenever I had seen them. The vibrant bushes were nothing more the soot.

Deeper into the woods things got slightly better as the fire hadn't quite gotten this far. The trees were poorly, most of them brown and dead, but at least they were standing. It began to grow misty and ahead I could see it was increasingly foggy.

"Evelyn!" Lucas was shouting. "Get back here! You're wasting time, what are you doing?"

I heard a far off sob coming from deep inside the skeleton forest, and all of a sudden I knew what her plan was. Lucas must have figured it out too, as he stopped his careful walking and began to sprint forwards, regardless of what he had to hurdle. I followed, and I dived further into the fog. I soon lost my way and couldn't see Lucas or Evelyn any more.

The Boundary was around here somewhere, I could hear it buzzing, but the fog had me completely incapacitated.

"You guys!" I called, voice sounding both far away and very close.

There was a muffled answer from Lucas, but I couldn't place where he was. I turned, trying to figure out where I had come from, but everywhere looked the same.

Gosh, Evelyn could be a pain sometimes.

There, over to the left! I could see light where the fog had thinned.

"Over here!" I shouted as I went blindly over. "Evelyn, Lucas!"

Ah, there was Lucas. Of course he had found— Wait...Lucas hadn't been wearing grey, he had been wearing off-white...then who...?

"Hello Penny," D greeted me amiably, turning around. There was nobody, absolutely nobody else it could have been.

My breath caught in my throat. D was *here*, standing right in front of me, which at one point had been stressed as impossible.

It – for I could find no gender in the voice, no characteristics that suggested male or female, although it was leaning towards the latter and was fully cloaked in a garment that hid its face from me, and which seemed to melt in with the creeping fog. I suppose I should have been scared, awed, or at least interested, but I could only feel anger. This was the person who had tricked me, who was in league with the Master, who hadn't helped me help my friends.

"You," I spat, utter loathing in my tone.

"Me," D replied, unaffected. "Are you not pleased to see me, Penny?"

"Pleased? Pleased?" I laughed somewhat hysterically. "You must not be familiar with rejection, because I ripped up your letters and threw them away, then refused to acknowledge your existence."

"I would beg to differ." D shrugged. Unless I was going around the bend again, it almost looked like the cloak was flickering, ever so slightly, like a shadow when the sun starts going in. "You did take my advice when I offered it, you still trusted I was telling the truth when I gave you those letters and told you to defend yourself. Surely you do not disregard me that much?"

"I hate you, though," I growled, unable to come up with a better retort. "You started the fire, you lied to me so many times, and I don't know why I was stupid enough to listen to someone allied with Him."

D laughed, an awful sound that made my blood run cold. "You say his name with such a reverence, and it's actually very amusing. He is human, he is mortal, and he is not worthy of the fear you have of him."

"But you are?"

"Depends," D chuckled with a tilted head. "What are you afraid of?"

"What do you want?" I snapped, irritated and nonplussed. Evelyn and Lucas were out there somewhere, stumbling through the fog so very close to the Boundary, and all D was doing was bragging. That, and there was something about the shadowy presence which shook me to the core.

"To discuss the weather," D replied airily. "To sightsee. To have a cup of tea and talk about old times. Or, more importantly, talk about the future. Not that it exists, but still makes for interesting conversation."

"I'll leave," I threatened.

"All right." D lifted a cloaked arm to gesture my dismissal. "Makes no difference to me. After you lose, we'll have plenty of time to talk."

I stood there, debating. D had been horrid to me, and probably whatever they had to say wouldn't apply to my friends, which went against our pact. Yet I was intrigued as to why D had shown his face, and why, if it had been possible to talk like this, D had communicated lies through letters first.

"Fine. But I still hate you."

"You're not my favorite person either," D pointed out frankly. "But it doesn't matter. Have you any idea what those letters spell, by the way? Senseless babble, out of all the things they could have said…"

"Are they okay, the others?" I interjected forcefully. "Where are they?"

D just shook a cloaked head and laughed again, saying, "If I told you, it would ruin the mystery, now wouldn't it? No point in that. They're perfectly alive, if that's what you're worried about."

I clenched my fists, seething in frustration.

"Who are you?" I snapped, jabbing a finger in the direction of that flowing cloak, half obscured by the fog. "You clearly aren't a previous habitant like you claimed, and you clearly aren't...normal. The Master is *afraid* of you, you know my dreams, you won't let me tell my friends, and you jump between helping me and hating me so fast it's ridiculous! You said it was impossible for me to meet you before, but now you're popping up everywhere and even speaking inside my head! You're making this even more complicated, so if you don't mind, either speak or get out, because I've had enough of being manipulated by people like you! Being in the dark *sucks*!"

D, stood there silently for a moment, then burst out laughing in that terrible, grating tone. The cloak shook, but still the face remained hidden.

"Penny, you are funny sometimes! You act so formidable, so in control...but you really don't know much about anything, do you? This game we've been playing is nearly over, and you still haven't the faintest idea what's going on. You are in no position to command like that!"

I wanted to scream. I was about to yell something rude when D began talking again, laughs subsided and replaced by a drawling monologue.

"I lied to you about who I was, because I don't think you're ready for the truth. I still don't. Letters are easier to communicate with, and easier to keep secret, so I wanted to try that first. As for Madon being scared...probably a tad harsh, but we, ah, know where we stand with one another. What I came to say was that the fairy tale you found under Avery's bed is a mixture of truth and fantasy, but the part you must take heed of is clear – only one of you will make it out. And it *has to be you*. Madon and I have...disagreed over this. Trust me, it isn't anything personal, and it isn't out of the kindness of my heart, assuming I even have one, but there is something else in the equation that makes it imperative you win. That is why I have been trying to help you, and you alone. It has to be you."

I stepped back, stunned. The Master didn't want me out, but D did. And if D had the influence I suspected, then I would be the one getting out of here whilst my friends stayed behind.

I should have been happy to have assistance with freedom, but instead I had a sinking feeling that had nothing to do with the chilly winds beginning to blow the fog away. It was cheating, giving them no chance. Whatever made me special, whatever made them unworthy, it wasn't fair.

"I don't want your help," I managed to hiss.

"Too bad." D sighed carelessly. "You're getting it. And, Penny? There's nothing you can do about it."

The wind blew violently for a moment, catching D by surprise, and for a moment the hood retracted enough to give me a glimpse of the face. I felt a shock of recognition, but before I could register anything, I stumbled back—

The baby cried as it was taken away, realizing suddenly that it wasn't in Mother's arms anymore. The man holding it was rough, not at all gentle, and the blankets were wrapped uncomfortable around its chest. The man looked down just in time to see the baby's eyes fly open in fear, and he nearly dropped the thing in shock. It was somehow emitting static, shocking his hands so painfully that it took all of his resilience not to drop it. No wonder it had to be put away.

I know who the baby in your dreams is. And it isn't you.

"It's you," I breathed, regaining my footing and staring at D in alarm. "I was wrong, they weren't my parents. They were yours."

D for once said nothing, seeming as unnerved as I was.

"But I don't understand. Why did you look like me as a baby?"

"Dreams mean nothing," D snarled. "They can be too easily

altered in a world like this."

D cast a wary look at the sky, which was now clearing at an impressive rate, before turning and ripping away so powerfully I felt my vision black out. I could feel the foul mood pulsating throughout the clearing, and I felt pity for whomever the wrath was directed at. The identity of whom I had a good idea.

Madon. We end this, one way or another.

*

Evelyn and Lucas were arguing near the Boundary a mere twenty feet away, apparently unaffected by the previous events. At first, I thought the intense emotion on Evelyn's face was anger, then I noticed the tears.

"What's going on?" I asked, and my voice sounded hollow. They were all right, but it didn't really matter anymore: they were going to lose.

"I'm finished," Evelyn whispered, rocking on her heels. "I can't take this anymore, so I'm going to join Fred, wherever he may be. But Lucas..." At this she flicked an annoyed glance at the glowering boy. "Lucas won't let me. He thinks we should all keep trying our best, when I don't even want to get out, I don't care about freedom, and I don't want to face the unknown alone! Tell him, Penny, tell him that it's not my fight anymore!"

"This is mad," Lucas defended through gritted teeth. "We don't know that stepping through will do anything but kill you."

"What if I don't care?" she shouted, tears streaming down her pale cheeks.

"I care!" Lucas yelled back. "God, Evelyn, we've lived together for fifteen years, you can't expect Penny and me to simply let you die!"

"That's not what I'm asking! I just want to be with Fred again, and for you all to have a shot at winning without me hampering you!"

"You're not hampering us," I choked, finally finding my voice. "Trust me, Evelyn. It won't make any difference whether you go now or later, so let's spend all the time we have left properly. You don't have to go like this."

"What's that supposed to mean?" Lucas frowned, eyes narrowing in suspicion.

I didn't fidget or stutter, simply staring at the ashy ground with defeated acceptance, and his eyebrows shot up in realization.

"It's planned out?" he whispered, staring at me and begging me to tell him he was wrong. "There's nothing we can do to change who gets out, is there?"

I hesitated. It was a power struggle between D and Madon, that much I had gathered, but either way they weren't leaving it to fate to decide. So I shook my head, and felt something in Lucas's confidence shatter.

"Do you know…who?" he queried, though I could tell that he didn't really want to know.

"Evelyn!" I screamed, suddenly realizing what our third member had been doing during our brief exchange.

Lucas completely misunderstood me. "No way! I thought…I thought it would be you…maybe Avery…but never her! I can't imagine—"

"No, you idiot!" I shook my head desperately, dragging him down the creek a couple of yards so he could see Evelyn standing at a section of the Boundary and slowly stepping towards it, so close that the hem of her dress singed and I could smell the tips of her stray curls burning. She was crying softly, of course, but staring resolutely at something over the Boundary, something we couldn't see. Three guesses what.

I ran and toppled her to the ground, feeling my elbow burn as it brushed the static fence. I knew she wouldn't make it in the end, but letting her go this way was simply too dangerous – we hadn't actually seen someone cross the Boundary and live to tell the tale.

"Get off me!" she shrieked, wresting away from me. "Fred! Penny, he's waiting for me, please just let me go to him!"

"It isn't real," I snapped, trying to stop her from advancing to the Boundary, which was crackling and sending out shocks of static. "Snap out of it! Lucas – give me a hand."

We were covered in dirt, our hair was riddled with twigs and dead leaves, and my arms were aching with the effort of withstanding her scratches and desperate attempts at escape. Lucas grabbed her wrists and together we managed to haul her into a standing position.

Evelyn's eyes were black, puffy from crying, and she had a shallow cut on her lip where I had accidentally slammed her into a splinter of wood.

I stood my ground, my only concern for my friend, though there was a massive void, which was growing larger by the minute.

We stood there for what felt like eons, Lucas holding Evelyn's hands securely behind her back, whilst she half-heartedly tried to tug away from him with a transfixed gaze at the illusion of Fred, and me standing forcefully between her and the Boundary.

No one dared move in the fear we would all topple over. Evelyn slowly stopped resisting, but we refused to drop our defenses until she broke from the obsession with the illusion.

Eventually, she looked down. We stepped away uncertainly, and I remembered that time way back when I had seen them all as monsters and they had treated me with the same caution.

"He's gone," she managed to say. No tears, only a defeat that nearly broke my heart.

So, in that deadened and mist-ridden forest, we held each other in a hug and didn't let go until the sun peeked through the clouds at midday. We didn't have much time left together, and I planned to spend every minute of it protecting what little we still had. If I was the one to go, fine.

But that didn't mean I would let D win.

26

"Do we even need to bother anymore?" Lucas asked me in a defeated tone.

"Of course we do!" I insisted, shocked that he would even consider quitting. "When I said they're trying to control it, I didn't mean the winner is set in stone, just...favored."

"Who's they?" He frowned, twiddling his pen between fingers and not meeting my eyes. "How come you seem to know these things?"

"It doesn't matter. Honestly, they're more of a hindrance than help. So let's get cracking this code, right? Evelyn?"

Evelyn was hovering over by the window, staring out at the rain and whispering softly to herself; I couldn't be sure, but it sounded like words of comfort or reassurance. She'd been distant and melancholy all day, whilst Lucas had been stonily impassive. It seemed to only be me who was actually desperate to work out the letters our friends had given as assistance, only me who believed the trials weren't won or lost yet.

"For goodness sake," I snapped, standing up and surveying my gloomy friends with distaste. "Will you have a look at yourselves for a minute? Drowning in self-pity will do nothing except let Avery win, because guess what? He's the one who's the favorite to get out."

I was lying through my teeth, but it achieved the desired reaction. Evelyn stood still for a moment, silent, and Lucas nearly choked to death on a handful of walnuts we had saved from luncheon.

"Blast," Lucas wheezed, stunned.

Saying things can make them a reality, be careful! D reminded me in my mind, but I shoved the voice away.

"This is why we need to figure this out!" I implored. "Or else Tressa will murder us for letting him win."

"R-O-D-U-I-S-E-A-T-W." Lucas frowned, needing to hear no

more. He bent down over the paper with immense concentration, with his tongue hanging out.

Evelyn shyly glided over and perched on her stool, wiping puffy eyes clear and peering over my shoulder for a glimpse of the riddle.

"Joining us?" I laughed, squeezing her hand. "I'm glad."

"Oh, it's not because I don't want to lose," she corrected firmly, voice wavering.

"No? Just developed a love for puzzles?"

"Actually, it's because Avery is a bloody menace," she said a matter-of-factly.

I laughed so hard my sides hurt, but it felt good! She never swore, not ever, and to hear her use it purposely in such a demure tone was just hilarious.

"Use…dart…" Lucas muttered over my giggles, so immersed in translation that he hadn't even noticed Evelyn's brief moment of humor. "No, that doesn't work. OWI don't spell anything, do they?"

"Unless the 'I' was actually an L?" I suggested, light-hearted now we were actually doing something and in better spirits. "Then it could be 'use owl dart'."

"That makes no sense," Lucas sighed, and I groaned in exasperation. Could they not be slightly, or even falsely cheerful for five seconds?

"Wait or sued?" Evelyn suggested without much confidence, bored with her petty skills already and impatient for it to be resolved. "So, we can take our time or risk being taken to court? I think that's what the word means anyway; there was this book on laws…"

"No, you're right. But I don't know if that's it, doesn't seem clear enough somehow," Lucas said. "And I can't think how it would make sense in this context."

"Rot as u die?" I suggested with a snort. "A little dire, but still something I could see Avery sending us as a morbid taunt."

"Penny!" Evelyn groaned. "That's disgusting, and not helpful at all! Don't be silly!"

My good mood melted away and I frowned bitterly. Yes, there wasn't much to be happy about, but no, being miserable wouldn't make it any better. I shook away the frown. I was determined D and Madon wouldn't see us give up, and I wanted to show them that they couldn't control what happened next.

"This is serious," Lucas scolded, his eyes still furiously searching the scrambled letters for sense. "Avery can't win. He can't."

I folded my arms and tried to make a word that made sense, but simply couldn't focus.

It's not as if there's— D began in my mind, fainter than before but still strong enough to make me flinch from the sensation.

Get out of my head! I screamed back. *I don't want your help! Leave me alone!*

I felt a shudder as the telepathic voice withdrew, and a twisted emotion that was somewhere between annoyed and hurt – which was ridiculous, considering we hated each other with a passion.

"Penny?"

"I'm fine," I snapped, sounding unnecessarily chilly. "Get back to decoding."

"What's going on with you?" Lucas demanded in an equally cold way. "You're acting just like Tressa and Avery before they—"

"I'm nothing like them!" I shouted, balling my fists and turning away to the window, where the rain was pounding at a rate that matched my growing frustration. "I'd never do what Avery did!"

"What about our pact? Did you follow it? Have you kept nothing from us? You have all this information from nowhere, all these special powers, you disappear and zone out as if you're talking to someone who's not there."

Lucas wasn't particularly angry. He spoke evenly, firmly, and

I nearly blurted everything out to him.

"Do you know what?" He sighed when I didn't respond. "I'm going to take these letters, and I'm going to figure them out by myself. You're welcome to copy them down, but I'm not sharing if I find out the answer, and I'm not going to help in any way. We've tried doing this together, and it clearly hasn't worked, so from here on in, it's every person for themselves."

And with that, Lucas scooped the things from the desk, and stomped calmly from the room. Evelyn's jaw dropped open in surprise, and (of course) her eyes began to well up with tears. I just ground my teeth and pushed my face against the freezing windowpane, feeling for the first time, truly alone.

"He didn't mean it?" she whimpered, turning her forlorn pout to me. "We…we can still work together, right? I want you to get out more than Avery, so I won't be much of a threat to you, promise!"

I turned from the window to see her face quivering at me hopefully, and for a moment I considered simply running up and hugging her, telling her to hold on a few more days until she could be with Fred.

But I didn't. I just muttered, "No. You heard Lucas. Go fend for yourself, and please don't do anything stupid."

Suddenly, the room felt very claustrophobic. In actuality, it was freezing cold, not a warm mantelpiece to be seen, but I had never felt it to be so stuffy.

Without hesitating, just in case I decided to stay, I pushed past Evelyn and barreled out of the door towards blessed fresh air – the smoky smell was killing me.

"Don't leave me alone!" she shrieked, grabbing onto my arm and sobbing.

"I'm sorry," I replied, shrugging her forcefully off. "But Lucas is right. This isn't working anymore."

"Penny!" she screamed, her pleading cries ricocheting of the walls in haunting echo.

I knew Evelyn feared isolation perhaps above all else, but I couldn't stay anymore. I mentally couldn't handle these downcast, doomed people right now, though those grief-stricken sobs nearly melted my heart and forced me to turn back.

Past the ruins I ran. Across the burned lawns. Steering away from the miraculously untouched graveyard. I lopped down on a scorched tree trunk, which had fallen onto its side, with little regard to the rain which was soaking my hair to a flat cap and ruining my only dress.

"Is this what you wanted?" I shouted to no one, listening to the fury in my voice reverberate through the estate. "Are you happy now?"

The rain poured harder, stinging my skin, and I chucked a rock at the sky just in case it hit someone sitting there.

Of course, there was no one there. There never had been anyone there. Only us. We had never done anything to deserve this. And I didn't even know who my parents were anymore! How was it that D had a mother and father and I didn't?

I touched the faint scar on the side of my head where the Master had slammed me against the wall with a flush of anger. Damn them all to the deepest pits of hell where they belonged, those murderous, secretive, manipulative, *stupid*...whatever they were supposed to be. Whoever they were.

Exhausted, hungry, and really quite cold, I flopped back down on the burned tree and let my head fall into my hands, eyes dry although I dearly wanted to cry.

Then I realized that there was a massive hole in the trunk, just big enough for a smallish person to squeeze inside if there were to play hide-and-seek...it was the cedar. The cedar I had always favored and loved, which had granted me safety every time I had chosen to hide inside of its ancient trunk. Now it was nothing more than a charred corpse in a dead world, devoured by a fire that seemed to be consuming more than just the physical aspects of this deranged estate.

I turned to look again at the manor. To my surprise, it seemed even more dilapidated than it had a day ago. The brick had crumbled more, the roof sinking more, everything seeming to slowly be falling apart as if it were a lit candle. Slowly melting.

I whirled around and jogged a little ways into the woods. Rain slapped my face, but I didn't let it deter me. In fact, after a few minutes of being pelted with a torrential downpour, the weather seemed to give up and simply stopped, leaving everything to become eerily quiet save for the rhythmic drips coming from the deadened, overhanging branches.

I snatched a fallen stick from the ground. It was about the length of my arm, and scorched black on one side. Tentatively, I held it out in front of me, using it both as a means of getting through a forest of collapsed limbs and as protection if more nightmares were lurking in these woods.

I shivered, my breath foggy in the chilly air. I efficiently prodded the dead undergrowth out of the way with a satisfactory *thwack, thwack…*

Then came a loud buzzing noise that nearly destroyed my eardrums, and a rip that threw the stick from my hands before disintegrating. I lurched forwards with a small shriek, stumbling quickly to the side before I tumbled through the Boundary.

It had moved! It had come inwards about ten feet, shrinking the forest considerably, and giving me a brand new fear.

"You can't do this!" I yelled angrily at the sky, looking through the Boundary towards the path I had once walked, and now would never be able to walk safely again. "This is cheating! This isn't fair!"

For once, there was no snide response in my mind, only silence.

How long would it be before the woods were gone entirely? Then the lawns, then the manor itself? How was it possible for the Boundary to *move?*

My toes began to burn, and I jumped backwards in alarm –

even as I stood there, it was advancing inch by inch.

I ran back to the lawns, hoisting my skirts and hurdling the obstacles until reaching the cedar I sprawled back onto its trunk, completely out of breath and feeling rather faint. Ashes danced across the grey world on a light breeze, the same color as the sky, the crumbling manor, the tall silhouettes of the woods, the ground. Everything.

R-O-D-U-I-S-E-A-T-W...what could it possibly be?

A curtain twitched, and I spotted Lucas quickly moving away from the window. It was a shame it had come to this, but still inevitable. I wouldn't tell them about the Boundary.

"Fine, I admit it. I need help. I hate you, but I need help," I hissed under my breath, waiting for D to respond.

Whilst I waited, I casually created a rip near the window Lucas was now back staring out of, so that it shattered into spider-webbed cracks and provided no transparency. Ha.

Don't kick a dog when it's down, D said tiredly in my mind. *The manor is destroying itself without your help.*

"Hello," I greeted with a practiced coolness. I was not begging, I was not relenting, I was simply accepting help that had previously been offered. Right? "You wanted to help me, and now I need—"

Stop there, D halted me mid-sentence. *You're now separated from your so-called friends, who have decided not to help you after all...funny, seems I predicted that a while back. And also, just courtesy rules, don't tell someone you hate them when you need their help, it's just not polite and isn't—*

Then, just like that, the drawling voice cut off. I searched my mind for traces of the other consciousness, but there was nothing. Then, like a light flickering back on, I felt it again.

That...that wasn't supposed to happen, D muttered in irritation, sounding slightly nonplussed but cool as usual. *This whole thing is so unstable it's hard to even keep connected...damn it Madon!*

I clasped my hands over my ears as though that would

quieten the shriek D suddenly let loose, waiting with my teeth gritted for the fury in my head to stop and become coherent advice.

Don't you ever trust him, D snarled viciously, between many colorful phrases that made me blush from the ferocity of the language. *You want advice? In exactly four hours, when the sun sets, I want you and the remaining two to come to the fallen cedar. Then forget any affection you have for them, and win the trial, all right? No excuses. Oh, and don't waste time on the puzzle, because it's easily the stupidest thing they could have thought to tell you. Let Lucas waste his time, but don't you make the same mistake.*

"I can't promise you all of that," I managed to croak. "I won't ever be able to forget them. But I'll try to win, if you can promise me they'll be all right afterwards."

You don't promise, then neither do I. Besides, I couldn't care less about what happens to them – they'll live after they lose, but I'm not interfering after that.

"So what exactly happens at dusk, then?" I asked, trying to be single-minded about winning. My friends would be fine, was that not all that mattered?

I could almost feel D grinning inside my head as the voice answered, *Well, you could say it's the finale. By the time the sun rises tomorrow, we'll have our winner.*

27

Four hours. Once that would have seemed like forever, but now I couldn't even grasp just how little time I had left.

I would have to tell them, else they wouldn't be given a sporting chance, although it pained me to have to fight them. I could never do what D wanted and forget my love for them, and in asking for me to do so, I knew that some sort of conflict would be involved.

Not knowing what to do with myself (should I prepare in some way – make amends whilst it was still possible?), I sat down on the cedar and lapsed into a melancholy state of thought. The ashes whipped silently around on a wind that was attacking the crumbling manor walls without mercy, and as I watched, a few more bricks tumbled in defeat to the ground.

Three hours.

I heaved myself off the trunk and set about walking the edge of the forest, listening to the crackling of the Boundary as it edged closer to our dying land. I managed to do several laps around the manor, thinking about many things, one of which was D.

Two hours.

My legs ached from walking across such an unstable surface, and I had a headache from being near to the Boundary for so long. I leaned against the unstable manor walls, mind turning now to the outside, and what it might possibly be like. Assuming I even got out, of course. When I pulled away from the wall, I noticed that a fine dust from the disintegrating bricks coated my dress.

One hour.

The sun had passed its peak, and through the thick layer of grey clouds I could see it sinking over the western woods. The wind picked up, seeming to whisper meaningless taunts in my ear, and I decided it would probably be best to go indoors for the moment.

I crossed over the ruins, a graveyard of colorless rubbish, which had once been our splendid past, and up the faded staircase, which didn't seem so grand with the shattered remnants of a pearl chandelier decorating the creaking wood.

Evelyn was curled up in what was now our room with her head resting against the glass, not crying, but shaking. She didn't notice as I peeked in the door, so I let her be, casting a weary glance at the black chalky letters scrawled on the wall – hopefully D was right and they spelled something useless, because I hadn't the faintest idea what they could possibly mean.

Lucas was in his chamber, writing feverishly on a scrawl of paper, nearly hidden behind a massive stack of books he had piled on his desk. I tried to tiptoe away without him noticing, but he was more alert than Evelyn by a mile, and I cursed under my breath as his head whipped up in surprise.

"Penny."

"Lucas."

"What are you doing here?"

"Nothing."

"Mm. Yet you must have come for something?"

"I wanted to see where you were."

"Why?"

"Why so nosey?"

"Why can't you just tell me? Or is this another secret?"

I gritted my teeth. The sarcastic, bitter argument was so unlike us, and I hated it. Although he had a point...

"All right, I am keeping secrets. Though I might remind you that it wasn't my idea to go our separate ways, it was, in fact, yours." I sniffed primly, hands on hips and wearing my best hurt pout. "Luckily I'm in a particularly forgiving and generous mood, so you may know that it would be beneficial to come down to the grounds in roughly half an hour."

"Beneficial?" Lucas laughed without humor. "To whom?"

I didn't reply, flashing a sickly sweet smile and turning from the room, knowing without a doubt that curiosity would propel him to come anyway.

"And work on your dramatic exits," I heard him mutter as I shut the door. "Your attempts are frankly quite embarrassing."

I stood in the corridor for a few minutes, wondering what to do with myself yet again for the last thirty minutes of relative normalcy I had left.

"Evelyn?" I called into the room, shivering from the blast of cold air that rushed out as soon as I set foot in the room. "Just wanted to say meet me outside in a few minutes, okay?"

She ignored me, though I could tell from the way she flinched at my voice that she'd heard perfectly well.

Great to feel loved, I sighed to myself.

Though I knew that she too, unsure of what else to do, would follow my instructions and meet at the cedar to face whatever was coming. Thirty minutes passed much slower than the last three-and-a-half hours had, but apparently wandering up and down a desolate corridor, accidentally ripping my gown to shreds on the rubble of the collapsed roof was a good pastime, because darkness soon began to fall and I made my way back to the cedar.

The mist rolled over the black grass in a haunting way, swallowing the forest in its density. The sky was a deep purple, tingled with darker splotches of clouds, and the ashes had settled with the wind, leaving it seeming almost peaceful. Deadly, alien, but yes peaceful. I sat on the cedar, which looked white in the light, and waited. Lucas was the first to arrive, arms folded and pride injured.

"I came. What's going—"

I held up a hand to quieten him. Somehow, his voice seemed to ruin the beautiful evening, and I wanted to savor it whilst I still could, even if it was dying.

Evelyn scuffled over a few minutes later, head down and mute when I greeted her.

We waited, and after a while I thought that maybe D had tricked me and nothing was going to happen.

There has been some resistance from a certain someone, D defended himself as I thought that opinion. *But he's no match for me.*

As if to prove it, there was the biggest, widest rip I had ever felt, so huge I could see the space opening even though it was not my own rip. From the gasps Evelyn and Lucas uttered, it was clear they could see it too.

I didn't think that I had passed out, but clearly I had, because there weren't three of us anymore after I blinked. There were four.

"Stop gaping like dumbstruck goldfish," Avery muttered dryly. "There are easier ways to die other than choke on this god-awful air...what the bloody hell happened?"

Evelyn was white as a sheet, eyes nearly popping out of her head. Lucas had his fists clenched in a barely concealed fury, like me at the moment.

Avery looked rather worse for wear, his shaggy hair matted and clothes just as grubby as his thin face. Otherwise he was perfectly healthy, standing with his arms crossed with a deliberating expression that was clearly trying to decide whether to approach us to explain, or run in the opposite direction.

"You," I snarled. "You filthy, traitorous, backstabbing little toad..."

"Hey!" He raised his arms in surrender, backing away. "In my defense, I knew that she was going to be all right and that the only way to get out of that arena was for one of us to—"

"Stab someone?" Lucas finished for him, livid. "So you could get a free ticket to the end?"

Avery nodded, shrugging. "Pretty much."

I punched him square in the face, sending him sprawling backwards into the dirty ground. He sprang back up in surprise, wiping the blood from his nose.

"You cut her," I spat. "You don't do that to friends, no matter what prize you get! You let them win, you let the trials win!"

Despite the fact I had him pinned to the ground by his throat, Avery managed to wheeze, "But you did too, didn't you, Penny? You listened to D and used it against the others…"

I dropped him as if he was poisonous, recoiling in shock. Avery knew D.

Lucas had been watching my reaction with amusement, seemingly mildly disappointed that I had decided to let Avery go. Evelyn was being sick in the woods, and emerged with a greenish tinge to her face.

I mentally reached for D, demanding an explanation, but I got nothing except silence in return.

"You need to figure out who the bad guy is in this fairy tale," Avery hissed at me, shaking slightly as he stood up. "There are several choices, and I'm thinking that you didn't pick the right one."

"I know what I'm doing!" I shouted back.

"Sure." He rolled his eyes. "I can tell by the way you're all aimlessly standing there waiting for something to happen that you're perfectly in control. Enjoy yourselves."

"Where have you been, Avery?" Lucas asked, frowning.

"Right here, actually," he answered conversationally, watching me with a cautious side-glance. "It was really weird…I kept drifting in and out of consciousness but I was always somewhere in the manor. You couldn't ever see me though, so I just hovered around the breakfast room. I was blacked out for most of the time, so I haven't really any idea why things are the way they are. I take it Freddie tripped over the Boundary?"

Evelyn's breathing suddenly came very fast, and for a moment I thought that she was going to attack Avery like I had. Luckily for him, she had more restraint.

"Oops, I forgot. You two were a thing, weren't you?"

"Do you have a death wish?" Lucas snapped. "Or are you oblivious to what you're saying?"

"I think I know what I'm saying much more than you do, actually. You haven't figured out that at certain times, stepping over the Boundary will pull you into the mirror world, like it did me? And until everybody has done that, no one can go free."

"Well...we knew about half of that. What's the mirror world?" Lucas asked, the desire to know overriding his anger.

"You'll know when you lose." Avery grinned, flashing a toothy smile. "Oh, don't look so horrified. I wouldn't dream of taking on Tressa if I thought that I'd have to spend the rest of my life living with her after one of you lot got out."

"Over my dead body," I challenged, my eyes boring into his. D promised me things, but what had it also promised to Avery?

"It won't come to that," Lucas put it with a worried look at the tension, which was almost palpable between us. "For now we need to figure out what's going on, then—"

"Shut up a minute," Evelyn whispered, and shockingly, we did. "I...I..."

I followed her line of sight, and nearly passed out again.

Tressa and Fred, standing off to the side, were slowly becoming visible through the mist.

Fred's face was still covered in soot and he waved to Evelyn with a forlorn look of utter longing on his round, handsome face. He shook his head as tears began to spill down her cheeks, and mimed wiping them away which only made her cry harder.

"Why aren't they coming over?" she sobbed, hiccupping like crazy and unable to stop staring at him. The duo seemed faded somehow, as if they weren't quite with us, and they remained silent without moving to greet us in any way.

"They're halfway between the mirror world and the Boundary," Avery explained, waving sweetly at Fred, who suddenly stopped smiling and froze. Tressa was ignoring him completely, arms folded to hide the blood which still stained the bodice of her dress.

Fred made an uncharacteristically rude gesture, which summed up everything he couldn't say, then beckoned for Evelyn to come over to him. She nodded weakly, swallowing and walking as if her legs were made of jelly.

It just about broke my heart as they half hugged, not quite able to touch and forced to stand about a foot apart. Evelyn was hysterically apologizing, but Fred simply smiled sadly and made a heart with his hands before rolling something across the grass towards her feet. There was a small rip as it passed from wherever they were trapped, to us, and she stooped down to pick it up.

"Fred..." she choked, but Tressa stepped forwards firmly and mimed shoving her away.

"Come, lovebird, show us what the losers gave you." Avery sighed, bored. Fred, Lucas, Tressa and I flinched in anger, but no one gave him the satisfaction of reacting further than that.

"It's...a...a...n-note," she hiccupped, barely understandable.

Her fingers were shaking so much she dropped the slip of paper twice before Avery sighed, stomped over, and snatched it away in irritation.

He was about to read it when I grabbed it, saying, "What's to stop you from reading it then rushing off and not telling us?"

"Then I think I should read it," Lucas pointed out honestly. "You're not exactly Miss Trustworthy either. Plenty of skeletons in your cupboard."

I handed it over without argument, wanting to get it over with.

"It's instructions," he gasped. We waited impatiently whilst he scanned the tiny handwriting, which I recognized with a jolt as D's. "We have to get to the attic, activate the machine..."

"So whoever gets there first and pulls that lever will rip way everyone else to the mirror world, and therefore be the winner," Avery summed up, seeming quite confused underneath the facade of superiority. "However the heck that's supposed to work."

I looked over at Tressa for guidance, but she shrugged in evident befuddlement with look of longing. How terrible it must be to know that you had no chance.

"Then we can be together," Evelyn realized with watery hope, flicking a longing glance at Fred.

To my surprise, he didn't look pleased at all. Contrarily, he shook his head frantically and pointed behind us at the collapsing manor, mouth moving in desperation to form words we couldn't hear.

"You want me to get out?" she whispered with sad realization. He nodded, relieved. "But then...I might never see you again."

"Doesn't matter," he mouthed, and made the heart shape again.

Tressa patted Fred on the shoulder and he jumped. They were both fading away again.

"Don't leave!" Evelyn cried, making to catch hold of his hand, but by the time she reached him they had vanished completely.

"Not what I expected," Avery admitted sullenly, kicking a chunk of dust so it puffed in the night air.

"Shocking. He doesn't know everything after all." I rolled my eyes. "Though I thought the lever was gone now..."

Does it matter? D shrieked in my mind, making me start. *It's whoever gets there first, and you're just standing there? Run!*

I flicked an unsure glance at my friends, before sprinting away towards the manor. Lucas and Evelyn called my name, but I didn't stop, feeling the night air whip my cheeks into, my heart pounding like a bass drum. This was it.

28

Avery cursed and dashed after me, but I only pushed faster. After a while, the footsteps stopped, and a quick peek revealed that he had ceased to pursue me. There was nothing but darkness behind.

No lights were on inside the house, so everything was in pitch darkness. I couldn't see a thing, much less who was behind me, and for a moment I had to stop to get my bearings.

I heard a crunch of leaves behind me.

"Don't hit me," Lucas whispered as I whipped around, expecting to see Avery. "Evelyn's disappeared to who-knows-where, you and Avery went sprinting off…"

"This is individual," I reminded him, still miffed by his previous decision to split up.

"I know, but we might as well stick together for now. I have a feeling this isn't going to be as simple as a race."

"Or it might be." I shrugged. "So stop bothering me or let's go."

Someone – or something – shrieked in the night, making us both jump. I skirted away from the woods, accidentally bumping into Lucas because I couldn't see a thing. Perhaps it wouldn't be too bad having someone to navigate with, just in case some horrendous monstrosity was sent to challenge us.

"Uh…but I'm sure it won't hurt to call a truce for now," I suggested airily, receiving an exasperated, albeit relieved, sigh from Lucas. "You're right, something very strange seems to be going on."

"Glad you've come around," he muttered. "Any plans?"

"Yeah. Get to the lever before anyone else."

"Perfect."

With that understanding, we pushed on towards to manor. The trees loomed up as massive shadows against a darker sky, as still and silent as death itself.

I focused on breathing, knowing that it would only be a few minutes until we were back inside, running at steady pace.

Yet after what seemed like forever, I could still not see the house, and I was getting quite out of puff.

"Have we been going in circles or something? This doesn't seem right," I panted, surveying the area with confusion.

The cedar hadn't been that deep in the forest, yet a quick glance seemed to assure that we were still in thick woodland. I didn't really know the individual trees, and in the dark it was impossible to tell exactly where we were.

"I can hear the Boundary." Lucas frowned, stopping beside me. "I thought we had been going out of the woods, not going farther in?"

"This is absurd," I groaned, leaning against a tree to catch my breath. "Why do they have to make everything so blooming complicated? It could have been so simple, you know, 'just get to the attic first', but instead they have to go and twist everything! Urgh!"

Focus, D spoke mildly, though seemingly preoccupied.

The voice was very faint and tired, and cut off after those two syllables. No help, as promised, no hints whatsoever.

Lucas raised an eyebrow but said nothing, exhaling slowly.

"Climb up a tree," he said eventually. "When we were in the fire, you said that you could see most of the grounds; perhaps it would work again, even in the dark."

It was the only idea we had, and running around on a wild goose chase didn't seem smart, so relying on touch alone I found a large oak with scooping branches perfect for climbing. They felt slightly rotten and soft under my hands, but I didn't dwell on it, scrambling upwards as if I had been born to do so.

I perched precariously at the topmost branch and waited for my eyes to adjust. By the looks of things, we weren't that deep in the forest but had done almost a full circle of the grounds since we left the cedar. The manor stood tall and black in the distance, which I took as a good sign, since surely, if anyone had made it already, they would have found a way to light a candle.

"Head that way," I shouted down to Lucas, pointing towards the open lawns. "We're only a few lines back!"

I slid downwards, wrapping my arms around a particularly sturdy branch and dangling my legs about seven feet from the ground. I could jump down, and save myself the time of descending.

"Penny!" Lucas yelled suddenly, and I saw his bright blue eyes widen in fear.

Before I could ask what the matter was, there was a terrible snapping sound and the rotting limb began to break away from the tree. I sucked in a breath, searching for a nearby branch to shift onto, but it was only a few seconds before the limb, which had been as wide as I, broke loose and crashed downwards with me clinging on for dear life. The air whooshed past me, and I screamed at least once before there was a heavy thud and pain exploded in my shoulder.

Almost as soon as the pain came, it was replaced by a surge of anger that boiled through my veins and caused my vision to flash like a strobe.

Lucas pushed the wood from my arm and offered a helping hand, but I just lay there and let the fury take over. My fists clenched tight, and my breathing became heavy, and…oh how my shoulder hurt!

I yet out a yelp of pain and unclenched my fists, feeling the muscles spasm and unleash myriad needles that seemed to dig in all over my shoulder blade, ripping and searing wherever they touched.

The anger hadn't been mine, it had been D's. Which meant the fall hadn't been an accident, and there was only one other person I knew who could manipulate the Boundary in such a way. Oh, rapture, a power struggle! And guess which lucky winner got to be in the middle?

"Splinters," Lucas winced, regarding the shards, which covered my upper arm. "And a lot of bruises, I'll bet. But not broken, or you wouldn't be able to go about swinging it like that."

I didn't ask where Lucas got his medical knowledge from, since it was the same answer as always. Perhaps I should have read more.

"Let's just keep moving," I hissed through gritted teeth.

My shoulder burned as if it were on fire, but every second I took now would allow Avery, and even Evelyn, an extra second to beat us.

What about Lucas? I asked myself. I'd have to cross that bridge when I came to it.

We jogged forwards in the direction I had seen was the right way, occasionally bumping into things, but otherwise making remarkable time. Except the lawns still weren't visible, and every time I thought we had nearly done it, another line of trees appeared. I was starting to feel quite hysterical, faint from pain and exhaustion. There was no way this could be possible!

Then footsteps echoed to my right.

Someone was coming.

Evelyn's lavender dress rustled through the trees, gone as soon as I tried to place exactly where it was. Then again, I saw it, to the left. In front of me now...no, behind. I pivoted, a frown creasing my forehead.

"Evelyn?" I whispered, though some sense deep within me told that it wasn't really her.

Lucas gingerly bent down and picked up a stick from the ground, tensed and ready.

She laughed, but it seemed to come from everywhere at once.

"Give it up," she ordered teasingly, appearing a few yards behind me and walking over, twirling a purple ribbon around skeletal fingers coyly. "It's over. You're done."

Black eyes, pointed teeth stained in red, jerky movements,

translucent skin covering an emaciated body, she was a mind monster.

I thought of the advancing Boundary, how Evelyn would have run haywire looking for Fred or a way out, not knowing that our world was shrinking as we spoke.

Lucas and I slowly backed away, but the monster echoed our every step. The stick suddenly looked flimsy, much too thin. So, with an unspoken understanding, we turned on our heels and sprinted with everything we had towards what should have been the lawns.

And just like that, we were out of the woods and tumbling down on the blessedly open grass of the gardens. There was no time to celebrate though, as the Evelyn-beast was right on our heels.

I scrambled upwards and surged towards the manor, not even checking to see if Lucas was behind me or not.

Then a sharp pain exploded in my shoulder again, but unlike before, it didn't stop there. My mouth opened to scream, but there was too much agony, blocking out any noise I might have made. My knees buckled and I collapsed, gasping for air, ears ringing with the laughs of the impersonating monster.

"I don't understand how something as pathetic as you could cause so much trouble," a voice sneered in my ear. "It's simply too easy. You'd think they'd have picked a greater challenge for the simple amusement of it, but perhaps I underestimated their capacity for compassion. Either way, it works in my favor."

Madon. Through the wave of pain, I heard Lucas scream, and a thud as he fell to the ground.

I tried to shout for him, but remained mute.

Everything was turning a deep red, so I closed my eyes and curled into a ball, waiting for it to stop.

This had happened before.

I summoned up all the energy I had left, and ripped away the pain, which consumed me. I felt Him try to attack my attempts, but to no avail.

"You've gotten stronger," He observed dryly, arms folded over a slender grey jacket as I struggled to my feet.

"So have you," I retorted, focusing on not falling over again. "For a few days, I thought you were actually getting weaker."

"I was." He shrugged nonchalantly, and I realized just how ill He looked. Paler, tired, black shadows under His eyes, and even thinner than usual. Lucas was in a heap on the ground, the stick lying a few inches from his limp fingertips. His chest was rising and falling, but only slightly.

"What did you do?" I snarled, wrenching myself away from him to face the Master. "What have you done to him?"

"Nothing," He replied, enjoying the blatant lie. "I don't have time for this, there are other matters I must attend to. First, though, there is of course the problem that you represent."

I realized then that I was absolutely terrified. I searched for D, but there was nothing. Running would do nothing either, I wouldn't be fast enough to get away before the torture found me for a second time, plus I was too tired to rip myself for the moment.

"Are you going to kill me?" I asked softly, not really wanting to know the answer.

The Master cocked His head to the side, as if thinking. Then His smile turned into a bitter frown and He replied, "I cannot. All I can do is stop you from getting out."

"You killed Beatrix," I reminded Him with a soft anger. "Why not me? Why not stop Avery?"

"You still do not understand what this world is, do you?" The Master smirked, though there was no amusement behind the gesture. "You do not know why you are here? Your little pen pals haven't told you that much, have they?"

"They told me more than you have," I retorted, hardly believing that such daring words could come from me. "And we found the fairy tale—"

"The legend," He muttered, voice dripping with distain. "Don't tell me you actually believe that? Who do you think planted it there? Certainly not me? Your confidants have told you nothing but what they wanted you to think, regardless of whether it is true or not. In short, they have manipulated you so that you, and you alone, would get out without any thought for the others. They have altered your dreams, your thoughts, even your sight..."

"They? But D is only one person," I asked in confusion. I hadn't ever really trusted D, not properly, but I had grown to rely on the advice which it had claimed would lead me to freedom. Yet what the Master was telling me made some sense.

"Wrong," He corrected, removing His hat and casually walking over to where I was crouched by an unconscious Lucas. "They are two...people. Though I do not think that they warrant the title 'people'. No matter. You are wasting my time, as I must see to a certain other issue. We will speak again, I am sure."

There was nothing else for it. I ran with all I had left towards the manor. A static whine was coming from behind me, and I knew it wasn't the Master. The Boundary was closing in, and fast. I chanced a quick glance behind me, and saw Him also staring at it in numb shock.

It was invisible, only the shuddering static giving away its position as it swallowed the last few trees. My forest was completely lost forever. The beast that resembled Evelyn had been standing just in front of the tree line, held at bay by the Master, let out a haunting yowl as the Boundary rippled over its body, but unlike what would have been expected it didn't turn to ashes. It simply vanished.

I squinted, concentrating, and noticed with a sharp realization that the layers I had spotted before in the Boundary were much thinner, as if many had been removed, as if it were almost possible to move them.

You haven't figured out that crossing the Boundary at certain times will pull you into the mirror world.

Touching the barrier now wouldn't kill me. I would simply lose.

Casting a guilty glance at Lucas, but knowing he would be okay, I turned and kept running whilst the Master's attention was preoccupied with his shrinking domain.

Then the air shifted and I stumbled, feeling a different sort of rip lash out on my back. I tripped over a brick, smashing my head on the ground and nearly passing out for a moment. The Master was coming over, a mask of impassiveness on His face though I thought I detected a trace of weariness underneath.

D! I shouted in my head, but it was still empty. Could I even trust it – them – enough to ask for help anymore?

I tried to create a defensive rip myself, but my vision was swimming too much to focus. Pain was exploding everywhere…

"Penny!" someone shouted.

"Lucas?" I called, my tongue heavy and slurring my words. "You…okay…?"

But I couldn't move anymore to see. It was over. I had lost.

Muffled shouts…pain…a snapping noise…pain…nothing.

I gasped and sat bolt upright, then turned and vomited all over the brick. Lucas had awoken again, and chucked his stick at the Master so that he lost concentration.

"He doesn't want you to get out, Penny!" Lucas yelled in explanation. "There must be some reason, but whatever it is…it's bad for Him, and therefore good for us."

The Master Himself seemed torn between retaliating to Lucas's attack and going after me, with the Boundary adding only more confusion to the whole thing.

Decisively, He created a rip that sent Lucas sprawling backwards into the Boundary before turning to me, power still crackling.

Lucas wasn't finished that easily. He rolled away, jumped back to his feet, running over to where we were standing in determination.

"She lied to you so many times," the Master hissed, turning to Lucas. "She didn't tell you anything about the letters, did she? Admit it, your logic makes no sense, and throwing your own life away for her now won't do a thing except postpone—"

But Lucas wasn't interested in the monologue.

"I think Penny is the only one who can bring down this place from the outside," he interrupted, speaking rather loudly as if I might not be able to hear him. "Which is why you don't want her to go free. Oh, and before I go, you might want to know that *I* know exactly who her letters were from. In fact, we all did."

With that, Lucas gave me a short nod, and hurled something small and sharp at the Master's head before diving into the Boundary, promptly vanishing.

I stood there dumbly for a moment, trying to figure out how D could have possibly communicated with all six of us (and how Evelyn could have kept it a secret), then realized I had a few seconds of opportunity before He chased after me.

Lucas had thrown a shard of glass from a broken window, and it had slashed a deep cut on His cheek, now bleeding profusely. I watched for a few stunned seconds as He stared at the blood dripping onto His hands with morbid fascination, too shocked to act.

Then I ran.

The Boundary was moving faster, so much that it was covering feet instead of inches at a time. Fast.

The wind was a tirade of whispers, some taunting and others encouraging, blowing in seven different directions.

A rip came from behind to try to trip me again, but it was much feebler than before and I easily avoided it. My hair singed at the edges, and I noted with a small scream that the Boundary was only a few paces behind me. The Master was gone, but I still had to cover the dangerous ruins on the way to the door.

Hopping bricks and scaling beams, un-snagging petticoats

and trying not to panic, I reached the front steps and fell.

My body was screaming in protest everywhere, so much that I could barely think for the agony of it. This was all happening so fast, much too fast...

When I caught my breath and got dizzily to my feet, preparing to start running again, the first thing I noticed was that the front doors had been restored to their original positions. When I tentatively tried to open them, they were stuck fast.

All that was left now was Avery, the manor, and me. Everything else was untouchable.

29

I took a deep, steadying gulp of air. Final two – it was nearly over now. Everything seemed much too dark with the outside closed off, and my second feeling was one of near immediate claustrophobia.

Calm down, I cautioned myself. Do what has to be done, then get out.

"Avery?" I shouted, voice ringing throughout the empty halls. "Avery?"

No answer. I should have known he'd play like this.

Although, it was strange for him to be hiding from me when the key to escape was in this very building. Surely, he would be either upstairs ready to claim his victory or...or not inside at all! The prospect of having no competition was indeed a pleasant one, though I firmly reminded my active imagination that the chance was slim.

The floorboard creaked as I stepped forwards, making me wince. A candle, a light, something to illuminate this darkness?

D whispered weakly in my mind, *There, must be candles. Look up!*

"Are you all right?" I frowned, hearing the sickly faintness. "Where were you a few moments ago when I needed you? And...is it true that there are two of you? Why does everyone—"

We cannot share power anymore, there is not enough left. I must save my strength until the end, for you may need—

Just like that, the voice was cut off. I wondered if D really couldn't communicate, or if they were just avoiding the questions.

I swallowed any childhood fear of the dark, and crept deeper into the entrance hall with outstretched arms groping for some kind object that would give away my precise location. My footsteps creaked and clomped, so loud it seemed that Avery would have no trouble finding my whereabouts should he still be competing.

I stumbled into something hard, knocking the wind from my lungs. My hands blindly reached out, meeting with a smooth, textured surface that could only be a wall. If there was a wall, there would be a candle.

Trying to ignore the throbbing in my shoulder, I reached upwards and felt around for the little nooks that always held wax candles, which I had never seen extinguished until now. My hands closed around the metal holder, and I pulled the stump from its cove. I had triumphed, but realization quickly dawned and I looked at it miserably; the only matches I knew of in the house were buried under several feet of rubble in Beatrix's old quarters. And I certainly was not about to try and climb outside!

Right, I would have to scratch that plan. Don't panic, I thought. Think, just think. Actually, it rather made sense; when I had first discovered the attic, it had been in pitch blackness, so why not now? Naturally, they had to make it difficult in some way.

So I set about trying to find the staircase.

One of the benefits of having lived in one place for fifteen years was that I had a mental map of the place, and despite the ruins I could guess pretty accurately where everything was located.

There was the banister, scratched and polished wood carved supported by carved spindles. Thin carpet lined the wide staircase, which curved upwards.

I half-climbed half-stumbled up the stairs, pausing at the landing that allowed access to the breakfast room.

This was nearly it. I might never see the place in the light again, might never see my friends again. It made me sick to my stomach just thinking about it, but I clung to what Lucas had said; maybe I had the power to open the Boundary from the outside, and that was why the Master didn't want me out but D did.

Outside...I didn't even really want to think about that too much, as there were simply too many chilling possibilities that could drive one insane.

Up the final few stairs, dodging (or tripping) around a pile of what used to be the roof, I finally emerged on the top floor.

Someone ran into me – hard – from the opposite wing, and we both fell backwards onto the floor with an ungraceful thump.

"Avery," I gasped through a clenched jaw, palms curled in fists so to not let the rising pain show.

"Penny," he replied with the same uneven tone. "I was wondering when I'd see you again."

"How did you get in through the south wing?"

"The fire burned a great big hole where the hall used to be, so whilst you and Lucas had a little chat with Him, I climbed over the ruins and got in that way." He shrugged, getting up and rubbing a bruise on his forehead. "I take it Lucas...?"

"Yeah." I nodded briskly. "Do you have any idea what happened to Evelyn?"

"Last time I saw her, she was chasing some kind of illusion deeper into the woods. She was running pretty close to the Boundary, it's not hard to guess."

My head was spinning like a top, but luckily Avery seemed pretty worn out himself and not in a huge rush to move. We knew we were the last two left, so until someone made a run for it we were okay.

"How do you know about D?" I asked bluntly, needing to know.

Avery inhaled sharply, his body going rigid.

"I was rather hoping you'd forget about that," he admitted. "But that was just wishful thinking. To be honest, it wasn't much: they spoke to me a couple of times in my head (weirdest sensation ever) and told me what the fairy tale meant. They said I couldn't tell anyone, and then they told me to...well, what to do if a situation like the arena arose. Then I didn't hear anything else.

"Did you know that everybody knew?"

"Only when Tressa and I found fairy tale and it was clear someone was talking to her, too."

I nodded, thinking it rather strange that one of the biggest puzzles had remained unknown to me until the last few weeks. D was indeed a curiosity, and I still wasn't completely decided if they were bad or good.

"Did you know that there were two of them?"

"Of course. How else could they have such conflicting opinions and speak to multiple people at the same time?"

I chose not to respond to that.

Everything was so dark, I could barely see his shadow. Hesitantly, I took a light step backwards, testing to see if he noticed. When there was no reaction, I carefully turned around and bent my legs as if to start running.

Unfortunately, I was never known for my lightness.

Avery heard my feet hit the ground, and with an irritated sigh shoved past me down the northern corridor.

I would never have been able to outrun him on a good day in my blasted gown, so with an injured shoulder it was virtually impossible. So instead, I summoned up all my energy, and created the biggest rip I had ever attempted in front of Avery, which threw him off his feet. It was difficult, not being able to see, but I could still visualize and that seemed to work well enough.

The manor seemed to feel the shift, and promptly chunks of ceiling began to rain down in a storm of rubble on our heads.

Avery swore softly, throwing up his hands against a particularly large brick. I jumped away from a splintered beam in shock, unsure why it had had such a profound effect.

"Do you not understand what a rip is?" Avery shouted angrily at me, jumping to avoid a falling candleholder. "It moves *everything*, it was unstable enough already!"

"Excuse me for defending myself!" I snapped back, trying to keep the fear from my voice. "This isn't just a game, this is a fight for our futures, don't expect me to sit back and let you win!"

"Excuse me," Avery mimicked. "Well, I have to go and escape before the whole thing collapses, so cheerio and enjoy imprisonment."

I seethed in irritation, letting the dust rain down on my hair without flinching, and began to throw up another rip that would hopefully knock him unconscious.

Avery froze for a moment, then with a twisted grin made a weak rip open up right in front of me. It wouldn't have normally been enough to do anything, but the surprise of it tripped me over.

"You...?" I spluttered, wincing as chunks of wall began to crack and fall over, exposing gasping holes in the corridor. "You can rip too?"

"Of course I can," he smirked. "We can all play dirty if we want to."

"No, but...but...I thought..."

"That you were special? That you were unique? Sorry to break it to you, darling, but you're not," Avery taunted, dancing around the collapsing foundations. "D taught me a few things too."

"You told me I was important!" I shouted into the darkness, as if D would turn up and explain everything. "You made me believe I would win!"

Avery's smirk turned into a frown as he hissed, "You still don't understand. This place *isn't real*. It's controlled by the whim of a few cruel people, including your beloved D, and we're subject to whatever they decide to put us through. We never had any control, and we never will!"

"Unless we get out," I retorted sharply. "So watch me do exactly that."

My dramatic exit was rather ruined by the ground shaking as if via earthquake, sending a shower of rubble falling to the floor, including some heavy beams that would cause some serious damage if they were to hit our heads.

"This whole thing is coming down!" I exclaimed, finding it extremely hard to dodge things in the dark.

"Then I suppose we have to hurry."

Something very large landed right behind me and pinned my gown to the ground as I tried to move, and though I tugged with all my strength it simply would not come free.

The noise of rumbling foundations became louder, almost like a scream as everything behind me crumbled to dust; the Boundary was coming, clearly not in a form that would allow survival.

"Avery!" I shrieked in desperation, suddenly realizing how badly this could end.

My shoulder would not allow more than a feeble attempt, and the dress was not a material that was adept at ripping. I tried to use the supernatural ripping to move the debris, but I was too tired and flustered for anything substantial.

He wasn't coming for me. I would meet my end here, ousted by my own confidence and resulting ignorance. Avery would get out, the others would live in a ruined world forever, and I would be naught but a pile of ashes.

"Avery, please! I'll do anything!" I pleaded, trying to make out whether he had vanished up the hallway or not. I could hear the static behind me, creeping closer and closer by the second.

Then there was light. The Boundary had consumed the entire south and west wings, and as they crumbled to the ground as ashes, the full extent of the damage was visible.

Everything, starting from the woods, was gone, leaving behind only a grey wasteland covered with what looked like a soft down of feathers. The stark shadows of the forest were the only objects left, and above them a deep red sun shone although I had seen it set a few hours ago. It cast the place in a crimson light, illuminating my face of terror as the manor disintegrated in front of me.

"Avery, damn it!" I screamed, twisting away from the other-worldly scene. "Please!"

The hall, the common room, the chambers, the foyer, now the breakfast room, the servant's quarters, the library…I watched in horrified fascination as they were swallowed up, watched over by a sun as red as the blood being pumped triple speed by my hyperactive heart.

Avery was standing down the hallway, trying to force a door open. His wide brown eyes met with mine for a moment, hesitating. I knew, deep down, that he wouldn't come. If he did, neither of us would make it.

I closed my eyes and waited.

*

She looked slightly like Elisabeth, from my dreams. Different, but I couldn't place how. A little bit like me too, but mostly like her, only younger.

She wore an expression of incalculable tiredness, with bags under her eyes so dark that they seemed to be bruises, the sweat on her brow betraying her strained panic. A deep red light bathing everything around her suddenly jolted me awake.

I was still here, but was I alive? It didn't feel right somehow.

"You're an idiot, Penny," she was muttering under her breath. I felt as though I'd heard her voice before, and yet I couldn't have.

"Do I know you?" I asked, feeling dizzy and sick the moment I opened my mouth.

"No," she replied sharply. "But that doesn't matter. What matters is that you got yourself trapped at the worst moment possible, and now I have to risk everything to save your unworthy backside! Would it kill *someone* to cooperate for once?"

The buzzing had stopped, the sun had stopped rising, and as I weakly turned around, Avery had frozen too.

"Are you D?" I slurred in confusion, trying to sit up and see what she was doing.

"I'm Demitra," she replied briskly. "I'm half of D."

Then something came loose that had been pinning my dress to the floor, and I stumbled backwards in shock.

Somehow, Demitra had moved a block of stone that must have weighed a ton from my dress.

"That's a weird name." I frowned, raising an eyebrow. It was all I could think of to say, and I winced at how immature it sounded.

"I'm a weird person," she answered with a wink, then gritted her teeth and rested an arm on the debris for support. "I won't be able to interfere anymore after this, since you've used up all my energy, so get up there, and whatever you do don't let anyone get out except for yourself. Oh, and as soon as I move, so will everything else, so please don't dawdle."

"Wait!" I cried, catching onto her arm as she turned to leave – where to, I didn't know. "You're...you're D? But you're so...normal!"

"What, did the overlapping voices and shady cloak trick you?" She laughed without humor, yanking here arm free of my grasp. "All part of the act, Penny. All part of the act. It's like a giant play. You are all the unwitting actors, Madon's the director, and I'm the visual effects manager."

"So it was you doing the trials? Who's the other half of D?"

"My brother." Demitra sighed, glancing around at the frozen scene warily. "He was the one who monitored the contraption in the attic, so we knew when to begin the tests. We got mad that Madon let you start it early, you see, and he got mad that we started cheating by talking to you all. Very blatant favoritism, you see."

"But...but...why favor me? And why let Avery know what to do in the arena?"

"You have power. You're more useful outside of the Boundary

than in it. My brother, Deio, doesn't see that way, and thought that somebody ruthless would be better…"

"So he arranged it so that the person willing to abandon all morals and fight for their own gain would get a ticket to the end?" I finished for her, puzzle pieces falling into place.

"Exactly." Demitra nodded with a touch of impatience. Pausing time was obviously very exhausting. "Anyway, you didn't make it easy for me."

"Maybe if you'd appeared like this, rather than as a monster, I'd have listened."

"Fear factor, sweetheart," Demitra retorted mockingly. It was funny – she looked so young. Almost exactly my age. "An excellent tool when manipulating people to do what you want."

"But why—"

"No time," she interrupted, holding up a hand. "Just get out of here and answer all your questions yourself. Nobody but you can decide what happens now."

My mouth opened, but Demitra simply turned into the Boundary and vanished.

Just as promised, there was a shudder and everything began to move again.

I tried to ignore what had just happened, knowing it would consume my mind if I let it. Instead, I tore across what little space was left towards the door where Avery was standing, animate again.

Then I wrenched open the tiny arched door and shot up the narrow staircase before anything else could happen.

Avery shouted something at me, but I didn't listen. A minute ago, I had been facing death. Now I was sure to win.

The landing…I let my palms run over the wall to try and find the hidden door, light all gone again, hoping that it would be unlocked, or else we were all done for.

Avery answered that question for me, ramming into the wall with his full body and stumbling over the threshold when it opened easily.

The attic was mostly dust, filled with the red light, and nothing like what it had been the first time. Here, I had started the trials and contacted D for the first time. I shuddered.

The contraption was there, but on a much smaller and less showy scale. Two interlocked rings about the diameter of dinner plates, glowing with an odd energy. And of course, that antique lever which called us to pull it and become victor.

I had expected it to be a race between Avery and I, but there was one problem.

Evelyn was already standing there, face white as a sheet and hands clasped over the handle, prepared to pull it.

"Evelyn?" Avery and I gasped in sync. "I...we...you..."

"Shocking, isn't it," she choked, body shaking, "that poor, distraught little Evelyn could actually defy her heart to beat you all? No one thought I could do it, not you two or Tressa, the Master or D, they all cast me off straight away. Only Fred believed in me."

"Not true!" I contradicted, swallowing down a rising panic. "I never wrote you off! We just thought that being here with Fred was what you wanted!"

Evelyn laughed quietly, sounding not at all bitter or twisted like D, but genuinely upset. "I thought so too, but this is what he wants for me, and I know...I know that if I stay on his account he'll never stop blaming himself, regardless of whether it was my choice or not. I know I'd feel the same way if it was reversed. I've been here for ages, contemplating..."

I had to tread carefully. She had the lever in her hand, the slightest slip up and she'd win, we'd lose.

"Don't do this, Evelyn. Don't make yourself unhappy; you know what you and I want...and we can have it! I can go, you can stay with Fred," I coaxed, steadily taking a step forwards whilst Avery stood silently to the side, formulating his own plan.

"No," she whispered, torn. "You don't understand, it would

destroy Fred if he thought for a second—"

"Forget Fred," I interrupted. "What do *you* want? Really?"

She stood there, tears pouring down her cheeks, but did not step away from the lever.

"To be thrust into an unknown world alone?" I pressed, coming a few steps closer with each word. We didn't have much time before everything caved in, I could feel it in the shaking floor, but I had to tread slowly. "To never see him again? You'd never get it back, and you don't know what ordeals could be waiting out there. I have no one to stay for, not like you do. This isn't your dream, it isn't your future."

She bit her lip, puffy eyes not straying from the circles but grip slacking.

I softly put one hand on her shoulder, and the other reached out to take the lever.

Avery jumped in from the side, elbowing me out of the way and snatching at the lever too.

Evelyn jumped and before anyone could process what was going on, she gave it a hefty pull.

Evelyn disappeared. I screamed. Avery shouted.

Then there was an almighty rip, and the ceiling came down on us in a wave of static and rubble.

30

Tressa was shaking me awake, but I was simply too tired. I rolled over to shrug her off, pulling the duvet tighter around my shoulders and burying my face into the pillows.

"Get up, Penny. Wake up. Don't make me dump water on you."

"I'm tired," I mumbled groggily. "Go away."

"Though your minor issues do concern me, we have much more to discuss. Get up."

I tried to fall back into a dream that I had been having, but it was no use; I had been well and truly awakened. There was something playing on my mind, something important that I must have forgotten...

"Oh my gosh!" I yelped, jumping up and out of bed in a terrible fright.

I was in the girls' chamber, which I had seen destroyed by the Boundary and turned to ashes.

Everything was back in order, from the pots on my vanity to the delicate lace curtains hanging from the windows, which exposed a beautiful sunny day outside. When I caught my reflection in a pristine mirror, I noticed that my skin seemed fuller, my hair brighter, and my eyes less sunken as if that one short sleep had healed everything.

Tressa was standing off to the side, dressed in a brand new gown. Her face seemed less gaunt too, but there was still something very drawn in her expression.

"What...how...?" I gasped, swaying on my feet.

"You lost," she answered simply, reaching into the cupboard and throwing a simple cream day dress at me. "Evelyn's gone to who-knows-where, and everything has gone back to normal for the rest of us."

"No, no, that's not possible!" I panicked, letting the dress fall to the floor. "I was supposed to...not her...this can't be happening..."

I pattered over to the window and threw open the shutters, letting a warm breeze blow through the room and bathe everything in a bright, sleepy morning light. Tressa watched with an unreadable nonchalance as I poked my head right out and leaned until I was nearly falling.

The grass was emerald again, sprawling until it met the vibrant forests, which were budding with a mixture of evergreen and blossoms, as alive as I had ever seen them. Even the bricks had lightened to a soft beige, and the rhododendrons were full of multicolor flowers at the foot.

"How long have I been asleep?" I frowned, trying and failing to keep my voice steady.

"I don't know, I just woke up a few minutes ago. You weren't here when I fell asleep." Tressa shrugged.

"This is the mirror world?"

"Oh, Avery, always making ordinary things seem so wonderful. This is where we have been whilst you lot battled it out, and it's basically just a replica of the original. At first, we could see what was going on with you too, as if the worlds overlapped, but slowly yours faded away as if it were dying. It's gone completely now."

I nodded numbly.

Evelyn was gone to the wonderful world outside of the Boundary, and I would be stuck here. Forever.

"Penny! Come back!"

I was gone, pushing past Tressa and tearing down the corridor. I was beyond feeling, I was beyond reason. I was beyond fear.

Everything was perfect, better than I remembered, but it was off somehow. Everything that had been destroyed was flawless, everything seemed lighter and happier.

Barefoot and in my nightgown, I stormed down the staircase, down through the entrance hall, which had been in a state of disrepair what seemed like only minutes before, now glistening in full glory.

Out in the gardens, I stopped for a moment to take a deep breath, immediately shocked by how fresh and pure the air seemed now that all the smoke was gone. The clouds had left only sapphire skies and sunshine in their absence, and the heavens seemed to go on forever. It felt quite exposing, yet the gentle wind caressed with such tenderness that it was near impossible to feel anything but relaxed.

This isn't real. That was what Avery had said. Now I knew exactly what he had meant, and I could not agree more.

My feet did the thinking for me, carrying me across the lush grass to the woods, until I decided on impulse to alter my course just slightly.

There, over in the shadier part of the estate, was a small grey blur. It was so faded that it was quite difficult to tell what it was, though after a quick wracking of memory I realized that it was Beatrix's grave. The only part of the old world which was still visible in this one – there was not supposed to be darkness here, no reminders of before, yet even in death Beatrix had managed to cheat the overlords to remain for us as a constant memory of who our enemies were, and what they had done.

I bowed my head slightly in her direction, feeling a slight surge of anger and sadness at her loss once again.

Then I continued into the woods, batting branches out of my way and letting the mounting dread stay under control until I could just check…then I nearly ran into the Boundary. It was not buzzing with that strange static we had gotten used to, and for one ecstatic moment, I thought that it had gone entirely.

Just to make sure, I yanked a healthier-than-life leaf on a twig from a nearby tree, then chucked it at the Boundary with a nervous flinch. It did not disintegrate; it did not go through…it simply bounced off without creating so much as a shudder.

Tentatively, I pushed my palm flat on the invisible wall, half expecting the shock of my life, but instead all I felt was a temper-ature-free surface as smooth as granite and lifeless as dirt. Rock solid, unmoving, eternal. It was official. I was stuck here in this plastic paradise forever.

"D!" I shouted with terror masked underneath a rising fury. "Demitra, whoever you are!"

My breath came hard and heavy, until I couldn't contain it anymore. I lashed out at the wall with my fists, only succeeding in bruising them (my shoulder had miraculously healed). I clenched them in pain and with a little scream of frustration tried to rip a large rock from the ground, but I could not do it. Panicking, on the edge of hysteria, I tried to levitate a tiny pebble from the soil, but found nothing. I couldn't even see the blurry edges that allowed me to attempt a rip.

"No!" I cried in despair, tear flowing freely now, knees giving out from underneath me. "No!" Footsteps echoed behind me, but my body was so overcome with the shuddering sobs and boundless fear that I couldn't look up until someone placed a gentle hand on my shoulder and helped me to my feet. It was Fred, Tressa and Avery.

"It's going to be okay," Fred smiled comfortingly, giving my hand an encouraging squeeze. Underneath it though, I saw something else in his expression. Something beyond sadness, something like what Evelyn had worn after she thought she had lost him.

"Fred…" I choked, feeling selfish yet not fully able to reveal my emotions. "I'm so sorry…"

"She's free." He shrugged, clearly struggling to remain composed. "I didn't actually expect her to…you know…get out, but I didn't want her to stay on my account either. Ironically, now I feel terrible because she's all alone out there and I won't ever be able to help her or see if she's okay. I don't think there ever was an easy solution."

"Evelyn," Avery muttered bitterly. "Plot twist right there.

Never saw that one coming."

"But it came," Tressa reminded him firmly, flicking Fred a sympathetic glance as he turned away. "So I suppose we'll have to just accept that this is our future."

"I can't accept it," I said at exactly the same time as Fred and Avery.

"You don't understand," Fred blurted, whirling around to face us with a single tear coursing down his face. "I *doubted* her, which is why I let her try for winning in the first place, because I didn't actually think she'd succeed! It was my own confidence in her inability that led her to win, and really I should have just... I don't know if I'm guilty for sentencing her to a dangerous life or guilty for wanting her back in this prison when outside is probably much better..."

Avery said something rude under his breath, but luckily for him no one heard enough to react.

I was simply too numb with shock to do anything but stare past the Boundary into a world I would now never touch. Because I knew that I could have let everyone out, but Evelyn never could. If I had told them that, would they had trusted me enough to let me win on those grounds? How else could this game have been played so that it wouldn't have ended this way?

"By the way, did you lot ever figure out what those letters we sent spelled?" Tressa interrupted the pensive silence. "Sorry for the jumble, but it took way too much effort to do it all at once, and D said that if we made it too obvious the Master would take them away."

I shook my head just as Lucas nodded.

"'War outside,'" he quoted glumly.

I felt something in my stomach drop.

"What?" Fred yelped, stumbling into the Boundary and falling onto his back. "War? Outside? Where Evelyn is? What...how...?"

"D told us," Avery explained, corners of his mouth curling

into a smirk at Fred's distress. "No idea what it meant, but there you go."

Again with D!

Fred ran off behind a tree and was promptly sick.

"It was supposed to be you, Penny," Lucas whispered from behind me.

His voice was uneven and forced, just as everyone else's seemed to be. The finality hadn't sunk in yet, and I hated to think of my sanity when it did.

"But it wasn't," I hissed softly, jaw clenched and rocking on the balls of my feet. "I messed up somehow, and now we're here forever and Evelyn is alone in the middle of some war."

Abruptly, I spun on my heels and tore from the forest again, letting tears blur my vision and anger fuel my speed. In what seemed like a matter of seconds, I was at the foot of the manor again, hair wild from running and face flushed with emotion.

The sun glinted off the stone walls, painting them golden, filling them with warmth. And there, blipping in and out of focus, was Demitra and a boy I took to be her brother. She was staring at the manor and screaming so loud it was silent, and he had a look of incalculable rage on his face.

"Penny," she snapped, turning around. Flickering so fast it was dizzying. "How could...now I can't...you've done!"

Her mouth was moving, but words came out intermittently.

"War outside?" I shouted back, bubbling with loathing. "What is that supposed to mean?"

"The year...1939..." The brother, Deio told me, remarkably calm in comparison. "World...Two."

"What?" I took a step back, stunned.

"...You!" Demitra snarled, probably cursing. "The war was...discourage the others...wanting to get out...chance for you!"

The flickering was faster, more violent, and I was so transfixed that I didn't notice the others gather around me in surprise.

As if noticing her predicament for the first time, she gaped at her hand with a look of utter horror. Then with one final scream, this one very much audible, they both vanished.

Avery shook his head in disbelief. "After all that, they were just a couple of teenagers."

"Looks can be deceiving," Fred muttered.

"A world war?" Lucas shuddered. "In a place nearly a century advanced from us... Poor Evelyn. I didn't tell her, when I found out, since I didn't understand... Oh lord, I've been an idiot."

"We all have," Tressa admitted in a small voice. "Some more than others."

Avery didn't shirk or apologize, but gazed at the spot where D had vanished with an odd expression. "Maybe the war really was only a way to discourage weaker people from winning. Like the arena."

"Only Evelyn knows now."

I just stood there, shaking, until long after my friends had all dispersed. D was gone, and Madon had got His way, presumably making him the sole Master of the Boundary again. There was only one thing to do now. I wandered to the foot of the manor, a shadowy area where the accursed bushes were once again thriving.

I plucked a blood red rhododendron from its stem, then lifted it slowly to the sky.

"You don't own us," I spat to the controllers, who I knew were watching from wherever they were. "You think this is over now you've sent Evelyn off to a warzone and left us to die here? It's never over, you hear? Never!"

My voice rose to a high pitch, echoing off the walls. A dark cloud was appearing from over the northern woods, a reminder of who was in charge and what they were capable of, but there was clear sky left still.

"Like you said," I added darkly. "The rhododendrons weren't

here for no reason. They mean 'beware'. Only this time, it's aimed at you, because I'm not giving up. Ever."

I thought I saw a figure staring at me with hollow eyes from over by the blurred grave, but when I blinked it was gone.

I dropped the flower, empty and exhausted.

Then I cast one last look at the forest before wandering back to see where my friends were, and decide what we would do next.

What I didn't notice was the flower slowly sinking into the ground behind my back.

The challenge had been accepted.

31

I blink. Once, twice, three times, just to make sure it's real. Then I repeat the procedure, because surely, my eyes must be playing tricks on me?

I pulled that lever not really thinking about the consequences. All I can remember is Penny trying to convince me to give her the victory, trying to quash my guilt...and then Avery startling me into pulling it for myself.

I think something must have happened in between then and now, but I simply can't remember. It takes a moment to even remember who I am.

Then it comes to me.

I am Evelyn, and I have just done something that has changed everything.

Groggily, I pick myself up from the ground and survey the area. It's familiar, and yet it's not, because I suddenly do not know where I am anymore. Yet I do...

I notice the slight difference in elevation to my left, where we used to play cricket, and that sunken pocket of land where the graveyard used to be. Yes, this is inside the Boundary. But it's so drastically different that I hardly recognize it anymore. For the trees are nearly all the same species, as tall and gnarled as I remember, yet spaced all differently, and extending over ground that should have been lawns and, of course, the manor itself. Now it is all gone and covered by forest.

I inhale air, which seems changed, though I cannot place how. Then I look up and see the sunlight filtering through the thick canopy in a way that creates miniature spotlights all over the floor, where, in some places, a curious blue-purple flower covers the ground.

Something screeches at me overhead, and for a moment I think Penny is about to jump out of a tree, laughing at my confusion...

I scream. It's not Penny, or Avery, or anyone else making such a strange sound, but a beastly creature unlike anything I have ever seen before! Black feathers covering its entire body, a pointed beak where a mouth should be, screeching as it unfurls powerful wings.

Think, Evelyn! I cry to myself. What was in those books of yours about this place? What would Lucas say it was? Did they hunt humans?

I back against a tree as something else rustles in the undergrowth, heart pounding, then flinch away screaming as something very tiny, with a million legs scuttles by my head on the tree bark.

Everything is alive with monsters here!

I wrap my arms around middle, biting my lip and forcing myself to stay calm.

What would Fred think?

With that single thought, I nearly lose it. Fred, who had told me I should, and more importantly could, succeed, Fred who had lost his own chance so that I might have mine...

"Where are you?" I call frantically, running about quite irrationally as if the manor might appear again alongside all my friends.

I don't really want this. I have never wanted freedom the way Penny had, but now it looks to be my future. And I don't like it one bit. Another beast, this one fluffy, squeaks indignantly as I nearly step on it and shoots up a tree as if it were an extension of its own body.

Frightened past reason, I huddle my knees into my chest and focus on taking deep, steady breaths.

What have I done?

I don't know how long I stay like this, weeping in terror at everything that moves around me, then even more so at the prospect of being alone forever.

Then, finally, I wipe away my tears and stand up. The sun has set, and it really is quite beautiful in here when one doesn't think about what might be crawling around as company. I cannot waste away my life feeling sorry for myself. Fred knew that I could survive, and so it must be so. It has to be.

I begin to walk forwards, unsure. When I reach the tiny creek that is still very much present in this world, it takes all my willpower to convince myself that the Boundary doesn't exist anymore. So I do what no one has been able to do before; I cross to the other side.

Immediately, it feels alien, though there is no difference. I jump back across four times just to make sure it's real, then continue on my way. I was never one for adventure, and I just cannot summon that adrenaline, that feeling I know Penny would have been exploding with right now.

A few yards on, and feeling suitably nervous again, I come across what can only be a large path. So large in fact, thoughts of giants cross my mind.

I start down the path, deciding that it must lead somewhere. And I have no intentions of still being stranded in the woods at night, when all manner of nightmares could arise from its depths. Hopefully, the people here are human!

It isn't long before I start seeing oddities in the landscape. Deep holes in the ground, closed off by rickety wooden structures, a few with peculiar contraptions cluttered around the area. Most are coated with rust and seem a long time abandoned, so I don't pay them any more attention than a vague curiosity.

Then I notice that the trees are starting to thin out, but unlike the Boundary it seems very artificial, as if someone has come and removed them on purpose. Stumps scatter haphazard clearings, many around the queer holes, and the road becomes more compact as if it has been used more in this area.

"Lucas, you never said anything about this," I whimper to no one.

I had been expecting those grand cities we had seen in

pictures, expecting friendly people to come up to me and explain everything.

It crosses my mind that the people might actually live in these holes, but since the thought of living underground brings chills to my skin, I decide to keep searching for a more civilized settlement.

Then I come out onto a hilltop. From my vantage point in this artificial clearing, I can see for miles around; rolling hills as far as the eye can see, most covered with thick woodland but a fair few only open grassland, strands of trees acting like natural borders between fields. The clouds dip down into a valley, where through the fog I think I can see light. A city perhaps.

Decisively, I hitch up my skirts and start down the steep hillside. My heart is pounding from fearful anticipation. What will I find in the valley? And, more importantly, what will happen when the finality of this sinks in? How will I possibly stay rational knowing that I shall never see…?

"You have a determination that is quite often overlooked by everyone, including yourself," Fred had told me once. "I think that if you properly set your mind to it, you could accomplish anything."

"I'm not one for that sort of thing," I had sighed contentedly, laying my head on his shoulder. "I prefer to keep things as they are, simple and perfect."

"You are so very unlike everyone else, Evelyn." He had laughed. "But just think of all the wonderful things out there you could discover! Imagine, getting out of this place, seeing what the world has to offer! You and I, we could do it!"

"No," I had replied simply. "I want for nothing here."

"Oh, Evelyn. What are you like?"

I bite my lip to keep from sobbing out loud, knowing that I should be as composed as possible for my introduction.

Who'd have thought, Fred? I groan to myself. You were right, but not about the part where both of us got out.

I will be brave for you.

I lose my footing on the sharp gradient, sliding down the hill and dirtying my rear. Panicked that my first impression shall be sliding ungracefully into someone, I grab hold of a tree and dig my heels into the ground.

Then, rather embarrassingly, I stumble to keep my footing and fall backwards into one of the holes, this one without a fence.

I catch hold of a root, hyperventilating, and look down.

I scream. The bottom is so deep that I cannot see a thing, only a darkness that surely never ends.

I try to hoist myself up, but my arms aren't strong enough. So I scream, and scream, and scream, until my throat is sore and my hands are beginning to slip.

Just when I think it's over, something grabs my elbows and yanks me upwards until I am safely lying on solid ground.

I am about to get up and thank my savior, when my head is forced back down by something cold and round. It clicks, and though I do not know what it is, I guess that it is a weapon.

"Please..." I croak. "I..."

The person holding the weapon bends over me in obvious confusion, and for the first time I see his face. Human. Odd-looking, covered in hair, but human.

"Please help me," I beg in a rush. "I don't know where I am, what to do, or anything! I don't—"

He seems flabbergasted, and glances behind me to where someone else must be standing. I turn my head, following his gaze, and see that the fog has cleared in the valley.

I squint, trying to make out the distant shapes. Then I start screaming again.

"What *are* those things?"

"You mean the trucks?" The man frowns. "They're the new army recruits, heading for training up north. Who...where are you from?"

I just shake my head, staring at the procession of machines

snaking through the valley. My heart is pounding so loud nothing else can register, but alongside the overwhelming fear, there's a new emotion. Determination. A different world, a different time, different people... Well, maybe that's the perfect recipe for a different me.

"Just hang on," I say to the sky, surprising myself with how calm I sound now, although my body is still trembling. "I'll find a way."

TO BE CONTINUED

Acknowledgements

First and foremost, thank you to everyone at JHP for making a longtime dream of mine come true. Especially to editor Maria Moloney, who put in countless hours to make this book reach its full potential. I can't thank you enough – you rock!

Thanks to my not-so-little sister, Annabel, for convincing me that *Boundary* wasn't just a pile of rubbish. Without you, it would have gone down with my last laptop, never to see the light of another day.

Also, to all the authors who offered feedback: thank you!

And of course, the rest of my family; Mum, Dad, and little-little sister Clara. Thank you for being so wonderful, despite the fact I didn't even speak about writing until six months ago. You have to admit, it's a better career choice than a mermaid.

LODESTONE BOOKS

Lodestone Books is a new imprint, which offers a broad spectrum of subjects in YA/NA literature. Compelling reading, the Teen/Young/New Adult reader is sure to find something edgy, enticing and innovative. From dystopian societies, through a whole range of fantasy, horror, science fiction and paranormal fiction, all the way to the other end of the sphere, historical drama, steam-punk adventure, and everything in between. You'll find stories of crime, coming of age and contemporary romance. Whatever your preference you will discover it here.